WOMAN
LAST SEEN IN HER
THIRTIES

OTHER TITLES BY CAMILLE PAGÁN

Forever is the Worst Long Time

Life and Other Near-Death Experiences

The Art of Forgetting

WOMAN LAST SEEN IN HER THIRTIES

CAMILLE PAGÁN

LAKE UNION
PUBLISHING

Published by Lake Union Publishing, Seattle

www.apub.com

ISBN-13: 9781503936997 (paperback)
ISBN-10: 1503936996 (paperback)
ISBN-13: 9781503949287 (hardcover)
ISBN-10: 1503949281 (hardcover)

Cover design by David Drummond

Printed in the United States of America

First edition

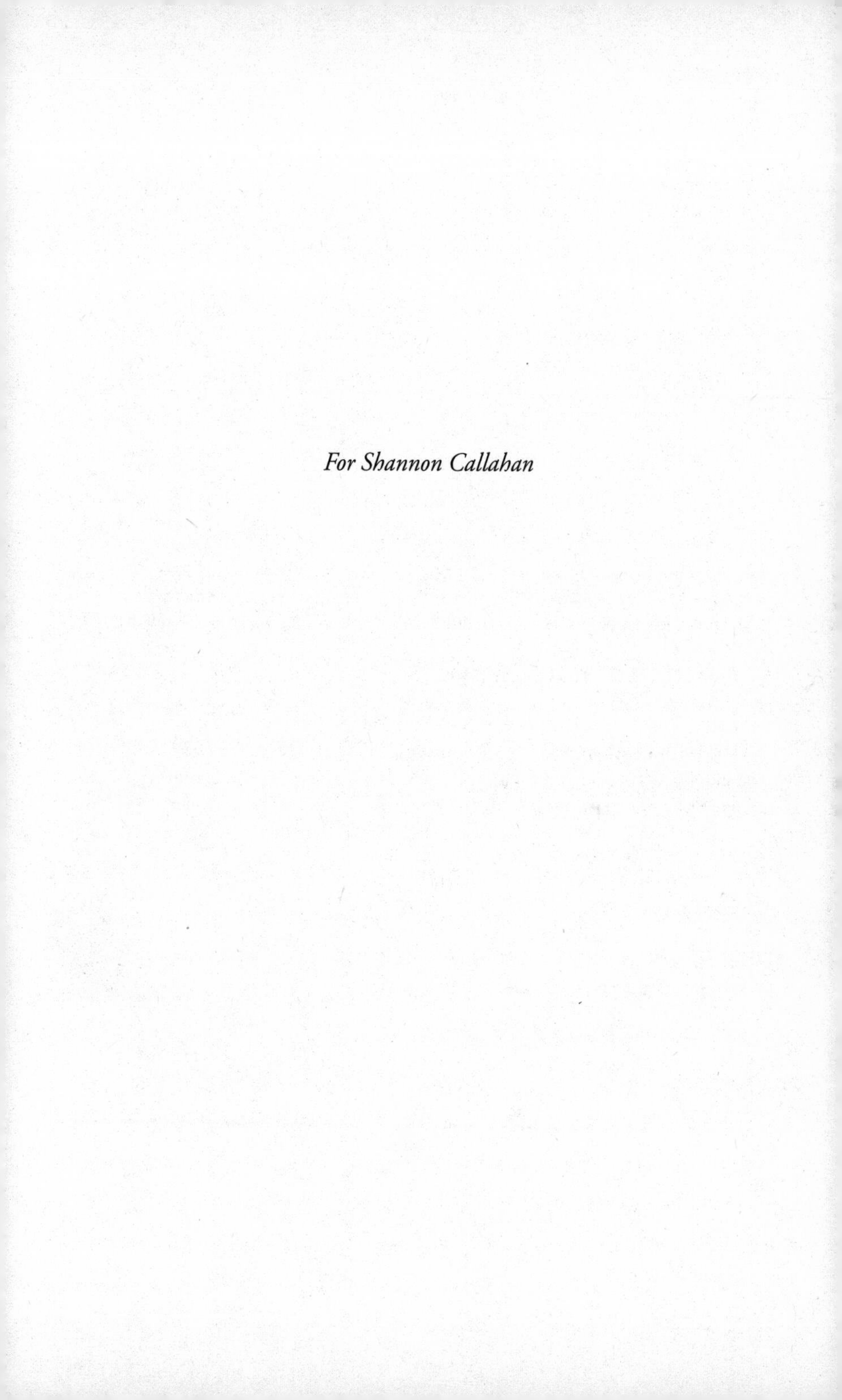

For Shannon Callahan

ONE

It's an age-old story: woman meets man, man woos woman, woman spends her best years believing their love is the everlasting kind. The pair watches with teary eyes as their progeny take flight from their suburban nest, knowing they'll return in times of crisis or when their laundry needs to be washed and folded.

Woman embraces aging with hair dye and ample amounts of wine. Man faces his impending mortality by convincing himself that a younger woman is the answer to his waning energy and flagging libido. Certain their sparkling future is worth the collateral damage, the May-December duo ride into the sunset as our heroine stands in the shadows, stunned by this unexpected rewrite.

Yes, mine is a tale as old as time. Beauty replaces the beast.

~

"I don't understand," I said to Adam, who was filling my favorite suitcase with the last of his clothes. "Why would you do this to us?"

"I told you, I'm not in love with you anymore." He zipped the suitcase and hoisted it off our bed. "I don't think I have been for a while now."

"That's what everyone says when they're infatuated with someone new," I said, resisting the urge to suggest he take an aspirin for his shoulder. It had been bothering him for months—which I now suspected was less about him hunching over his keyboard and more the consequence of him holding his lover up against the wall while they copulated—and I had just seen him wince. "It won't last."

"You're not listening to me, *Maggie*." He said my name like a curse, which seemed incredibly hurtful considering how often I chose not to mention I was aware he had just passed gas.

"I've spent decades listening to you, Adam, when maybe what I should have been doing was talking more. We can go to a therapist and try to figure out how to communicate better. We can *fix* this." I was starting to sound as frantic as I felt. We were planning an anniversary trip to Rome! We had less than a decade until retirement! We swore until death did us part! He couldn't just *leave*.

Except apparently he could, because he was wheeling our best suitcase toward the door. I wanted to yank it right out of his hands, but something else was starting to sink in. Unfortunately, it felt a lot like reality. "What's her name, Adam?" I called suddenly.

His face was blank as he turned back to me.

"The woman you're sleeping with?" I said. "The woman you're abandoning me for? I want to know her name."

His composed expression exploded into anger. "Does it matter?"

I sat on the edge of our bed, my eyes welling with tears. This was my reward for thirty-two years of love and companionship? "Have you been lobotomized? Of course it matters. If you're going to trade me in like a used car, I need to know the name of your new ride."

He shook his head, like I was the one disappointing him. Then he said, "Jillian."

"Jillian?" I don't know what I had been expecting. Jezebel, perhaps. But Jillian: that was the name of a sunny, blameless woman with interesting hobbies. Not one who slept with my husband. "Jillian *who*?"

Another blank look. "Smith," he finally mumbled.

"Awfully generic."

"Awfully common," he said, the edge returning to his voice. "That's her name."

I exhaled, not so much a sigh as all remaining hope exiting my body. "Where did you meet her?" I asked after a moment.

"I thought you didn't want to talk about it."

This was true. Three days earlier he had sat me down and announced he wasn't happy in our marriage; he hadn't been for some time.

I thought, *Not happy?* He had been bounding around like a man in his twenties for months, more energetic and alive than I had seen him in ages. He was still affectionate toward me, too. Just days earlier we had gone to dinner with Gita and Reddy, our closest couple friends. As Adam was telling us a story about a man at his health club who danced his way through his workout, he reached under the table and squeezed my thigh. My chest filled with warmth—he still had that effect on me after all these years. It was true that I had hoped for something more when we got home that night, but I didn't take it personally when he kissed me with closed lips and promptly passed out on his side of the bed. He had been having trouble in the arousal department, but I saw no reason to take this as an indication that he was about to obliterate our union.

When I stopped Adam in the middle of his "I'm unhappy with us" speech days after that and he agreed to sleep on it for a few nights, this seemed like further evidence that his angst was owing to some sort of testosterone lull or midlife mood swing. Of course, I spent those in-between days fretting. Was he depressed? Had the grief of his father's death a year earlier finally kicked in?

I'll admit I mostly assumed he was listless in the way a man can become after his sexual prime goes the way of the diplodocus. But that could be addressed with, say, a skydiving excursion (though admittedly the combination of heights and potential human error made that a no-go for me) or maybe light S&M (except if our parenting was any indication, this was equally problematic, as both Adam and I struggled to exert dominance over people we loved). Never in a million years did I imagine he was planning to leave me for another woman.

Clearly this had been a miscalculation on my part. "Just answer the question," I said.

Now he looked away from me. "At a coffee shop."

"Where?"

"Near my work."

"How old is she?"

He shook his head and muttered, "Thirty?"

Thirty. Thirty! "Christ on a cracker, Adam Harris. What kind of message are you sending to Jack and Zoe by dating a woman who is closer in age to them than us? Forget clichés—it's practically a crime against nature!" I was staring at him as I said this, and damned if he didn't flinch and turn the other way. "What about our plans? What about our vacation, and your mother moving in with us?" Adam's mother, Rose, had recently been diagnosed with early-stage dementia, and he and I had been planning to tell her she could come live with us for at least a few years while we were still able to care for her. After all, with both of our kids finally out of the house and on their own, we had more than enough space, and Rose said she couldn't bear the thought of being in a nursing home with a bunch of senile old folks. "What about our retirement, Adam?" I said, and now I was practically yelling. "What about *forever*?"

"I'm done planning, Maggie," Adam said, still facing the wall. "I want a different life."

And then he left.

~

A different life? Was this code for a lover with undappled skin and perky breasts? Whatever Adam meant, he really meant it, because a few weeks later I was served divorce papers, which I stashed behind the cache of *Martha Stewart* Livings in the spare bathroom, should anyone using the toilet desire more realistic reading material.

I did not need to comb through the legal documents to gather that the entire thing had been premeditated. Adam had hired a divorce lawyer before he told me he had accidentally fallen for someone, as though he had failed to uphold his marital vows by missing a step on fidelity's ladder. He had found a rental apartment while I was still researching hotels in Rome, and had consulted with his mother's accountant to ensure his father had left ample funds to cover her stay in an assisted living facility (affirmative). And while I couldn't be certain, Zoe's and Jack's surprise seemed feigned when I called to break the news about the separation. Had Adam already told them—or had they sensed that our marriage was crumbling even as I was busy stepping over the cracks? The details were paralyzing, and I routinely found myself staring into the refrigerator or behind the wheel of my car with no knowledge of what I was doing there. (The sole silver lining of our separation was that I now had some insight into Rose's mental state.)

Yet I spent the first few weeks after Adam's bombshell waiting for him to wake from this nightmare he had dreamed up for us both and realize the only compassionate, logical thing to do was to come back. After all, both cheating and leaving were completely out of character for him. Adam was not just a loving and devoted if occasionally overworked husband and father; he was also the sort of person who cared deeply what others thought of him. He would not want our friends, neighbors, and family whispering about his incredibly stupid decision. And so each time there was a knock at the door, I rushed to answer. Every time the phone rang I prayed the name on the screen would be Adam

Harris, who was calling to beg for my forgiveness and ask if he could come home. (How could he go from speaking with me every single day to not at all? My mind boggled.)

But when a ceaseless string of disappointments began to make it clear Adam had no plans to return, I went numb. Don't get me wrong: I did all the things one might do following a catastrophic loss. I went days without showering, cried in inappropriate places, and couldn't bring myself to eat a single doughnut (which the *Diagnostic and Statistical Manual of Mental Disorders* should probably add as a criterion for clinical depression). But I did so feeling as if I were acting out a part in a movie I hated, rather than living my actual life.

"Mom, don't *worry* about Dad. He's a *giant douche*. You're *going* to get *through* this," said Jack, who sounded like he was stoned, but was nonetheless saying all the right things as I snorted back tears on the other end of the line. My baby. Unlike his older sister—who made it seem like I was interrupting her Very Important Law Job every time I called—Jack called *me* to check in.

And bless him, he was mostly right. I made it through the second month, then the third, and after securing a prescription for sleeping pills from my doctor—who as a physician was required to inform me they were addictive, but as a divorcée promised they would get me through my grief- and anxiety-fueled insomnia—I survived another two.

Somehow five blurry months passed, and I found myself standing near a checkout counter at the grocery store, feeling guilty about spending much of my anemic paycheck on an overpriced lump of mozzarella, a couple of hothouse tomatoes, and a bottle of cheap end-of-season rosé to replace the one I had finished the night before. I had just grabbed a plastic-wrapped cookie from a display rack when something metal slammed into my lower back.

Pain shot up my spine, and I lurched forward while moaning in what I hoped was a demure fashion. As I slowly righted myself, I saw a ridiculously fit man wheeling a shopping cart away from me. His cart,

I noticed, was filled with cans of protein powder and enough organic produce to deplete my entire checking account.

The man glanced back at me briefly, confirming my suspicion that he was responsible for the ramming. "You just ran into me," I said feebly.

He shrugged, no longer looking at me, and continued on his way.

My eyes smarted with equal parts humiliation and discomfort. When had I ceased to be a human and metamorphosed into a windowpane? Maybe people had been looking right through me for years, and I was only now realizing it. Ladies and gentlemen, the Amazing Invisible Woman has finally been spotted!

I must admit I was wearing the costume: black shirt, black pants, and bare face mapped with fine lines. And to think I had been waltzing around oblivious to my own superpower all this time.

The zinging pain in my back began to give way to a hot, uncomfortable sensation, at which point I detected the first rumblings of the seismic shift about to take place.

"Hey!" I yelled after the man. "You *hurt* me!"

To my right a child was staring at me, her mouth gaping open. Her mother, wearing a sheepish smile intended not for me but for our fellow shoppers, pulled the child by the arm to indicate she was to keep moving. I remembered that stage—trying to prevent a young Jack from pointing at a man in a wheelchair as my face burned, or silencing a small Zoe when she decided to identify and announce the flaws of those around her (a behavior that would regrettably follow her into adulthood).

"Please kill me if I ever act like that in public," I heard a college-age woman mutter to her friend as they stood by the salad bar.

"Don't get between her and her cookie," her friend said, and they erupted in a fit of laughter.

"Pardon me?" I called. "Would you care to repeat that?"

They looked at each other and made exaggerated grimaces implying that I was cuckoo for Cocoa Puffs. But I had a daughter; I knew what was wafting in the air between us, and it was more enticing than the smell of fresh muffins, fried chicken, or even a just-opened bottle of the most luscious pinot noir.

It was fear.

"Oh, girls," I said, taking a painful step toward them. My spine still ached, and I wondered if I would end up with chronic lower back pain, which I read could be triggered by even a seemingly minor injury. I regarded the young women's slender thighs, clad in ninety-dollar yoga pants their parents had paid for, as they inched away from me. "You're young and full of hope. You can still pout your way out of a parking ticket and don't have to worry that if you're hurt in public you'll be left to fend for yourself even as some tartlet accuses you of overreacting. But one day that will all change, and when it does you'll see my face smiling at you from somewhere up in the sky, because I'll probably be dead then. Here," I said, grabbing the cookie from my groceries. I tossed it into one of the women's baskets; to my delight, it actually landed on top of her cardboard salad container. "Enjoy it while you can."

I didn't stop to take in their reaction, nor that of other gawkers. No, I marched to the checkout counter and purchased my sad dinner, barely suppressing a grin all the while.

My elation was short-lived. When I pulled into the driveway of the building our family had once called home, it hit me yet again that no one was inside waiting for me; no one would call out my name as he or she or they walked through the door at any point that evening or the next morning. I was, then and what seemed would be forevermore, alone.

I let myself inside. I poured rosé into a large water glass and drew the curtains closed. Then I cried until my eyes stung, sipping my lousy pink wine between sobs. As I was walking to the bathroom to get some tissue, I caught a glimpse of myself in the oversize mirror in the dining room and did a double take. It was not that the red-nosed suburbanite staring back at me was so terribly offensive. It was just that . . . well, I hardly recognized her.

Where was the bright-eyed girl who had dreamed of a happy nuclear family and actually lived to see her dream come true?

Where was the doting mother who crawled between the mattress and box spring and let her children jump on her and scream with delight as they pretended to flatten her, even though it meant risking a ruptured disc?

Where was the wife who believed her husband meant it when he said, "So long as we both shall live"?

I wasn't sure when the woman once known as Maggie Halfmoon had vanished, but I had a strong suspicion she had last been seen during her thirties. And that was every bit as frightening as my husband walking out the door on the life we had created together.

Because how could I possibly face the world alone if no one could see me?

TWO

Things I have worried about more than twice:

An air-conditioning unit falling out of a window and onto me or someone I love; why I cannot seem to remember the names of my children's friends' mothers when I bump into them (Jennifer—it's always Jennifer, unless I say Jennifer, in which case it's actually Susan or Karen); whether I will accidentally snort a brain-eating amoeba while swimming in any given lake; the speed at which my hair, north and south, is turning gray; ill-intentioned strangers with guns; well-meaning acquaintances with guns; if my children are happy, and how much of their happiness, or lack thereof, has anything to do with me; whether wanting and sometimes having a second glass of wine means I drink too much; and if our family will suddenly go broke, in spite of savings and retirement accounts indicating years of mostly careful money management. Other anxiety triggers include identity theft, all correspondence from the IRS, Lyme disease, being stuck at social events when I want to go home, and airbag recalls (which unflaggingly involve whatever make, model, and year of car I am behind the wheel of).

I had never, however, worried Adam would leave me before he did just that.

Not *once*.

How could this be, wondered the women of my book club when I admitted, after breaking down in tears over a discussion of Nora Ephron's *Heartburn*, that Adam and I were no more—and worse, that I had not seen it coming? Surely this scenario must have crossed my mind once or twice, they gently insisted; most of us had been meeting for a decade, so they were familiar with my proclivity for unlikely disaster preparedness. It was as simple as believing he loved me so much he would never hurt me like that, I told them, and for this confession I was rewarded with the knowledge that every woman there, regardless of current marital status, had imagined in detail the worst-case scenario I had never anticipated and was now living through.

What I did not tell the women of my book club was that Adam had been my one sure thing.

"If you marry—and I'm sure as sugar not saying you should—choose a man who loves you just a little more than you love him," my mother told me when I was growing up. She knew of what she spoke: my father had promised to make her his wife after she moved from Virginia to Michigan with him, only to run back home without her the minute he learned his seed had sprouted. She was just nineteen at the time. While she had other boyfriends over the years, she never trusted a man enough to share her life with her, because, she said, she couldn't find one who loved her enough.

My mother was right about most things, but I thought her advice on love was tainted by my father's betrayal. Anyway, it wasn't as though a person got to *choose* whom she loved, I told myself when I fell for a senior named Ian Rausch halfway through my freshman year at the University of Michigan. Ian was pale to the point of translucence, and the Parliament Lights he chain-smoked emanated from his every pore, but he had moony brown eyes and wrote poetry, and I loved him on sight. He was going to hike through Central America after graduation, he warned me after he took me to bed for the first time—this was Ian's idea of a date—so I wasn't to get too comfortable. But the sex was fantastic and Ian wrote poems about me, and I didn't yet understand that neither was the same thing as love. So I bought a Spanish-English dictionary and told Ian that if he wanted a traveling companion, I was ready and willing. Then one evening I knocked on his door, and a woman wearing only a t-shirt answered.

Ian left town at the end of that summer, though I later heard he only made it as far as Texas. I spent the first half of my sophomore year recovering from him, and the second half rebuilding my grade point average, which had suffered from my lovelorn lack of focus and was threatening to end my full-ride scholarship. By the time I slid into my seat in a political science seminar one frigid January morning my junior year, I had begun to think that maybe there was something to my mother's advice.

I found myself behind a herd of men, the likes of whom had sat before me in almost every class I had taken. As usual, they all seemed identical: wealthy, white, entitled. Yet for whatever reason, one man's profile—the regal slope of his nose, the outline of his full lips, his smooth neck emerging from his cable-knit sweater—piqued my interest.

Maybe it was pheromones; maybe it was fate. But I had been staring at him for a few seconds when he spun around and smiled, like he had been waiting for me to notice him. "Hello," he said to me. "I'm Adam."

I smiled back. "Maggie," I said. And then I turned my attention to the role of executive power in a constitutional democracy and barely gave him another thought.

Adam sought me out after class; he would later tell me that seminar had been the longest fifty minutes of his life. He had electric green eyes and a soccer player's lean build, and I was immediately attracted to him. But whereas he declared our first kiss earth-shattering, it would take several gentle pointers before I felt the same spark when his lips were on mine.

Once we made it to bed, however, Adam proved to be a far more generous lover than Ian had ever been. And there was something addictive about how he enveloped me in his safe, secure existence. It was not just that he took me on actual dates and surprised me with novels, nice cardigans, and all sorts of other thoughtful gifts. It was that he made me feel like he had been waiting his whole life for me. Not once did he talk about dating other women; I can't even remember him so much as turning his head to check out another coed. He told me he loved me two months into our relationship. When I finally realized I was in love with Adam, nine months after we began dating, it was not the same euphoric, libidinous tingle I had felt for Ian. It was deeper, more satisfying—and mildly terrifying. I was too young to settle down.

"Maggie, you'd be God's own fool to lose that boy," my mother told me. We were standing in the kitchen of her apartment at the end of my senior year; Adam had wanted to meet her, so we had driven his old green Volvo up to her most recent place in Flint. It was an apartment—a tiny one, but at least it was not a trailer or a few rooms in a friend's place. I hated myself for feeling glad about that, because I knew Adam wouldn't have cared either way.

"I know, Ma," I said.

"I mean it. He loves you almost half as much as I do, which is an awful lot," she said, her eyes trained on the potato she was peeling.

"Are you making an observation or telling me what to do?" I remarked.

"You may know more than me on some counts, Margaret Louise, but not this one," she said quietly. "He's a sure thing."

But how could I decide on a single person with whom to spend the rest of forever at twenty-one years old? What if I was wrong, or one of us changed our minds—or simply changed? "Stability isn't everything," I argued.

My mother looked at me with her golden-brown eyes, which were almost identical to my own, and in an instant my childhood came back at me. Stashing my few belongings into a garbage bag and fleeing our latest home in the middle of the night because my mother couldn't scrape together the rent. Not knowing if my ramen cup would be my last meal for a while. The half a year we spent living with her grandparents in a coal-mining town wedged between the hills of Kentucky and Virginia, until my mother ran into my father at the Piggly Wiggly and hightailed us right back to Michigan. My mother had made sure I always felt loved, but aside from that love, she had been unable to provide much by way of stability.

"Isn't it?" she said. Then she began to cough. She had cut back to a half pack a day, but the damage had long been done. I lightly patted her on the back, waiting for the hacking to pass; when it finally did, we went back to talking about lunch.

Three decades later, I cursed myself for so much misdirected catastrophizing. I had not been crushed by an air conditioner (yet). My children were mostly happy, even if one made me feel like an afterthought, and the other relied on his parents' charity to make it in a loosely defined creative career in New York City. Neither Adam nor I had been diagnosed with cancer, heart disease, or any number of conditions that he in particular had a strong genetic predisposition to. We had been through lean times, especially after Adam left his partner-track position to open his own firm. But we had never been unable to put food on the table or pay our bills.

Come to find out that all that time, I should have been expending my mental energy on my so-called sure thing.

My mother had died of lung cancer nineteen years earlier, when she was just fifty-four. I would have given anything for her to see even a few more months of life. But as I got into bed one balmy night at the end of September and leaned over to smell Adam's pillow—which I still could not bring myself to wash, let alone throw out—and then pulled it close to my body, feeling as alone as I ever had, I had a terrible thought.

At least my mother had not lived long enough to learn that my sure thing had been nothing but a fairy tale.

THREE

"Maggie? It's Rose."

Of course it was. It was early October, and though I had not heard from Adam, his mother continued to call me every two to three days, just as she had for years. I started as a lifeline to her son; somewhere along the way I became her daughter. Rose knew where to place nine different pieces of silverware at a single table setting and exactly how much to discreetly tip the service people who helped her with domestic tasks large and small. I had grown up in dingy rentals and didn't learn it was proper to pass the salt and pepper together until I was already out of college; I still had no idea what to do with all those forks. No surprise, it had taken Rose and me several years to warm to each other. But after my own mother died when I was thirty-four, I had readily accepted Rose as the next best thing.

I wedged the phone between my chin and shoulder. "Hi, Rose. How's life at Mountainview Manor?" I asked, referring to the inexplicably named assisted living facility on Chicago's north side, which was ninety miles from the nearest mountain but offered a clear view of Lake Michigan.

Rose sniffed. "This place makes me want to stockpile antidepressants."

"I thought you were only taking vitamin D?" I asked.

"I know where to find pills if I need them. Larry over in 14-B is sweet on me."

Through the kitchen window, the leaves on the trees resembled an autumnal rainbow. I must have been gazing at them for a while, because Rose said, "Maggie? Maggie, are you still there?"

"Yes, Rose. I'm here. Sorry."

"I asked how you were doing. And don't gussy it up on my behalf. Tell me the truth."

The truth was that no sleeping pill could prevent me from waking most nights around three, remembering that half of the bed Adam and I had shared was empty, and wandering around the house until five or so, when I passed out on the sofa or Zoe's old daybed. The truth was that I sometimes wondered how long it would take for someone to realize I was missing if I were to walk into Lake Michigan with a few large rocks in my coat pockets. That when I was at work or grocery shopping or otherwise following the routines that predated Adam's departure, I sometimes pretended nothing had changed. And each time I arrived home to an empty house, it was as though my life had just been demolished anew.

"I'm okay," I said to Rose. "I'm getting through it."

"All right. You know I'm not one to push." She paused. "Have you seen Adam?"

"No." I had driven past his law office a couple times, hoping to catch a glimpse of him and maybe even Jillian, heading out for coffee or a midday tryst. (No such luck.) I *had* technically seen him during a meeting with our lawyers, which had become awkward after I insisted that there was no reason for us to meet when we had not both agreed to a divorce. To Adam's credit, he'd had the wherewithal to look sheepish, but then I'd made the mistake of asking him where Jillian was, and his face had turned red. Our lawyers had exchanged knowing looks and rushed through the rest of the meeting. "Have you?"

"In fact I have," said Rose. "He came for a visit the other day."

I watched a well-fed squirrel chase a smaller squirrel around the base of the oak tree in the yard. "Did he bring his girlfriend?" I hated that I was weak enough to ask this, knowing that against her better judgment Rose would tell me if he had. But I could not stop thinking about Jillian Smith and how she was probably offering up her supple body to my husband at that very moment.

Not that I actually knew what Adam's paramour looked like. Of course, I had Googled her the same day Adam left, but my search had been as confusing as it had been comprehensive. There were half a dozen Jillian Smiths in the greater Chicago area, at least three of whom were around thirty. Two worked fairly close to Adam's office in the West Loop and therefore could have bumped into him at his favorite coffee shop. Was he making sweet love to the curvy blond marketing professional who liked posing for duck-faced pictures with her parents' aging Maltese—or the slim, glamorous public policy advocate who didn't appear to have a social media presence outside of LinkedIn? Did I even want to know?

(Of course I did.)

Rose sighed. "Oh, Maggie." I waited for her to continue, but there was an extended silence on the other end.

"Rose? Are you there?"

"What's that? What were you saying?"

My heart gave a little lurch; Rose was having more and more of these moments lately, and while any one was innocuous enough, their sum total pointed to a future in which she would no longer be fully present. And yet I pushed on, which suggested I was the one whose neurons weren't firing at full speed. "I was asking if Adam brought his girlfriend."

"Now, Maggie, we both *know* he wouldn't dare. You're the mother of my grandchildren. I won't tolerate such impropriety."

I found myself tearing up. "Thank you. That means a lot to me."

"Don't thank me. That's how it's supposed to be."

I wiped my eyes even as my mind wandered back to the elusive Jillian. Yes, it had to be the brunette public policy advocate who had stolen his heart. Although Adam had given up his dream job of being a public defender even before we had children and took on a sizable mortgage in a town with astronomical property taxes, I still thought of him as a Robin Hood at heart. We used to spend hours talking about politics and social justice, though eventually these topics gave way to our children's lives and how to spend our retirement.

But Jillian Smith, Yale BA ('08), Duke MPP ('11), was surely riveted by Adam's fresh, enlightened take on inequality—while Adam was no doubt riveted by her flat stomach and pert breasts, which hung in their original position because she had not birthed two small humans, or so I was assuming. Regardless, I did not need to see Jillian in the flesh to know Adam had no problem getting aroused with her.

The doorbell rang, pulling me out of my mental cave. "Rose? I have to run. I'll call you in a few days," I said, knowing full well she would beat me to it.

"You take care of yourself, Maggie. And come see me soon."

"I will, Rose. Promise."

Linnea, my Realtor, was standing on the porch with a clipboard in hand. Linnea and I weren't friends, per se, but we had known each other for roughly a million years and had survived a particularly brutal stint on the PTO together. She had heard about Adam leaving from every other person in town and offered to do me a favor by charging only half her standard commission on the condition that I leave glowing reviews on a variety of social media platforms, most of which I had never heard of. "Remind me to talk to you about curb appeal," she said by way of a greeting.

"Can't wait," I said as she marched through the door.

The house had to go. We had moved in twenty-four years earlier; it should have been nearly paid off. But we had remortgaged during the early aughts when Adam was setting up his own law practice, and we still had an ample monthly payment. I was employed, but on a part-time basis, balancing the books and doing the odd secretarial task for a local dentist. What I made each month was enough to cover hygienic essentials and groceries—not the ownership and upkeep of a large house. I was receiving temporary support and would get alimony after the divorce was finalized. Moreover, Adam had agreed to pay for my health care premiums through the end of the following calendar year. However, unless I wanted to fork my entire monthly check over to the mortgage company, a much smaller home was in my immediate future.

It's not like I thought I'd die in the place; Adam and I were going to sell after Rose had lived with us for a few years and we were ready to retire, or at least slow down our (i.e., Adam's) pace. But I wasn't ready to rush that plan. Just because Adam was done with our life didn't mean I was.

"The place is spacious, but it's a bit . . . dated," said Linnea as she strolled through the hallway into the dining room.

Our house was one of those brick and aluminum-sided cul-de-sac numbers that was last considered stylish when I was a teenager, which is to say long ago. But it reminded me of the Brady Bunch house, and as the only child of a single mom who usually worked two jobs to make ends meet, that house and its residents had been the stuff of my dreams. Though Adam and I had two children, not six, and I had usually played the role of Alice rather than Carol, our door was always open and our home was happy and full.

Adam hadn't cared about the house itself one way or the other. He wanted it because it was in the right neighborhood and boasted his idea of a perfect yard: immense, partially shaded, and abutting a wooded park where the local kids, including ours, liked to chug beer that had been stolen from various fridges, including ours. When we first moved in, Adam somehow believed that being a partner-track lawyer would still afford him enough free time to play ball with his kids. Instead, I learned to pitch and catch while encouraging our markedly unathletic children to be good sports. By the time Adam opened his own practice and could set his own hours, Zoe and Jack had already lost interest in softball and, to a lesser degree, their father.

I followed Linnea's gaze from the living room, with its worn beige carpet and pale peach walls, to the three-season room, which was decorated with a sagging sofa and a tiled coffee table. She was right, of course.

"Nothing that can't be fixed," said Linnea, sensing my despair. "Rip up the carpet, have a painting crew come in, maybe . . ." Her eyes landed on the tired brown La-Z-Boy we had inherited from Adam's father. Initially I had been certain Adam leaving it behind was a sign he intended to return. (How trusting I was! How tightly I clung to the hope that my husband would recall and uphold the vows he had made before God, a priest, and more than a hundred people, most of whom his parents had invited to our wedding and I have not seen since!) "Buy a few pieces of modern furniture to fill out the place," she finished.

"So you're saying I have to spend money to make money . . . even though I have no money."

Linnea nodded her head vigorously. "Exactly."

~

"Terry," I said to my boss a few days later, "do you think you might give me a raise?"

"Mmm-hmm," he said, staring at an X-ray affixed to a light box. Terry, a.k.a. Terrance Krutcher, DDS, had been looking at the image for so long I suspected he was sleeping with his eyes open, so I didn't feel bad about interrupting him.

"Really?" I said, rising from my chair. Terry had set me up at a small desk in the back of the office where he reviewed X-rays and stored molding materials for night guards and the like. That I was not given a more sanitary workstation or permission to work at home should have been the first clue I was not going to get more money out of him, but I was trying to utilize the last shred of optimism I had left. After all, since I was the bookkeeper, I knew Terry paid the cleaner the same amount he paid me.

"Mmm-hmm," he said again.

"Thank you so much. Two more dollars an hour would make a big difference. I promise I'll make it worth your while."

Now he spun around to face me. "Oh. Oh my. I'm sorry, Maggie, I thought we were discussing something else," he said, peering at me over his bifocals. "My budget is set in stone for now. I could give you, say, an extra half an hour of work every week if it might help."

An extra six dollars a week would buy me two-thirds of a glass of wine at the Italian place Gita and I liked to go to. "I see. Even though I'm now managing credit card payments and helping Chrissy?" I said, referring to the receptionist, who was the sort of wickless candle that mistook herself for a hundred-watt bulb.

"I'm sorry, Maggie; it's not personal. If money's an issue, you could try Craigslist," he said, turning back to the light box. He retrieved the X-ray and started for the door. "I'm told there are lots of positions for seasoned bookkeepers," he called over his shoulder. "Not that I want you to quit, you understand, but I would be happy to serve as a reference for you if you got another part-time position, provided you weren't going to work at a competitor and it didn't infringe on your time here."

"Thanks," I mumbled, but Terry was already gone.

I didn't *have* to work there. In addition to my QuickBooks wizardry, I had a master's degree in social work, a field that paid better and was infinitely more interesting than dental billing. But I had left social work in the early nineties after one of my clients, coming down from a two-day high, held a knife to my neck and demanded I give him everything I had, including the pink plastic bracelet that had been Zoe's Mother's Day present to me. I complied, but not before the man left a shallow cut several centimeters from my jugular. I was pregnant with Jack at the time. With Adam's support, I quit the same day. As much as I loved my job, it wasn't worth my life.

Initially I assumed I would find a safer social work position, or perhaps pursue a related career once Jack and Zoe were both in school full-time. But someone needed to be home for sick days and to let the repairmen in; someone had to stock the fridge and shuttle the kids from one activity to the next, and it sure wasn't going to be Adam. Our family could have made do if I had returned to work, but Adam liked me being home, and I liked being needed by the people who mattered to me most.

The position at the dental office was mostly a way to bring in some extra money for retirement while occupying my time after Jack went to college. I was well organized and good at math, and compared to helping recovering addicts get their children out of foster care, bookkeeping was a cinch.

It was also riveting as watching cement set. But as I stared at the 3-D model of a jaw that had been discarded at the end of my desk, I realized I would rather be at the office than at the house. At least I had been able to preserve one small aspect of my preseparation life.

~

When I got home that evening, I wandered from one room to the next, admiring what Adam and I had built together. It may have been a little outdated, but every paint color, piece of furniture, and knickknack had been our choice—and I, for one, still loved it. When I was finished with my tour, I poured myself a teeming glass of tempranillo, drank the entire thing while standing at the kitchen counter, and served myself another because no one was there to judge me.

It had been six months since Adam left, and his absence still felt like one of the legs of the chair I was sitting on had broken off. I was just barely managing to balance, but selling the house or giving Terry the heave-ho would be like yanking out another leg, at which point I was sure to find myself on the floor.

Yes, I thought as I drained my second glass of wine, I would find a way to hold on to the house, at least for the time being. I would keep going to work and calling Rose and, when need be, crying over drinks with Gita.

Adam may have wanted something different. But the last thing I needed was another change.

FOUR

I have always loved Thanksgiving, the way it involves neither religion nor wrapping paper, and for nearly two decades Adam and I had hosted dinner for our extended family and anyone else who wanted to swing by with a side dish. Adam was a lousy cook but a good companion, and he would stand beside me all day long, slicing and dicing like a sous-chef with two left hands and slipping me an occasional glass of wine if I started to stress.

Gita told me I should come to her house this year. "You can bring the kids, and even Rose if you want," she said. I laughed and said I was too much of a creature of habit to give up my beloved holiday ritual, but in fact I was dead serious. I had no intention of breaking our family tradition.

"I'm calling about Thanksgiving," I told Zoe one evening at the beginning of November. I had waited until nine to phone her, and this had resulted in her actually answering for a change.

"Yeah, about that," she said. "Jack and I talked, and we thought maybe you could come to New York, just this one time. The three of us could do something at my apartment, or we could even go out. There's a French place around the corner from my apartment that does a nice prix fixe dinner."

Bad enough that I would have to plaster on a smile while Adam was eating another woman's pumpkin pie. But trade my turkey for a stranger's coq au vin? I would rather starve. "That's very sweet, love, but I was still planning on you and Jack coming home."

"We haven't bought tickets, though . . ."

"Well, you better hop on that tonight, because they'll be more expensive every hour that you wait. I can't promise it won't be strange here without your father, but it'll be a chance for us to spend time together and for you to sort through some of your things in case I do have to sell the house." I sniffed; my lawyer told me there was a distinct possibility that the court would compel me to sell the home where my children had thrown epic fits and attempted to murder each other.

"Mom, have you been drinking?" asked Zoe.

"Why on God's green earth would you ask such a ridiculous question?" I closed one eye to assess the volume of the bottle of pinot noir before me on the kitchen counter. It was practically half-full; could I not call my own daughter without being harassed?

"I wouldn't blame you if you were. I just—"

"Want to chastise me? Yes, Zoe. I am aware."

"No, *Mom*," she said, using the exact tone Adam used when he made *Maggie* sound like a curse word. "I'm just worried about you. You don't have to act like this isn't hurting you."

"I think you'd be better off worrying about the white collar criminals you're wasting your energy representing."

"That's not very nice."

It wasn't, and that's because it was true. When Zoe was little she preferred doing whatever I was doing to playdates with her friends. But by high school she had become prickly, as though I, Mom-God, had personally devised each of her problems. She no longer erupted in hormone-fueled rages, but her laser focus on her career made it difficult for us to see eye to eye; I simply could not understand how my brilliant daughter could funnel her intelligence into the dark art of corporate law. Even Adam, who ended up as a tort lawyer like his father before him, felt there was something ethically sticky about Zoe defending pharmaceutical companies' price-gouging practices.

I sighed. "I'm sorry."

"Just because I don't make the choices you made doesn't mean mine are bad. You don't hear me criticizing you for giving up your career for Dad."

"Zoe Halfmoon Harris, that is both unkind and untrue. I did it for all of us—and I for one don't regret it."

"Sorry. I didn't mean anything," she said, and although she sounded apologetic, we both knew she did indeed mean every word. In third grade, Zoe announced that she thought it was "weird" that I didn't have a job like some of her friends' mothers. Little had changed over the years; she seemed unable to comprehend that willfully derailing oneself from a career-oriented track was not synonymous with being incompetent, unconfident, and unfulfilled. It was true that I found bookkeeping largely thankless, but until Adam left, I had loved my day-to-day life—not just the domestic minutiae, but the flexibility to drop everything and have lunch with Adam, or fly out to see the kids in New York, or run Rose to the doctor. Most of my hours were my family's, which was how I liked it.

"So about Thanksgiving—"

"What about Dad?" Zoe interjected.

The wine I had just sipped made a wrong turn in my throat, and I sputtered. When I could speak again I said, "What about him?"

"Well, is Grandma Rose going to come over?"

"Yes," I said. While Adam's brother, Rick, and his wife, Heather, had declined my invitation, Rose said she would be there, with or without Adam. "What does that have to do with your father?"

"It's just—well, it's going to be weird without him. I talked to him about it, and he sounded pretty blue about being alone."

Was he? Good. I wasn't sure why Adam wouldn't be with Jillian—she was probably celebrating with her family, who didn't know about her home-wrecking ways—but I was glad his lousy decisions were not leaving him unscathed. "I hope you're not suggesting that you're going to have dinner with him instead of me," I said, more sharply than I had intended.

"Hey," said Zoe. "I'm not the enemy here."

I refilled my glass. "No, you're not." Then I took a drink of wine, even though the room was starting to tilt ever so slightly.

That was when it came to me. On the advice of Gita and my lawyer, I was trying not to reach out to Adam. I had largely succeeded. But once in a while I gave in to my impulse to try to convince him to come back and called him. He mostly ignored me. One time, though, he picked up. "Our lawyers told us not to talk," he said before I could even say hello. "You're not going to convince me to change my mind, so please stop calling."

I remember thinking that he sounded like someone I barely knew. A stranger, even. It was too easy to be cold and callous over the phone; Adam had told me this very thing when explaining why lawyers screamed at each other during conference calls only to laugh together later over drinks. Face-to-face, it's hard to pretend the other person isn't a human being.

And face-to-face, Adam couldn't possibly pretend I wasn't still his wife and the mother of his children. After all, that was the whole reason he was steering clear of me—wasn't it? To fool himself into thinking he hadn't wreaked catastrophic damage on our family? To ignore the truth lurking in his heart, which was that he had left behind the best thing he had ever had?

"Do you know if your father is planning to have dinner with his girlfriend?" I asked Zoe.

"Of course not, Mom," she said, more gently this time. "You know he never even mentions her."

"I'm very glad to hear that." I dabbed my eyes. "As it happens, I just had a fantastic idea. Please ask your father to join us for Thanksgiving, even if it's just for dessert. I'll ask Jack to ask him, too. We can celebrate as a *family*, just one last time."

"I really don't think that's a good plan, Mom."

"It's not like your father and I are on bad terms." We were on no terms at all, really, but that was beside the point.

"That's not—"

"Please, Zoe. I need normal this year. I know it won't be completely normal, but it's almost as good. If you and Jack tell your father this is what you want, he'll agree."

She sighed. "Fine. But I'm on record as thinking this is a bad idea."

"Oh, Zo-bear, you're the best. Thank you. This really means a lot to me."

"It's okay." She paused. "Mom?"

"Yes?"

"Take care of yourself, okay?"

I promised her I would. Then I kept my promise by pouring myself a tall glass of water to try to minimize the hangover I would inevitably suffer the following day and offset at least a bit of liver damage. As I sipped it, I thought about how Adam could barely look at me when he told me he wasn't in love with me anymore. He probably couldn't stand to see the way he was hurting me—or admit that he might be wrong. Oh, Adam. As much as I didn't envy myself, my heart ached for him. What was he going through, to have dug his heels in after making such a shortsighted decision?

To be clear, if I had discovered he had cheated on me and concealed it in order to preserve our marriage, it would have destroyed me. I would have tried to forgive him, though it probably would have taken us years to repair our bond. But for him to *leave* me for someone else—well, that meant that he was in so much pain that he was willing to go to the most drastic extreme to feel better. Surely hitting fifty had taken a toll on his ego, but maybe he, like I, was bereft over our children leaving home. Or perhaps decades of a financially rewarding but psychologically unfulfilling job had finally gotten to him. He himself had claimed he wanted a new life.

I couldn't remember if it was the Dalai Lama or Oprah who had said it, but the first step to healing was radical honesty. Yes, yes, it was. I drank some more water, even though I could hear all that liquid sloshing around in my stomach, feeling more hopeful than I had in months.

Maybe if I could help Adam face the facts—and by the facts, I meant me—he would finally see that an old wife and a new life were not mutually exclusive.

FIVE

After graduation, Adam went to Notre Dame for law school. I headed to Chicago, where Adam had grown up and where we intended to settle down, to get my master's in social work. We managed to spend most weekends together and generally regarded the difficulty of being apart as a requirement for the future we were building. My graduate program was a year shorter than Adam's, but rather than joining him in Indiana, I decorated our apartment, took a position as a caseworker for the state of Illinois, and continued to visit Adam when I was able. Two weeks after he received his law degree, we were married.

As much as I relished being Adam's girlfriend, being his wife was worlds better. He worked long hours and I usually did, too, and in retrospect I wonder if that didn't make the time we had together that much more charged; those early years, we made love whenever we had an opportunity or could create one. We traveled—to California and Spain and small towns up and down Michigan's west coast—and went to parties and friends' weddings, spent time with our families, and talked and talked and talked. I had never thought of myself as much of a conversationalist; more often than not, when I opened my mouth a random worry would pop out, branding me as a pessimist (which I was, but I didn't want *others* to know that).

It was different with Adam. Politics, pop culture, our families, the many wonderful and unpredictable facets of life—we discussed it all at length. Adam saw my cynicism and anxiety as signs of an intelligent mind. Maybe because of that, I soon stopped worrying about how I was coming off and got used to the idea that some people simply weren't for me.

Just when I thought things were as good as they ever would be for us, Adam said, "Maggie, I want to start a family the second you're ready"—and so we did. I had Zoe when I was twenty-six, and Jack just before I turned twenty-nine. I was under no illusion motherhood would be easy, even though I wasn't a single parent like my own mother. And indeed there is a several-year period that is mostly a blur in my mind, punctuated by the occasional memory of a first word or trip to the emergency room.

Oh, but my thirties were glorious. I emerged from days of dirty diapers and sleepless nights a competent, fulfilled caregiver to two smart little humans who loved and needed me more than anyone in the world. I don't have many photographs of myself from those years; mostly I was the one on the other end of the camera, documenting soccer games and holiday parties and vacations at the lake house we rented for a week each summer. In the few pictures I'm in, though, I'm not being vain when I say I looked as good as I ever had or would again. Beyond the fact that I was slender and in my sexual prime, there is simply a glow you take on when you're happy about where you're at in life.

Sadly, there was no serum or surgery that would transport me back to that time. But I *could* take a cue from whichever Jillian Smith was sleeping with my husband (I was certain it was the public policy advocate, but was attempting to keep an open mind) and begin taking better care of myself. As long as Adam and I were still married, there was a chance for us to stay that way. And if I was going to make a go at salvaging our relationship, I would have to give it my all.

~

"I can't see Adam looking like this," I told Gita. We had just returned from a brisk evening walk around our neighborhood. I wasn't a fan of vigorous exercise, but Gita swore sweating had kept her from falling through depression's trapdoor during a terrible breakup she went through before meeting Reddy. I was fairly certain I had already survived the worst of my separation, what with the doughnut aversion and spontaneous sobbing, and that my return to crullers and cabernet was proof I was on the other side. Gita remained unconvinced.

She regarded me from across her kitchen island. "You do need your roots touched up, but give me an hour and I'll give you a full month of good hair." (In addition to being my closest friend, Gita owned a salon and was my colorist.)

"Har har."

"If we're being serious," she said, pushing the glass of wine she had just poured for me across the granite counter, "I would argue that you shouldn't see Adam—period."

The wine was crisp and dry, and made me feel slightly less bitter about exercise. "Well, I am, so I think you should be a little more supportive."

Gita walked around the island, took the glass from my hands, and set it on the counter. Then she hugged me. "Oh, Maggie, don't be such a toad," she said, and I let out a reluctant croak. "I'm so supportive it's ridiculous. I just wonder, what are you trying to accomplish, being in the same small space with the man you're trying to get over?"

I wasn't trying to get over anything; I was trying to get my life back. But this was my secret to carry. Even my closest friend in the world could not understand that the void within me was one only Adam could fill.

When I didn't answer, Gita added, "You don't even know if he'll come, do you?"

I shrugged. "Jack said he said he would consider it." When my son told me this, I hopped around the kitchen triumphantly, more buoyant than I had been since before Adam had left. He would not have considered coming to dinner if there weren't still a chance our relationship could reverse course. "So I'd like to look at least semidecent. I'm not expecting miracles, but this," I said, motioning to my lint-covered t-shirt, "won't do."

Her face lit up. "Nothing a trip to Nordstrom can't fix."

"You know how I feel about shopping."

"I do, but a department store is preferable to dragging yourself from store to store in the mall. And Nordstrom carries sizes for real women."

"As opposed to the fake kind who fit into clothing between the sizes of subzero and twelve."

"They have a plus-size department and a great petites section," said Gita in a voice that told me I was not to insult her favorite pastime.

"So helpful of them to categorize women by body type."

"Toady, stop being so cynical and trust me. You could use a pick-me-up, and you probably need to go down a size, too."

I glanced at my waist. It was true; for the first time since perimenopause, my clothes were loose. "Go buy some outfits that make you feel good about yourself," insisted Gita.

But my goal wasn't to feel good about myself; it was to make *Adam* feel good about me. He had the body fat of a professional athlete and a full head of hair. He was well groomed, wore nice clothing, and saw the dentist every six months. I, too, had good teeth and was not balding—but that's roughly where the commonalities ended. I had not taken particularly good care of myself over the years, and it wasn't like I could get a free pass by wearing a pin that said, *I look like this because I have been caring for everyone else.*

I understood that tearing off my apron to reveal a slinky black dress would not be enough to make my husband fall in love with me again. But as his affair with one Jillian Smith had demonstrated, he preferred the company of a woman who tended to herself. On that front, I had my work cut out for me.

~

Gita offered to help me shop, but her work schedule didn't sync with mine until after Thanksgiving—which was how I found myself standing in the center of a sea of garments alone. I felt dizzy: So many colors! So many styles! So much mental energy required to choose items that were flattering, fashionable, and age appropriate!

I fingered a crisp white blouse. It was a welcome contrast to the black shirts overpopulating my closet. But I could locate every size but my own, which would prove to be the case with the next half-dozen shirts I selected.

At last I spotted a billowing purple blouse with a small flower pattern. It had a bohemian garden-party vibe, though I'm not sure the manufacturer would have described it that way, and it came in my size. I eyed the tag sewn in the back of the shirt. Viscose? Wasn't that a fancy name for thread spun from petroleum by-products? Whatever it was, I could not justify spending a full week's wages on fabric of an indeterminate origin.

I looked around, frustrated and frazzled; I could feel my blood sugar starting to dip to a level that would send me straight into the arms of the devil (that is, Cinnabon). With relief, I located a protein bar in my purse and broke off a large piece, which I popped in my mouth.

"Can I help you?" asked a saleswoman, approaching from behind. She was several decades younger than I was and wore a thin smile that said her mind was somewhere else entirely.

"Ywesth," I said through a mouthful of chocolate-flavored cardboard.

"Great! Well, let me know if you need anything," she said, and disappeared as quickly as she had surfaced.

I said yes! I glanced around with the wild eyes of a child whose mother has just gone missing. What now? I was about to go into full-on meltdown mode when I spotted another salesperson, this one also young but male. "Yoo-hoo!" I called, and then cringed because Zoe said I sounded *so old* when I said that. "Excuse me!"

I swear the salesman's head twitched in my direction. But rather than turning around, he glanced down at something—probably his phone—and started striding toward the other side of the store.

Big mistake: I was not going to waste my time or money in a place where I had been deemed nonexistent. There must be one or two semi-nice items hanging in my closet that I could wear to Thanksgiving dinner.

The nearest exit was just past the makeup counters, which I usually sprinted past in order to avoid aggressive perfume spritzing. I was gearing up to do my best Jackie Joyner-Kersee when a woman wearing a pink smock smiled at me. Maybe because she wasn't armed with a malodorous bottle, I found myself smiling back.

"You have fantastic eyes," she said. "Any interest in trying our new Bare Naked Bombshell mascara? It would make them pop even more." My skepticism must have been obvious because she added, "The name is silly, I know, but the product itself works wonders. Look," she said, motioning to her own eyes. "Normally my lashes are so short and pale you can't tell they're there."

I wasn't into makeup, but Gita, who knew about these things, said it was a shortcut to confidence. Prior to my separation I wasn't necessarily lacking in confidence. True, I didn't like the way the skin above my eyes had begun to sag, nor the ever-deepening fault line in my forehead—but when I caught myself being self-critical, I redirected my thoughts to more pressing matters, like my mother-in-law's failing health. Now I felt less certain about my priorities. Even if Adam had mostly been motivated by his own internal struggles, I couldn't help but wonder about the role my appearance had played in his deciding to pack that last suitcase and go.

"Okay," I said, regarding the woman's eyelashes, which had to be falsies. "I'll try it."

She clapped her hands together. "Fantastic! Let me take you to my station."

I followed behind her and sat on a high stool as she pulled various pots and palettes from a set of drawers beneath a makeup display.

"Just mascara, right?" I said, looking at the array of makeup she had retrieved.

"Well . . . I would love to try our Breakaway concealer and foundation on you, and maybe a sweep of First Crush Baby blush and a tiny bit of the Barely Believable eye shadow trio. And just a hint of Come Hither gloss. I think you'll really love how natural it all looks. But it's completely up to you." She stared at me with big, hopeful eyes.

I sighed. It was a shame that putting on a bold face meant covering it with chemicals. "Let's have it."

She worked remarkably fast; it could not have been more than seven minutes later when she held a mirror in front of my face. "Well? What do you think?"

What I thought was that my wrinkles were no longer the first thing I noticed. The brown sunspots Adam used to call freckles were hidden beneath a layer of Spackle that was the exact color of my skin. My cheeks were flushed like I had just emerged from a windstorm or a roll in the hay. And my eyes? They were enormous.

Best of all, I still looked like myself—only better.

"I'm impressed," I said slowly.

"But?"

"But it seems like an awful lot of makeup. I don't know if I'm the kind of woman who uses a dozen different products just to face the world."

"I only used six, but even if it were triple that, is that really so bad? It's no one's business how much makeup a woman wears. The point is to make you feel good about yourself, not make other people feel good about how you look. Though you know, you don't really *need* makeup—you're gorgeous." She smiled at me. "From the look you're giving me, I'm guessing it may have been a while since someone told you that."

When was the last time Adam had paid me a true compliment? I couldn't remember. My throat tightened, making it impossible to speak.

"Don't worry, the Bombshell mascara is waterproof," the woman said kindly, and handed me a tissue.

"Thank you," I said, dabbing at the corners of my eyes. "That's very nice of you. Though doesn't you saying nice things about my makeup-free face hurt your sales quota?"

She laughed. "Yeah, it occasionally takes a toll. By the way, I'm Dionne."

"Maggie," I told her. "Dionne, do you think you could help me pick out only the most important items? I'm on a bit of a budget."

Before leaving the department store, I told Dionne about my miserable shopping experience. She confessed that she did the majority of her shopping online. "Your bedroom is the only dressing room you should ever use," she whispered. "I read reviews to see how things fit, stick to styles that look good on me, even when they're not on-trend, and return everything that doesn't work. Make sure you go through your wardrobe first so you don't end up with fourteen pairs of identical pants."

When I got home, I rifled through my clothes. I had never been interested in fashion, but I used to put more of an effort into looking put together. I wasn't sure when that had stopped being true, but judging from the contents of my closet, which I had mostly accumulated during the past ten years, I had approached my children leaving for college like a Victorian-era widow in mourning. Here was a black sweater that made me look like a charred sausage; there was a black cardigan that pilled the minute I put it on. Both of my go-to black t-shirts were worn out, and the yoga pants I wore most days sagged in the rear and had faded to a dingy gray. Almost everything was dark and joyless, and not a single piece of it played up my backside or long legs, which were the two parts of my body I truly took pride in.

At the end of the funeral procession that was my closet, I spotted a soft pink button-down I had bought around the dawn of the new millennium. I had worn that shirt to dinner with Adam, to PTO meetings, and any other time I wanted to feel good about myself. That was, until Adam told me offhandedly he didn't really like pink. Green, yes, blue, definitely, and black and white, he said when I pressed, were always a safe bet. He wasn't trying to be unkind. But I had already been wearing that shirt for several years when he admitted he didn't care for pink, and I was crushed, because I didn't want to wear something my husband disliked.

Well, the pink shirt still fit, and while it was well worn, I happened to like it. I left it and my least offensive garments on their hangers and threw everything else in a pile to be donated. Then I went online to look for new clothes.

Our savings account was off-limits until Adam and I finalized our financial agreement, and my checking account had just been depleted by my trip to the makeup counter. I hated to use a credit card—my mother always told me not to spend money I didn't have, and this advice had served me well. But these were drastic times, so I reluctantly pulled out my plastic to buy a couple of blouses, a pair of slacks, a blue dress in a forgiving jersey knit, and two pairs of jeans. None of these items screamed, "Look at me!" But even if Adam were wild about leopard print and plunging necklines—and I could no longer say for sure that he wasn't—my goal was not to be screamingly visible.

No, if all went as planned, these tasteful separates would call to mind my wardrobe from decades past, which would in turn remind Adam of the woman he had fallen in love with.

Except . . . what if it didn't work? What if Adam really had found the fountain of youth in the arms of a younger woman? No dress or tube of lip gloss would help me compete with that.

My mother had told me I'd be a fool to let Adam go. But as I closed my computer, I found myself considering the distinct and all-too-real possibility that I would not be making a winning touchdown in what very well may be the last seven seconds of my marriage.

And then what? What if I really did have to sell the house, start my life over as a divorcée, and subject myself to the horrors of dating, knowing that even the Adams of the world were not immune to the siren song of fresh tail?

I left my computer on the bed and walked to the kitchen to retrieve a bottle of pinot grigio from the fridge. After uncorking the bottle, I served myself a generous pour. But as I began lifting the glass to my lips, one word rang through me:

No.

As I stared into the straw-colored pool of delight mere inches from my mouth, there it was again: *No.*

Wine would relax me, but for once I didn't want to relax. What if my anxiety was trying to tell me something? (Wasn't that what I had always argued when Adam told me I worried too much—that worry was an evolution-honed defense mechanism that kept our entire family alive and well?) What if my pain actually served a purpose, and soaking it in thirteen percent ethyl alcohol would keep me from ever finding out what that purpose was? How many cocktails and glasses of cabernet sauvignon had washed down disappointment before I had a chance to taste it? And anger and sadness and shame—and at what cost? After seven months of numbing my worst feelings, I was ready to feel them, even the ones that made it seem like life was nothing but a big fat cosmic joke.

And the thing was, I knew better. I did. Unlike Adam's father's funeral, which was recent enough to still be archived as a short film in my mind, I barely remembered my mother's memorial service. I was just thirty-four then, but it wasn't time that faded the details. It was that my head was somewhere else entirely (and not because I was drinking).

I simply pretended what was happening wasn't, really. I must have secretly believed that denial would allow me to slip from one reality—in which my mother was gone, in the most permanent sense of the word—into a more tolerable world.

Of that day, I did remember the newly budding trees through the window of a church I had never been in before. I remembered the tiny pink flowers on Zoe's spring dress and being irrationally upset when she smeared chocolate on its smock during the luncheon following the service. I remembered staring at Adam's fingers woven through mine, and his gold wedding band, which I had chosen for him. Notice I do not mention the sorrow. Because though it was there, lurking beneath the surface, I was determined to power through it. After all, I had small children to care for; I had a husband whose employer demanded sixty hours of his time each week. I could not afford to luxuriate in my sadness, or so it seemed.

Grief came back for me, as it will. Six months after my mother died, woe rose from the ground on what would have been her fifty-fifth birthday. A year later it twisted my stomach when I reached for the phone to call her, only to remember she was no longer among the living. Even years after her passing, grief stabbed me while I was in the midst of mundane acts, like tucking Jack in at night or trimming Zoe's hair, as my mother had done for me. My mother's death taught me that when you think you are bypassing heartache, all you're really doing is borrowing happiness from another day.

Yet there I was, trying to drown my separation in wine. I regarded my glass one more time and emptied it into the kitchen sink. As the pinot grigio disappeared down the drain, leaving only the sharp fragrance of Italian grapes in its wake, I found myself thinking that in spite of my makeup and new clothes, this may have been the first sign that a newly improved Maggie was beginning to rise from the ashes.

SIX

"Mom, you okay?" Zoe asked. It was the evening before Thanksgiving, and she had arrived home a few hours earlier. Now she was at the dining room table, sorting through a box of her old photographs and yearbooks that I had retrieved from the basement. Jack had flown in with her but opted to spend the night at Adam's apartment so Adam wouldn't feel too alone. I was not thrilled about this—if anyone was too alone, it was *moi*—but I bit my tongue; the last thing I wanted was for the kids to join me in counting tallies on my separation scorecard. Anyway, maybe Jack would be able to help ensure Adam showed up for dinner.

"I'm fine," I told Zoe, pushing my lips into a smile as an invisible vise threatened to crush my temples. Normally I would have marinated my worries with wine, but I hadn't had a drink in two weeks. It was hard—harder than I had thought it would be, even though I was more alert when I was awake and better able to sleep through the night. But it took a long time to actually *fall* asleep with so many sober, anxious thoughts floating through my mind, and a mug of tea just didn't symbolize that I had made it through another day the way a glass of wine did. Yet I stuck with it, because with every day that I allowed myself to wade in the flood of emotions that seemed to come from not drinking, I grew a little stronger and surer.

"You look a little nervous," said Zoe, looking up from the photo she was holding.

"Well, I'm not!"

"Okay, Mom," she said, as if I were the child. "But it's not too late to change plans. We could have dinner with just us, and then Jack and I could see Dad the next day."

"Grandma Rose is coming here, though," I said.

"And she still can. That doesn't mean Dad has to be here." With her brown hair in a knot on top of her head and her long legs folded like a pretzel, Zoe looked more like a dancer than a lawyer. She narrowed her eyes. "Please tell me this isn't about you getting back together with Dad."

I sighed and sat across from her. "Yes? No? I'm not sure, Zoe. You know I still love your father very much."

Her face softened, and she handed me a photo. "That doesn't mean you should take him back."

"You'd really rather see us divorced than me forgive him?" I asked, staring at the photo. In it, Zoe and Jack were floating on inner tubes at the lake where we had vacationed each summer; they must have been about nine and twelve at the time.

"I guess not," she admitted. "But I don't like what he did to you."

"That makes two of us. But as of right now, it's all conjecture on both our parts. Anyway, the whole point of this is to have at least one more Thanksgiving with all four of us together."

"Fair enough." She took the photo from me and put it back into the box. Then she stood. "I hate to say it, but I need to squeeze in an hour of work."

"The night before Thanksgiving?" I saw my daughter a total of five days out of any given year. Maybe fewer now that she was a practicing lawyer.

She pulled at her topknot. "I have to comb through a bunch of files so I can answer a complaint for a partner Friday morning. Come on, Mom. Don't look at me like that. I won't be the grunt forever. In another six months there will be new associates to field the worst of it." Her phone began vibrating on the table. She picked it up, skimmed the text, and stuck it in the back pocket of her jeans. "See? Even tonight, there's more to do. But I'll be back down in a bit, and we can brine the turkey or bake pies or whatever."

I was already done with the prep work, and I doubted Zoe would be finished with her files anytime soon. But she was home, and that was what I had wanted. "Okay, sweetheart."

She bent to kiss my cheek. "Thanks for understanding. I thought for sure you were going to make a comment."

"Me? Never," I said, arching my eyebrows exaggeratedly.

She laughed and I joined her, grateful that this hadn't turned into an argument.

Zoe paused at the doorway. "Hey, Mom?"

"Yeah, Zoe?"

She smiled. "It's nice to be home."

After she went up to her old room, I lay on the sofa, thinking about how I would see Adam in less than twelve hours. It would be our first encounter since the awkward meeting with our lawyers at the end of the summer. The contours of his body were as familiar as my own; his voice was the soundtrack of my life. But as I stared up at a hairline crack in the ceiling, I let myself acknowledge—just for a moment—that I no longer knew the thoughts that were rattling around in his head, if I ever had at all. It was almost impossible to anticipate what the next day would bring. And that was enough to make me wonder whether I was making a colossal mistake.

~

The next thing I knew, it was morning and Zoe was standing at the foot of the sofa. "Morning, Mom," she said.

"Oh my word," I said, sitting straight up. I must have fretted myself right into unconsciousness. "I'm so sorry. We were supposed to hang out when you were done with work."

"Don't be sorry." Zoe handed me a mug of coffee, then turned on the television and plopped down on the other end of the sofa. "I figured you were pretty exhausted, so I put a blanket over you and left you there. I almost didn't wake you this morning, but I thought you'd want to catch some of the parade." Watching the parade was what we had always done, even after the kids got older. "You feeling okay?"

Aside from cottonmouth and an ominous, unspecific feeling of dread, I felt fantastic. "Yes, and thank you for doing that." I noted that Zoe was clad in workout wear, and judging from her flushed face and damp ponytail, had already gone for a run. Oh, to be young again.

"Good." She stretched out her leg and touched my thigh with her socked foot. "I got some bagels. You want one?"

Any other year I would have been the one to wake early and prepare breakfast. Just last Thanksgiving all four of us squeezed together on the sofa with coffee and the everything-but-the-kitchen-sink muffins the kids loved so we could watch the Macy's floats and bicker about whether the musical acts were a waste (Jack and I agreed they had to go, whereas Adam and Zoe felt they were cheesy but a necessary tradition). But I would not let myself wallow in nostalgia. I needed to show Adam that the past had passed and we could still start fresh, together. "Bagels sound wonderful," I told Zoe.

~

Jack came loping through the front door just after four. "Mom!" he said, pulling me in for a hug, and although I was pretty sure I smelled marijuana on him, what could I do but embrace my child?

Rose teetered in behind him in kitten heels and a tweed pantsuit. "Maggie, love," she said, letting me take her by the arm. "So happy to see you."

"Glad to see you, too, Rose," I said as I looked past her. There was no sign of Adam. "What can I get you to drink?" I asked as I guided her into the living room.

She sat gingerly on the edge of the sofa. Even at eighty, she could still wrap one thin leg around the other and tuck her ankle behind her opposite foot. "A little brandy, if you have it."

"Of course." Adam had left the bar and all its contents behind. Really, other than toiletries, clothing, and the contents of his home office, he had taken almost nothing with him to his new apartment. This seemed to be another indication that he was on a midlife *rumspringa*. I had faith that he would find the wider world, however alluring, ultimately less gratifying than the one he had taken leave of.

I had just walked to the bar when I heard Adam's voice. "Mom?" he said to Rose. "You doing all right?"

I swallowed hard and told myself to stay calm. Adam had cried in my arms when his father died, and I had let his tears pool on my shoulder long after I felt them seeping through my shirt. When he had a life-threatening bout of *E. coli*, I managed to get him off the toilet and to the hospital. And when he accidentally sent a disparaging email about a client to said client—severing a major, much-needed deal in the process—it was me he turned to for assurance that he was neither the first nor the worst person to make such a mistake. I knew just how human he was; there was no reason to be nervous about seeing him.

But then he appeared in the doorway, and every nerve in my body began to tremble. He was dressed in a deep purple dress shirt I had never seen before and a pair of gray wool slacks. Though the summer tan he'd had when I last saw him was long gone and he looked tired, he was as handsome as he had ever been. When his clear green eyes met mine, I wasn't sure my knees wouldn't let out.

"Hello, Maggie," he said. He leaned forward to kiss my cheek, and I held my breath as his lips brushed my skin. "Happy Thanksgiving."

"Happy Thanksgiving," I said. I could feel Jack and Rose staring at us. "Thank you for coming."

"You look nice," he said.

I glanced at my navy dress, which was suddenly worth every dollar of credit card debt. "Thank you."

"How have you been?" he asked.

"Fine." I could feel myself flushing; this felt almost like a first date. Or, say, an awkward run-in with an ex, though I quickly banished this thought. But Adam didn't seem unhappy to be here—and that was not nothing. "You?"

Before he could respond, Zoe appeared from the kitchen and ran over to hug him.

"Hey, sweetheart," he said, and if I wasn't mistaken, he sounded choked up. Yes, this was what I wanted: for him to have a gut-punch emotional response to being with his whole family again.

"Glad you're here, Dad," Zoe said. "Do you want a drink? Scotch on the rocks?"

"Sure. Thank you," said Adam. He looked around the living room. I wondered if he was taking in how little had changed since he had last been here.

"Mom, a glass of wine?" Zoe asked.

"I'm fine," I said, even though a glass of wine sounded better than a bag full of money.

"Maggie," said Adam, nodding toward the dining room, "a minute of your time?"

Like I could say no. I nodded and followed him into the room, where we stood in front of the windows. Winter had arrived early, and the ground outside was dusted with snow. I decided to be proactive and start the conversation. "Thank you for coming today."

He continued to look out the window as he responded. "I'm not sure what your motivation was in inviting me. It's going to be harder for the kids if we act like things are back to normal before we divorce."

But we weren't *going* to divorce. He just didn't realize that yet.

"You're here," I said. The space between my breasts was getting swampy. "Which suggests you didn't think it was the worst idea."

"I'm here because the kids and my mother strong-armed me into it," he said so evenly he could have been delivering a weather report.

"I wanted a chance for the four of us to be together—just for one more holiday. Could you give me that?"

"I—" he said, but just then Zoe appeared.

"I come bearing gifts," she said, handing me a glass of wine, even though I had declined, and Adam a tumbler with a generous pour of amber liquid. "Jack and I are putting the food on the table. Join us in a minute?"

We nodded and smiled at her as if to say, *See honey? Everything is just fine.* Then we looked at each other, our smiles already flatlined.

"Adam," I said, just as he said, "Maggie."

I swear I saw a new smile form on his lips—normally this was when I jokingly called him *Maggie* and he called me *Adam*—but it was gone as soon as it had appeared. "You go," he said.

"No, you."

He sighed. "Let's just make the most of dinner, okay? We're all here together now, so let's do our best to enjoy it."

Yes, let's. Let's enjoy it so much that you remember this wonderful thing you have and realize you can't just give it up. "That was the whole reason I did this in the first place," I said quietly, still holding the glass of wine I had no intention of drinking. It would have been so easy to take a sip, but I needed the extra fortitude that would come from surviving this night without my go-to anxiety aid.

Adam gave me a strange, unreadable look and headed back into the living room.

~

Rose seemed to be having a good night. Over appetizers, she told us a story about how she had once served half-cooked chicken to her late husband Richard and his boss, and both men had either not noticed or decided to eat it anyway. As she chatted, I picked at a bacon-wrapped date, which I usually ate by the half dozen. Then Zoe told us about a case she was working on. I stole glances at Adam as I pretended to listen. He seemed fine, if a bit stiff, but he joined in the conversation and even addressed me directly a few times.

"Sweetheart, any leads on design jobs?" I asked Jack as we began passing the main dishes around the table. He was wearing a flannel shirt and gray jeans that were tight to the point of being a danger to my unborn grandchildren. Attire aside, at twenty-four he looked so much like me it was uncanny. I sometimes wondered how this had affected the way I parented him. Had I favored Jack because he was my male clone, or had I secretly preferred Zoe because she was the spitting image of her father? Would I ever know, let alone adjust my behavior accordingly?

Jack scrunched up his face. "Oh, I'm, uh—it's kind of on hold. The skate shop just made me assistant manager. They say I can do their graphics, too."

"That's great," I told him, even as dollar signs dove off the side of my mental cliff. Jack had studied design in school and claimed he wanted to work in an ad agency. However, he had mostly held menial jobs since moving to New York more than a year ago, and Adam and I had been subsidizing him since. I thought this hindered his ability to grow up; Adam, however, argued that it was our role as parents to make sure he felt secure enough to take risks. Unfortunately, now that Adam and I were separated, Jack's semi-long-term dependence was a threat to my own financial security. I made a note to tell Adam it was time to reevaluate this plan. "So will you be getting a raise?"

"Um, no. They can't pay me more, but it'll be great exposure."

A person could die of exposure, not that I said this to my beloved son.

"I might even get to run my own store," he continued. "We were going to open a second spot in Williamsburg, but the market's way oversaturated, so now we're looking at Bed-Stuy. It's practically a done deal."

"*Practically* and *done* are at direct odds with each other," said Zoe, who was spooning mashed potatoes onto her plate.

"Guys," Adam warned.

I had just taken a bite of turkey when Jack turned to Adam. "Any news on the job, Dad?"

"Adam?" said Rose. "What's this?"

Adam looked up from his plate. "There's no real job to speak of, so no—no news."

Jack snorted. "Come on, Dad. It's not like you got fired."

I raised my eyebrows. "Adam? Is there something you want to tell me?"

He sighed. "There's not much to tell, to be honest. I'm just not particularly happy with my career, and I want to do some good in the world."

Breaking news this was not; I had been hearing some version of this exact lament since the Reagan era.

"I have an opportunity to start taking on pro bono work for the Innocence Collaboration," said Adam, referring to an organization that advocated on behalf of the wrongfully convicted. "My contact said they're looking for someone like me to join their staff in the fall, so this would be a kind of trial run." Adam had been interested in the project for years—it was exactly the kind of effort he and I both supported, and we had even once discussed creating our own nonprofit to do this sort of work—so I wanted to be happy for him.

And yet I couldn't. Because all I could think was that for all my decades of swearing that we would find a way to make it happen if he wanted to make the leap to a more fulfilling career, another woman had given him the strength to finally jump.

"I thought you were waiting until retirement," I said. He had been saving up for retirement since his first law job, with a goal of retiring at sixty; that way, he reasoned, he would still be young enough to do all the things he had been putting off. Like working for the Innocence Collaboration.

He allowed a small smile to surface. "I think it's a good time for me to try something new."

And how. I glowered at him for making such a terrible Freudian slip when something old was sitting right across from him.

Adam flushed as he realized his gaffe. "Anyway," he added quickly, "it's not going to replace my practice, at least not for now. I'm just going to scale back so I finally have a little free time to pursue other things."

Free time? I had carried the wine Zoe poured me to the table, but had not had any of it. Yet out of instinct I reached for the glass and gripped the stem so tight it was a wonder it didn't snap and slice my fingers open. Adam had been a workaholic as long as I had known him. He studied far more than he needed to in college; in law school, he would have missed his own mother's birthday if it had interfered with a deadline for the law journal. Even though he didn't feel passionately about tort law, he still put in more billable hours than any other lawyer we knew.

I understood that, and I married him anyway. His work ethic reminded me of my mother's—no matter what they were tasked with, they did it thoroughly and well—and it was one of the things I loved best about him. When I felt neglected, I asked him to make time for the kids and me—and he did. But mostly I let him do his thing, because I was not one of those spouses who expected their husband or wife to become someone else as time went on. That, I believed, was a quick-bake recipe for marital strife.

But now Adam was prioritizing free time—no doubt so he could spend at least some of it with Jillian Smith, who was overseeing his new career path.

"People change, Maggie," he said quietly.

I put down my glass and held the edge of the table, certain that I was seconds from stroking out. "Do they?" I said. "Or is that something they tell themselves to feel better?"

"What's for dessert?" asked Zoe with false cheer.

Adam looked at her, relieved. "I brought some chocolates."

"Great. And we have pie, of course." Zoe looked at me. "Mom, want to put coffee on while I get dessert ready?"

"I'll help," said Jack, who stretched his arms over his head but appeared to be in no rush to stand. Then he looked at me. "Mom?" he said quietly, and I understood that he was asking if I was okay.

I wanted to respond, but I was afraid if I opened my mouth something terrible would fly out. I don't know what I had expected. Adam had not argued with me or expressed animosity, which was about as much as I could have asked for. But he remained chilly, and fool that I was, I must have been hoping that seeing me would make him—well, thaw.

Rose suddenly stood from the table. She had only had the one brandy before dinner, but she was wobbling like a Weeble. "Richard," she said to no one in particular, "I'm tired. Could you please take me home?"

Adam gave me a knowing look—this was the very sort of incident that led us to take Rose to a neurologist in the first place—and for a moment it was like nothing had changed. He stood and took her arm. "Dad's not here, Mom," he said gently.

She smoothed an invisible wrinkle in her jacket. "Oh yes, yes, I know that, dear," she said. "You know how I can get."

"It's okay. Would you actually like to go home?"

Ropes of panic began to tighten around me. Adam had barely been here an hour and a half. He couldn't leave now—not when things between us were strained. I needed this night to end on a good note. I needed *us* to end on a good note. Preferably a good thirty to forty years from now, holding hands and lying side by side in bed, our bodies giving up their ghosts at about the same time (I had read this was not uncommon for two people who had spent three-quarters of their lives loving each other).

"I'm afraid I would," said Rose stoically. She turned to me. "Maggie, you've been a gracious host, as ever."

"Thanks, Rose," I said. "I appreciate your coming. Adam—"

I was about to thank him for coming, too, when he turned to Zoe. "Would you and Jack mind taking my car and driving Grandma home?"

Had he just suggested what I thought he had suggested? He actually wanted to spend time with *me*, alone? Maybe he was rethinking things even faster than I had ever allowed myself to dream of.

"I'd be happy to," said Zoe.

"Only if it's not too much trouble," warbled Rose.

Jack put his arm around her. "Of course not, Grandma."

"Great," said Adam. "We'll have dessert when you return. In the meantime, your mother and I can take this opportunity to catch up on a few things." He met my eye and pursed his lips into a sheepish half smile.

I knew this expression well. It was the one Adam made when he realized he had made a mistake and intended to fix it.

SEVEN

"So." Adam was standing in the foyer in front of the framed map of Chicago I had bought for him for his forty-fifth birthday. The map was drawn in 1870, the year before the Great Chicago Fire that reshaped the city, and Adam had said it was the best gift he had ever received. He was a cartophile—that was the word for a map enthusiast, he had told me when we were still dating. I wondered if Jillian, who had probably only ever oriented herself with a GPS, knew this about my husband.

"So," I said quietly. "I'm surprised you stayed."

His pinpoint pupils belied his casual shrug. "We haven't really had a chance to talk."

Not for my lack of trying. "No, we haven't," I said.

"How have you been doing?" he asked, making no indication that he intended to leave the foyer.

Awful, I wanted to say. Worse than after Jack had officially moved out of the house and into his New York apartment; worse than almost any other point in my life other than my mother dying.

But I was trying to put my best foot forward, and admitting any of this would be the opposite of that. Also, it occurred to me suddenly that I was not actually doing awfully—at least not in that moment. After all,

Adam was back in our house, even if he was lingering in the entryway. He was here to be with me, on purpose. "You first," I said.

"I feel bad," he said, and as I stared at him, I saw that he really did; in spite of his sharp outfit and manufactured pleasantry, he looked like a man who was slowly being flattened beneath the weight of his own self-loathing. As much as it pained me to see him like this, I was still glad he was suffering. Redemption was only possible after contrition and confession.

"Yes, well," I said, still standing with my arms crossed over my chest so I wouldn't leap toward him and embrace him.

"That's why I wanted to talk to you," he added, glancing into the living room. "I wanted to make things right between us."

My heart swelled. Adam was a man who clung to the principles of morality and justice, or at least he had been before he put his pelvis in charge of his life. But everything in his face told me he was again allowing his frontal lobe to guide him. He was returning to himself—and me.

"Should we go sit?" he said.

"Let's."

I had just sat on the sofa when Adam held up a finger. "One second," he said, and dashed into the dining room. I heard clanking; when he reappeared, he was holding two tumblers, one of which he handed to me. "It's the twenty-year Glenlivet Reddy bought me when I turned fifty," he said.

I almost blurted out that I was not drinking, but if I had, I would have followed it with an explanation of why, which would have led to a confession of just how low I had dipped since he left. I was trying to show Adam that I was better than ever—not a sad sack who had to give up booze. Anyway, wasn't this an alcohol-infused olive branch on his part? I could hardly turn down such a thing.

But Adam, who seemed to have mistaken my momentary hesitation for denial, frowned. "Come on, Maggie. You can't expect me to have both of these."

"You're right." I took the crystal tumbler from him; I would just have a small sip. "What are we drinking to?"

He sat on the sofa, and though he was not a large man by any stretch of the imagination, he sank into the cushions. When he came home again, we would need to pick out new furniture. "To peace," he said.

I began to give him a skeptical look, but as our eyes met, my tough front immediately gave way to longing. Even after the way he had hurt me, I loved him. And I had counted on him. How would I ever trust again if he reneged on the most important promise anyone had ever made me?

I wouldn't. And that hinted at a future even darker and bleaker than the one I occasionally allowed myself to picture.

I ran a finger over the tumbler's cut-glass pattern. "To peace." Then I tossed my scotch back, managing to swallow the majority in a single gulp.

Oh—

Oh my.

The amber liquid was at once searing and delicious. I finished the sip left at the bottom, then handed my glass to Adam. "Pour me another," I said. I almost added *please*, but it was probably the single word in the English language that I had used more often than he had during our marital tenure.

He took my glass, nodded, then drained his own. "Think I'll do the same," he murmured as he stood and disappeared into the dining room.

When he returned with a glass in each hand, a surge of warmth came over me. While this was perhaps one part liquor, it was also equal parts love, familiarity, and the sort of heightened desire one has when one has not known a man intimately in more than half a year.

"You seem like you're doing a lot better than the last time we saw each other," Adam said, handing me my glass.

Did I? I smiled softly and took a sip. "Maybe I am," I said, and then I had another sip, and a third. At dinner, I had unintentionally emulated Rose's favorite calorie-curbing technique and had mostly pushed my meal around on my plate. The Glenlivet hit me fast and hard, opening one of memory's strange chambers and pushing me into the past.

Adam and I were lying in bed one morning in his law-school apartment. I don't remember much about the apartment anymore, but he had dark blue flannel sheets that somehow made his small studio feel like the safest place I had ever been. The sun was streaming down through the high window, and Adam was tracing a finger up my bare spine. "What do you want most in life, Maggie?" he asked, his touch sending waves of goose bumps across my skin. "Whatever it is, I want to give it to you."

I remember that I could only offer myself as an answer, because I could not find the word for what I was feeling. What I wanted was what he had already promised and provided, except I wanted it forever: Shelter, in the most all-encompassing meaning of the word. A family. Love.

I pushed that mental door shut and looked at Adam, who seemed to be gazing at me not as the person who had left me, but as the steady, loving man who intended to grow old with me. His pupils had all but swallowed the green of his irises, and I let myself sink into that dark place. *You still love me, don't you?* I asked wordlessly. *Are you ready to again offer me whatever I want? Because I'm prepared to take it.*

Emboldened, I moved toward him on the sofa. Jillian Smith was now so far in the distance that she was practically the horizon itself. I, however, was Adam Harris' wife, the woman who had birthed his children and shared his life.

Adam reached forward and touched my arm, and his fingers were electric on my skin.

"Maggie," he said gruffly, and I could feel his gaze move from my face to my neck and down to my cleavage, which had been highlighted by my wrap dress and, per Dionne's suggestion, the slightest dusting of First Crush Baby blush.

Then I unintentionally glanced at Adam's hand on my forearm, and in doing so, at his stainless steel watch. The drive to Rose's retirement home was just forty-two minutes—thirty with Zoe behind the wheel. The kids would be back soon; I needed to move fast.

Adam's hand still on my arm, I inched even closer and let my own hand rest on his leg. His thigh was solid beneath my fingers, and he glanced up at me.

Was he . . . interested? Yes. Aroused? It wasn't out of the question.

But I also saw something different in his eyes—something I didn't recognize. Maybe he really had changed, as he had implied at dinner, and it was for the better. Maybe we both had. I had recently read something in the *Tribune* about a couple who had been married for fifty years. When asked about the longevity of their relationship, the wife said she'd had three different marriages with the same man; in order to survive, they had needed to change with each other again and again. Adam and I could learn to transform together.

"Maggie," he said quietly, taking my hand off his thigh and grasping it in his own. "There's something I need to tell you." His jaw was peppered with stubble, which reminded me of nights on the dock at the lake house we used to rent each summer. Adam let himself fully unwind while we were there. It only lasted one week, but it was glorious. The kids stopped going with us when they started college, and soon after, we stopped going, too. Adam said we would find another vacation spot—a smaller, more romantic place for just the two of us—but it had been years since we stared at a placid lake, feeling right about ourselves and the world. "About Jillian . . ."

The optimism I had been feeling seconds earlier evaporated. Adam and Jillian were serious. So serious that even though he and I weren't divorced, he had already asked her to marry him. Maybe she even had a baby on the way. Poor Jack and Zoe—this would be such a terrible adjustment for them.

He grimaced. "We're not together."

Thank God. "Why didn't you say so?" I said breathlessly.

"The thing is, there is no Jillian," he said. "Not really."

In an instant, the sofa beneath me was a waterbed. "What do you mean, *there is no Jillian*?" I could not manage to translate what he had said into anything that remotely applied to me. "Are you saying . . ." I stared at him, my mouth gaping open. Why wasn't he filling in the blanks and making this easier for me? "Does Jillian Smith not *exist*?" I managed.

"Jillian Smith exists. She's just not my girlfriend."

I continued to stare. This was good news—wasn't it? So . . . why wasn't I happy? "Adam," I said, "I honestly don't understand what you're telling me."

He rubbed his forehead. "We had coffee a bunch of times, and dinner a few times, too. We were friends at first, and then I guess it was like we were dating, sort of. But I—" He looked up and gave me a woeful look. "I thought about sleeping with her. I wanted to. She wanted to. It was literally the first time I ever actually wanted to cheat on you, Maggie. I couldn't do it, but wanting to felt like a sign, and the more I thought about it, the more I realized that I needed to end our marriage."

I'm not sure when or how, but I had risen from the sofa and had backed myself against a bookshelf. "You never even *slept* with her?"

He shook his head. "I kissed her. Nothing more."

"Why didn't you tell me earlier?" This came out as a scream-cry, as I used to describe my children's temper tantrums. Had Adam just informed me that all the erotic and not-our-style acts I had assumed he was doing with one Jillian Smith were but a torturous figment of my imagination? I could barely process the barrage of garbage coming out of his mouth.

"I'm telling you now," he said. "That's why I agreed to come tonight. I wanted to make peace. I don't want any more lies."

"No," I said, shaking my head. "This does not make peace. It makes—" I wanted to say war, but that wasn't right. What it made was my life even worse.

He hung his head. "I'm sorry, Maggie. I know I screwed up. I don't want things to end on this note."

End.

My eyes shifted from Adam to the crystal tumbler sitting on the coffee table and back again. The glass was thick enough to do serious damage if I lobbed it at Adam, and to be honest, I was considering it.

It would have been better, I thought suddenly, if he had dropped dead instead of leaving me. Then I could have enjoyed the pure, unadulterated grief of being a widow.

"Adam." A sob was lurking in my throat. "How could you possibly be so cruel?"

"I'm sorry," he said lamely. "I should have come clean a long time ago."

No, you should not have, I thought, my stomach churning. If he was really going to leave me, he should have stuck with his lie. Now I had two terrible truths to live with: not only did my husband no longer love me, there was no other woman to blame. I, Maggie Halfmoon Harris, had simply not been enough. And if I had not been enough for the man who had always claimed to love me more than I loved him ("Don't feel bad about it," he used to tease), then—well, there was no hope for me.

"Go," I said, pointing toward the foyer.

"I'm sorry," Adam said again.

It was like a bomb had gone off. Static reverberation rang through my ears; all I could see before me was destruction. "GO," I yelled.

Adam, who seemed shell-shocked himself, just stood there staring at me. So I ran to the closet, grabbed his coat, and threw it out the front door into the snow.

It was a wretched night, and the wind sent snow shooting into the house. I stood in the spray, barely feeling the cold stinging my skin. Because I could not speak, I glared at Adam and pointed outside.

There was hesitation in his eyes; he probably thought I was going to hurt him or myself, and at least one of these things was a strong possibility.

Then he looked at me once last time and marched into the dark. The kids still had his car, and nothing within walking distance was open on Thanksgiving. But his well-being was no longer my concern. Now—finally—I understood that.

The minute I shut the door behind him, I fell to my knees and put my forehead on the cold tile. I couldn't even cry; I just lay there moaning like I had been mortally wounded. In spite of my gift for imagining ghastly possibilities, I had dramatically underestimated my own worst-case scenario.

My husband hadn't replaced me at all. He simply didn't want me to be a part of his life.

EIGHT

The house I had been desperate to keep suddenly became the most unbearable place I could imagine being.

"You can come stay with me in New York for a while," Zoe had said the day after Thanksgiving. I had managed to pull myself off the floor before she and Jack got home from dropping off Rose, and I had not told either of them what had transpired with Adam. But they were smart enough to know that his walking around the neighborhood on an eighteen-degree night meant it couldn't have ended well. Now instead of gloating that she had told me so, my daughter was inviting me to disrupt her overpacked schedule.

"I really appreciate the offer, sweetie," I said to Zoe. "And maybe I'll take you up on it at some point. But I can't just call off work and fly to New York right now."

"Why not?"

"Because Terry is counting on me to be at work."

I could tell she was trying hard not to roll her eyes at me. "Screw Terry. For once in your life, Mom, it would do you good to focus on what you want."

I had done exactly that with Adam, and look where that had landed me. "Zoe Halfmoon Harris, that is not appropriate," I said.

She scrunched up her nose. "Yeah, well, screw Terry, and screw Dad, too. I don't know what happened between you, but I know it wasn't good."

No, it wasn't. I felt like I had been buried up to my neck in the sand and was watching the tide begin to roll in. But I didn't want to give my children reasons to resent their father. "I'm going to be fine," I told Zoe. "Just wait and see."

~

The afternoon after Jack and Zoe returned to New York, I drifted through the house like a ghost, a large glass of wine in hand. Five o'clock was hours away, but what was the point of self-care now?

Once bustling with noise and activity and real live humans, our home had become a museum of Harris family history. The faded red walls of Adam's home office bore dark rectangles where his diplomas had hung. Our bedroom was strewn with clothes, which I could not bring myself to hang in my half-empty closet; across the hall, Jack's bedroom was stuffed with belongings that he swore he would retrieve as soon as he settled down. Then I let myself into Zoe's room. The quilt Rose had paid someone to sew using fabric scraps from Zoe's old baby clothes was draped across her daybed. The sight of it made me want to weep. I had been so fortunate to raise two healthy, interesting children, but my fortune seemed to resurrect as loss. How had it all flown by so fast?

Zoe had taken most of the framed photos from her old dresser, but had left behind one of Adam, Jack, Zoe, and me, decked in outlandish Christmas sweaters that Adam's brother, Rick, had bought us as gag gifts.

It was a rare photo of me, and I had been ridiculously happy when it was taken. Of course I had; I had been with the people I loved most.

I was still staring at the photo when the phone rang. I assumed it would be Rose. But caller ID revealed a local number I didn't recognize, and I was curious enough to pick up.

"May I please speak with Maggie Harris?" The person on the other end sounded like she was going to ask me to share a few pertinent details about my identity so that an almost-legit-sounding company would claim to lower my mortgage rate while enabling a woman in Arizona to purchase bedazzled Victoria's Secret thongs using a credit card registered in my name.

"Yes," I said cautiously. "May I ask who *this* is?"

"This is Barbara Kline from Bridgewater Travel. I'm calling on behalf of Mark Johnson, who arranged your upcoming trip to Rome. Mark is no longer with the company, so I'll be working with you from here on out."

The woman may as well have reached through the phone and slapped me, and I stood there blinking. In the chaos of the past few months, I had completely forgotten about the romantic trip I had planned back when I was under the impression Adam and I were happily married.

"Maggie?" said Barbara kindly.

"Um. My husband and I—" *Don't have a future together.* "We can't go anymore," I said, and took a swig of my wine.

"That's a shame. Are you absolutely sure? Of all the trips I've put together, the Rome excursion is one of my absolute favorites. Even in December, you'll still have plenty of sun, and because it's not high tourist season it's one of the best times to see the popular destinations like the Colosseum and the Vatican." Barbara paused. "I'm sure Mark told you this, but unfortunately, the deposit is nonrefundable."

Rome was supposed to be our big trip—the one Adam and I had been waiting for. International travel was out of the question when the kids were young, and later their teenage schedules and Adam's unceasing workload made it only slightly more feasible, which is to say it never happened.

When Jack went to college, Adam and I had flown to Argentina for a week; the day after I arrived, Jack had a meningitis scare that turned out to be an especially bad case of the flu, and though Rose was able to step in and we didn't fly back early, I had been racked with guilt the entire time. That put us off long flights for a while.

But with the kids officially on their own, last year Adam and I decided we would finally do it up properly for our next anniversary. Rome was Adam's idea—he had visited with his parents when he was young and wanted to return. I was eager to see the frescoes painted on cathedral ceilings and dine on pasta that had been made that day.

Mostly, though, I was looking forward to a week with my husband in which legal caseloads and grocery runs and the countless humdrum demands of our everyday life were not present. It was supposed to be a chance for us to connect the way we used to and, I secretly hoped, to rekindle our flame.

"Are you sure my husband didn't cancel in time for a refund?" I asked Barbara. It wasn't like Adam to forget something like that. Then again, it wasn't like him to be a bald-faced liar and ruiner of lives, either, so what did I know?

"Unfortunately so. I attempted to contact him earlier in the month and didn't hear back. I've tried to call you a few times as well, with no success. Did you get the email I sent last week?"

I had not, probably because I hadn't opened my computer. Nor had I bothered to listen to my voicemail; I was too wrapped up in preparing for Thanksgiving and my ill-fated reunion with Adam.

I wandered from Zoe's room back into my bedroom and sat down on the bed. The mattress was a lumpy old queen. I had wanted to replace it with a king for years but had read online that a smaller bed was better for marital intimacy. (So much for that theory.) Lord, how I had come to hate this space.

I was about to tell Barbara that we would have to forfeit the deposit when Zoe's words came back to me: "For once in your life, Mom, it would do you good to focus on what you want." I still wanted to go to Rome. So why shouldn't I? "Since the deposit is nonrefundable, is there any chance you could change the reservation?"

"I may be able to do so, depending on availability. Are you and your husband eyeing a particular week?"

"Actually, it would just be for one person. Me." Adam wasn't the only one who had gone and lost his mind. But if there was ever a time to act irrationally, it was now.

"Of course," said Barbara, and if I wasn't mistaken, there was a hint of glee in her voice. She added, "I *love* taking trips on my own."

I had not traveled on my own for leisure since—ever. "Really?"

"Oh yes," she twittered. "There's nothing better than exploring by yourself. The places you'll go, the people you'll meet—you just don't have the same sort of serendipity when you're traveling in a pair. Of course, as a woman you must be careful."

Spontaneously signing on to a solo trip to Rome—which I would need Adam to pay for, even if he didn't yet know that—was 180 degrees from careful. But I had spent my whole life avoiding risk, and a fat lot of good that had done me.

"I'll do my best," I told Barbara. "How soon can I go?"

"One second." Barbara put me on hold. When she returned, she said she could arrange for me to leave in a week and a half if I was willing to pay a $200 change fee. (I wasn't, but Adam would have to.) Then she went over the itinerary to see if I wanted to adjust any of my plans.

Adam and I had settled on a relatively unstructured trip that included a few guided tours. I told Barbara I would skip the Vatican trip we had signed up for—I could see that on my own—but keep the ancient-ruins expedition. "You know," said Barbara, just before we got off the phone, "the last time I was in Rome, I went on this wonderful culinary tour in Testaccio. It's one of the best food neighborhoods in the city, and it isn't as touristy as Campo de' Fiori or Trastevere. You'll go to a traditional Roman bakery, a restaurant that only serves pasta, a cheesemonger—"

"Sold," I said. "Please put it on my husband's credit card."

I hung up feeling simultaneously triumphant and terrified. I was almost as excited about Rome as I had been about seeing Adam at Thanksgiving—but this time he wouldn't be there to deliver yet another unpleasant surprise.

Except . . . who *was* I, heading across the Atlantic on my own and sticking my almost ex-husband with the bill?

I didn't know anymore. But maybe I would find out in Italy.

~

When I got to work that afternoon, I told Terry I would need to take the second week of December off.

"I would have appreciated a little more notice," he said stiffly, holding up a crown for inspection.

I almost said I was sorry for springing my vacation on him, but it wasn't true. "Terry, I haven't taken a nonholiday off in almost two years, and this time of year is always incredibly slow. Besides, it's kind of an emergency."

He kept staring at the porcelain tooth. "Are you having a health problem?"

"Yes. Menopause," I said dryly. I wasn't sure what had gotten into me, but I was not in the mood for Terry.

He placed the tooth back in its case. "That's not amusing."

What was not amusing was that a medical professional either didn't know or didn't care that the question he had just posed was illegal. "May I have the time off or not?" I said.

Terry turned to me. "Maggie," he said, his voice as cold as his blue eyes, "I ask for very little from you."

This was untrue. In the past three years, Terry had required me to learn two new accounting systems—both of which, as I had warned him, were useless and quickly abandoned—on my own time. He also routinely asked me to stay an extra fifteen minutes to run a payroll report or do some other task that could have waited, and on every single occasion had to be reminded why my paycheck was slightly higher than normal.

Of course, Terry asked very little *about* me, and maybe that's what he had actually meant. Inappropriate health question aside, I could not think of a single occasion in which he had inquired about my personal life. To him, I might as well have been a Waterpik. Or, you know—invisible. "So is that a no?" I said, cocking my head.

Terry, who seemed taken aback by the way I was looking at him, cleared his throat. "Yes."

Something strange was brewing in me. It almost as though all of the anger I had bottled up after Adam left had been fermenting and was now far more potent. "I'm not actually clear on what your yes means, but I'm going to plan on not being here. I'll put in extra time this week and the beginning of next to make sure everything is set up so there are minimal interruptions."

He was peering at me over the edge of his bifocals. "I don't think that's the best way to keep your employer happy, do you, Maggie?"

I glanced around the office for a moment, considering my next move. Then I said brightly, "Well, Terry, as it happens, I'm finding that trying to keep other people happy isn't working out so well for me. And in fact, this place makes me the opposite of happy, and your patronizing response to my simple vacation request put that in stark perspective."

I opened my desk drawer, retrieved the pens I had purchased for myself because Terry stocked the kind that bled all over your hand, and carefully closed the drawer again. Then I removed my key to the dentist office from my keychain and put it on my desk next to a discarded X-ray. Terry was still staring at me over his glasses. I smiled at him like the crazy person I had become. "Best of luck to you, Terry," I said. "I quit."

NINE

"Oh no. I knew this was going to happen," said Gita, shaking her head.

We were outside our favorite Italian restaurant, and I had just told her about quitting my job. "What?" I said. "I'm finally taking control of my life. You should be happy for me."

"It was inevitable, really," she said, holding the door open.

The smell of fresh bread wafted at me as I stepped inside the restaurant. "You make it sound like a bad thing that I'm finally focusing on what I want for a change," I said. "It could have been worse. I could have told Terry to wade in a piranha pond."

Gita laughed the brief, bark-like laugh of a person who is humoring you, and told the hostess we needed a table for two.

"Going to Rome is great, and I'm proud of you," she said once we had been seated. "But quitting your job on the spot? What's next? You going to hitchhike across Europe and call me once you've located a yurt and a young lover to call your own? I mean, this seems awfully *Eat, Pray, Love* to me. I'm on board with the food part, but I'm less enthused about the rest."

"Don't be ridiculous," I scoffed. "I'd rather get a nasal piercing than meditate, and I'm certainly not looking for love. I'm not moving anywhere, either." I had liked Oak Valley well enough to remain there for twenty-four years; the town was socioeconomically and racially diverse, which was more than you could say for most places, and its proximity to Chicago couldn't be beat.

But as I looked across the restaurant at the table where Gita, Reddy, Adam, and I had been seated earlier that spring, I was filled with the most painful sort of nostalgia. Never again would the four of us dine together. Nor would Adam and I have breakfast at Jimmy's, the diner down the street that we both loved, or walk through the wooded park on summer nights, seeing if we could spot one of the cicadas that were filling the air with their mating songs. Adam may have moved to the city, but his memory was scattered all around this town.

No surprise, Gita had already considered this. "You could get a nice condo in Naperville," she said, referring to a nearby suburb. "Just don't hightail it out of Illinois."

A waiter had delivered a basket of bread, but the piece I had taken sat on my plate like a joyless lump. "You know I'm trying to keep my life as normal as possible."

"With the crap Adam just pulled on you, it would almost be weird if you didn't have a midlife crisis. Ditching your job without another lined up indicates you're well on your way. Especially for you," she said, arching an eyebrow at me. "Two weeks ago, you were freaking out about spending sixty dollars on a dress. Now you're telling me you're fine with living on spousal support?"

Fine? Not exactly. I broke into a cold sweat if I spent more than two minutes trying to do the math on what the next one to thirty-five years might look like for me financially. So mostly I tried not to and attempted to channel my mother instead. When money was really tight during my childhood, she would smile and say, "Don't you borrow trouble from tomorrow. Things have always worked out before, so there's no reason to think this time will be any different." And sure enough, she would find a way to pull us out of whatever hole we had slipped into.

No, I would not work myself into a lather about my financial situation. It may not have been a smart move, but the astonishment on Terry's face as I marched out of his office had almost been worth every penny it would cost me.

"It'll work out," I told Gita. "The minute I get back from Italy, I'll focus on getting a new job."

Our waiter appeared to take our drink orders. After the scotch with Adam, I had abandoned my quest to avoid alcohol. I had higher hurdles to clear, I decided, and besides, I was on my way to Italy, which happened to produce some of my favorite adult beverages on the planet, which I planned to partake in. After we ordered wine, I turned back to Gita. "Let's *pretend* I'm midlife and not two-thirds of the way through. I think I've already taken a ride or three on the SS *Crisis*, don't you?"

"Sort of, though that was what happened to you, not how you responded." Gita sipped her water. "Anyway, I don't think fifty-three is too late."

"Yes, well—" I had been about to make a remark about turning fifty-four in June when I stopped myself. My mother was fifty-four when she died, and that made me think of an entirely different sort of "too late." "I don't think I can afford to have a midlife crisis even if I were so inclined," I concluded.

But later, as Gita was telling me about her daughter Amy's medical school applications, I thought about what was keeping me from doing something drastic and arguably stupid. And the answer was . . . nothing. My husband didn't want me; my children barely needed me. I no longer had a job or anything tethering me to Oak Valley, or anywhere else. I was a free agent, and if I wanted to go behave like Adam—recklessly and without consideration for others—then who could blame me?

When Gita and I left the restaurant later that evening, snow was falling in wet clusters, coating the fences and trees in white. Beneath the lamplight, the five-block stretch of Main Street that constituted Oak Valley's downtown sparkled. At any other point in my life, I would have thanked God and my lucky stars for being fortunate enough to have landed in such a place.

Now I could not wait to get out of there.

~

A week later, I said goodbye to Gita and drove myself to the airport.

"We're going to have the *very best time*!" I heard a young woman squeal to her friends as they wheeled their enormous suitcases toward the check-in desk.

I wondered if they sold that sort of enthusiasm at the gift shop. There I was, heading to an international destination with warmer weather and a plethora of possibilities—and I was staring into the sea of faces at the security line, wishing Adam's were one of them. Maybe he'd had a come-to-Jesus moment, I thought futilely, and had called the travel agency and arranged to join me. Maybe he had suddenly realized what I had understood months ago: that there were few things as depressing as facing down the last decades of your life alone.

When I printed my boarding pass at one of the check-in kiosks, I did a double take: the pass said I was seated in 4C. It had to be a mistake, I decided as I went through security. But when I checked in with the gate agent, she informed me that no mistake had been made; my reservation had been upgraded, though by whom she could not say.

"So it *was* already paid for?" I asked her, envisioning a surprise bill when I returned from Italy.

The agent smiled at me. "There are no additional fees. Enjoy."

Barbara at Bridgewater Travel had confirmed that Adam—or at least his credit card company—had accepted all of the fees for the trip. Had he paid for the upgrade out of guilt? After all, he knew I had always wanted to fly first class but had never had the opportunity, or extra cash, to do so. Or was it just a lucky break? Even as I stowed my carry-on and took my seat, I kept glancing around to see if an agent was going to run up and tell me there had been a mix-up. *Don't borrow trouble,* I told myself as I settled into my seat, which was not so much a chair as a self-contained privacy pod.

"Champagne?" asked a flight attendant the minute I had clicked my seat belt.

I nodded, thanked her, and took one of the flutes from the tray she was carrying. I loathed flying—especially the first minute of the ascent, which I had read was when a crash was most likely to occur—but maybe complimentary bubbles could help take the edge off.

The wine was just okay, but I drank it anyway; I couldn't get over the fact that they used real glass in first class. I had just accepted a refill when a woman's head appeared from behind the divider between my seat and the one next to it.

"Howdy!" she said.

I wasn't in the mood to chat, but the woman, who had a warm, craggy face and gray hair that was cropped close and tousled in every direction, seemed harmless. Interesting, even. The hand she thrust at me was decorated with silver rings, several of which were studded with chunks of turquoise. "Jean Abernathy," she said as I shook her hand. "That's a good handshake you have on you."

"Maggie Halfmoon," I said. I almost added *Harris*, but stopped myself. I had left my wedding ring at home; might as well do the same with my married name. "And thanks. My husband always says a good handshake is important." Oh no.

"Lordy, I didn't at all mean to make you cry," said Jean.

"I'm not crying." I dabbed at my eyes and then took a sip of my champagne for good measure.

"Course you're not," said Jean. She had a southern twang, and I couldn't tell if it was her voice or the champagne bubbles in my head that made her remind me of my mother. "Listen, Maggie. I'll give you some space, but if you need me, I'm just on the other side of this here wall." She knocked the plastic with her knuckles, and I managed a small laugh. "Holler if you need me."

I told her I would. I finished my drink, trying not to begin crying again over my gratuitous use of the word *husband*, and leaned into the deep leather seat. I spent a few minutes feeling guilty about stretching my legs out on the foldout bed while passengers a few rows behind me were forced to slumber in the fetal position. Then I fell fast asleep.

~

When I came to again, the cabin was dark. As my eyes opened I was gripped with hunger. I couldn't remember when I had last been legitimately hungry. It had been weeks, at least. A dish of fancy nuts from takeoff was still on my tray, and I poured them into my hand. I had just popped the second almond in my mouth when a flight attendant appeared. "Would you like to begin with the cheese plate, Tuscan white bean soup, or beet salad with goat cheese and quinoa chips?"

"Cheese, please," I said, trying not to drool all over my fancy leather seat.

"Excellent. And would you prefer flatiron steak with polenta, steamed sole with Italian herbs, or manicotti with spinach?"

"Manicotti sounds great."

"Fresh bread?"

"Yes," I said, thanking God and whoever made the error that landed me in first class.

"And may I bring you a drink?"

My head was throbbing, probably from the champagne. But when almost in Rome . . . "A glass of red wine, please."

"Chianti, cabernet, or lambrusco?"

"Chianti."

"The food can't be beat, huh?" Jean's voice traveled over the divider as the flight attendant was delivering my wine.

I leaned forward so I could see her. She was tearing into a loaf of crusty bread. "I was just thinking that," I told her.

"Still can't get over it myself. I waited sixty-eight years to take a first-class flight, and now I see that I should have sold a kidney back in the eighties if that's what it took to get to the front. It's rare air up here." She grinned at me.

"Yes, it is. Do you know what time it is, by any chance?"

"Four in the morning. At least, that's Eastern time. Three a.m. Central. You from Chicago?"

I nodded. "You?"

She shook her head, which sent her silver earrings shaking. "Had a connection from Detroit. I'm from Ann Arbor." I must have looked dubious, because she added, "Since 1976, that is. I grew up in the south, in case you're wondering about the accent."

"I was. I'm from Michigan and went to school in Ann Arbor. But my mother's family is from rural Virginia. Lee County—you ever hear of it?"

"Lee County!" she hooted. "I grew up just over the hill in Big Stone Gap."

I smiled. "Just over the hill" was how my mother had described anything between five and fifty miles away. No wonder Jean seemed so familiar. "Is that so?"

"Sure is," she said, looking awfully pleased herself. "So what's bringing you to Rome, Maggie Halfmoon?"

"It's kind of a long story."

Jean lifted her drink, which smelled like it was a hundred proof. "It's kind of a long flight."

I eyed her for a moment. I didn't know this woman, but I'd probably never see her again, so what did it matter if I told her the truth? "My husband called it quits on our marriage," I admitted. "We were supposed to go to Rome together, but now I'm on a one-woman farewell tour. I guess it's my way of sticking it to him while trying to wrap my mind around our divorce."

"Well, good for you!" declared Jean.

Was it good for me? It certainly wasn't good for Adam. Though I *had* saved him from flushing our $900 deposit down the drain, even if it had also required adding another $800 to his credit card bill.

His bill! I thought suddenly. *Ours.* Our bill. Until we were divorced our finances remained a unit, and I would not feel bad about using a portion of them to do something for myself.

"Sometimes you've got to take a hammer to life's hard edges," Jean added.

"Isn't that the truth."

"It is indeed. Anyway, I know a thing or two about farewell tours. I was married thirty-six years and went through a butt-ugly divorce that ended up with my husband in the morgue."

I must have looked alarmed, because she held up her hands. "Not to worry—I didn't *kill* him. He was ten years my senior and had a heart condition that the doctors thought would do him in years earlier. My leaving was just the final straw, I suppose."

"Why were you splitting up?"

"Let's just say I was more than ready for a new chapter. It was terrible that it resulted in the end of Sam's story—that took me a long time to move past. But here I am, and so it goes."

I hoped that my flying companion's new chapter had not involved lying to her husband about a lover that she didn't actually have. "What about you?" I asked. "What brings you to Rome?"

"I'm spending two weeks in Rome. Then I'm heading to Florence for six months."

"No kidding."

"Yes indeed. I'm a painter." She reached into the bag at her feet and pulled out her phone. When she found what she was looking for, she held the screen up, revealing a photo of a canvas on which she had painted a dappled house with woods behind it. "Started in my fifties and have no intention of stopping," she said, flipping to a photo of another painting just as stunning as the first. "I manage to sell enough of them to make a living, and now I'm off to Florence on a fellowship." She laughed. "Judging by the expression on your mug, I'm guessing you thought they wouldn't pay to send a wrinkled bat like me to Italy."

"I didn't say that at all," I said, grinning at her. "I'm thoroughly impressed."

"Well," said Jean, instantly bashful, "I still can't believe I made it happen myself."

We chatted off and on for the next few hours. She was good company; though Adam was never completely out of my mind, neither was he at the forefront while Jean and I were talking. After we touched down at Fiumicino Airport and deplaned, she handed me a card with her contact information. "I'm sure you've got big plans for your week," she said, patting my arm. She was very tall, which I hadn't realized until we were shuffling off the plane, and wore flowing linen clothes that made her look every bit the artist she was. "But if you want to grab a plate of pasta or a glass of wine, shoot me an email. It's always nice to have company once in a while."

I thought of what the travel agent had said about the serendipity of traveling alone. "I'd love that," I told Jean.

~

The first few miles from the airport could have been almost anywhere. Through the window of my taxi I saw gas stations and strip malls, apartments and homes and schools, and flat wheat-colored fields.

But with one turn I was on a road flanked by two towering, ancient stone walls. "Welcome to Rome," said the taxi driver in accented English.

The walls became shorter as the road rose and deposited us into the city. I don't know what I was expecting—I suppose a modern metropolis with pockets of history here and there—but antiquity was everywhere. Most of the buildings were made of stone, and many were flanked with columns and were clearly thousands of years old.

Still, I thought perhaps we were just passing through a charming neighborhood as the taxi made its way toward Piazza Navona, where I would be staying. I soon realized all of it was charming. Rome was a wash of cobblestone streets, colorful homes and restaurants and shops, government buildings with stucco walls and terra-cotta-tiled roofs, and more regal, ornate churches than I had ever seen in a single place. My spirits rose: in a city like this, it would be next to impossible for me to run out of things to do. And if I stayed busy, I might actually be able to enjoy myself instead of running around ruing Adam.

I had reserved a room at a bed-and-breakfast hidden on a steep, narrow road off the center of a bustling neighborhood. Its door was tucked into the middle of a long wall; if the taxi hadn't deposited me directly in front of it, I might have missed it. A friendly front-desk clerk named Danilo checked me in and showed me to my room.

The room was small—as most hotel rooms in Rome were, the travel agent had warned back when Adam and I were planning to travel together—but it was bright, clean, and painted a lemon yellow that seemed to be the same shade as the sun streaming in through the wavy windowpane.

After I got settled in and freshened up, I slipped on an old trench coat and headed out. I walked for a few blocks, soaking up the sounds of shopkeepers yelling Italian to each other and watching attractive people zip past on Vespas and in small, brightly colored cars. I remembered arriving in Barcelona with Adam decades earlier and being disappointed that the hotel we had chosen was in a sleepy financial district that might as well have been Washington, DC. This was the opposite of that. It seemed I had been dropped into an advertisement for an idyllic Italian getaway.

There were dozens of different places to eat within a quarter-mile radius; after circling for a while, I settled on a cozy café. The café had two small tables positioned on either side of the entrance. The air was cool, but the sun was warm on my skin. When a woman behind the front counter indicated I was free to sit outside, I took the table to the right.

I sat unattended to for a few minutes, and then a few more. A young couple sat at the table across from me, and the waiter who had been ignoring me walked over to help them. *So my powers of transparency have followed me to Italy,* I thought with defeat. I was about to get up when the woman behind the counter yelled out to the waiter. "Pietro!" she said, and rattled off something in Italian that was simultaneously angry sounding and beautiful. Then she looked at me with a gap-toothed grin. "Sorry," she said. "Pietro is not good at his job, but he is the only one who showed up for work today."

I laughed, the tension instantly defused. "Thank you."

"What would you like?" she called, still behind the counter.

"A cappuccino, please, and a ham-and-cheese panini."

"Bene," she said, and nodded.

It had only been a few hours since I'd had breakfast on the plane, but I was ravenous again and grateful when Pietro delivered my food. Along with the coffee and sandwich I had ordered, he placed a small plate with two chocolates in front of me.

"A gift," he said with a flourish of his hand.

"Grazie," I said, reciting one of the Italian phrases I had memorized in preparation for my trip. I looked down and saw that light brown espresso had been used to create a sun in the center of the foamed milk atop my coffee. It was almost too pretty to drink, but I was already jet-lagged and would need the caffeine if I was going to adjust to the new time zone. I lifted the small mug to my mouth, took a sip, and almost

swooned as the milky coffee hit my tongue. What had I been drinking all these years? The cappuccino alone had been worth the trip to Italy.

As I looked up, I realized the gap-toothed woman behind the counter was watching me. She grinned again. *"Bene, si?"*

I had no idea how to say, "This is the flavor of heaven," so I nodded, almost tearfully grateful, and said, *"Molto bene."*

It was very good indeed. And for the first time in quite some time, I felt that way, too.

TEN

When I woke the next morning, the sun was streaming through the window and I could hear birds chirping in the tree outside. If I were in a Disney movie, a couple of mice might have stopped by to help me pull an outfit together. But alas, this was my life, so I untwisted my nightgown from around my waist, rubbed my sleep-crusted eyes, and thought, *Why would Adam choose* nothing *over me?*

Had I really been so intolerable? However humiliated and horrible I may have felt, I had been a good wife. I had always supported Adam and his ambitions, and had accepted him wholeheartedly for who he was, never pushing him to be or do what he could not.

I'm done planning, I heard him say. Well, yes, I *had* made plans—doing so was integral to my sense of control, which I had been trying to gain since my uncontrollable childhood. Adam had been the one to point this out to me back when we were dating, and he had praised me for it because he was a planner, too. The man had three calendars—two electronic versions and a paper daybook because he was paranoid the e-versions would fail him—as well as a running mental outline of how his life was to unfold.

Up until earlier that year, it had all been on schedule.

It wasn't as though he could claim he wanted fewer responsibilities. I paid our bills, made sure the fridge and cupboards were well stocked, and maintained communication with everyone in our lives, save Adam's clients and employees, so that he wouldn't have to unless he wanted to. I even had our car tires rotated and changed the furnace filter, for cripes' sake.

Now I was being punished for having made his life easier?

A knock at the door broke through my thoughts. Just outside my room, my breakfast had been delivered on a cart. I wheeled it inside, expecting little, but when I removed the silver lid covering the tray, a small feast awaited me.

The frothy cappuccino was almost as good as the one I'd had the afternoon before. I took a few sips and then topped a triangle of toast with hazelnut spread and ate every last crumb before moving on to a tiny cup of yogurt. The yogurt was thick and tasted just ever so slightly like honey. I ate a soft-boiled egg perched in a yellow porcelain eggcup, even though it pained me to crack its speckled shell with my spoon. I unwrapped a piece of chocolate (chocolate at breakfast—bless this place!) and washed it down with the rest of my coffee. After having spent months approaching food as a duty, my appetite had finally resurfaced. It had to be a sign that I was returning to myself.

~

I had thought Italy would be a chance to escape my troubles. By my second day, it became evident they were still trailing behind me. When a thin, dark-haired tourist strode past me in the gardens at Vatican City, I found myself wondering if Jillian Smith had any idea she had been co-opted in Adam's elaborate lie. Or maybe *she* had left him, I mused, pausing beside a manicured hedge to watch the woman walk away. He had said Jillian had wanted to sleep with him—but that wasn't necessarily the same as wanting to break up his marriage. Maybe she was married, too, but was a compassionate cheater who didn't chop down her family tree just because she wanted to stick her feathers in a new nest for a while. I didn't know why I cared—she and he and they were all a thing of the past—but it seemed that maybe Jillian Smith would know what had driven Adam to this point.

I spent the afternoon on the ancient-ruins walking tour, thinking more of the same. Our last stop on the tour was Torre Argentina, the Roman cat sanctuary where cats lazed about in the spot where Julius Caesar had gasped his last breath. A couple that had been canoodling every step of the way was necking against a wall with a large placard that said "Do Not Touch" in five different languages, and I was so busy trying not to think about when Adam and I had last made out like that in public—I wasn't sure, but it was sometime during the previous millennium—that I missed the first half of the guide's story of Caesar's fateful betrayal. Of course, I already knew a thing or two about fateful endings (*et tu*, husband?).

When I got back to my hotel that night, I emailed Jean to see if she wanted to get together the following day, with the hope that having an actual person to talk to would yank me from my mental sludge (the two and a half glasses of wine I'd had at dinner, however inexpensive and delicious, had been ineffective in that department).

Jean was game, and so we agreed to meet for lunch at a restaurant run by one of the city's renowned *Pizzaioli*, or pizza makers. I had never been a big fan of pizza, which was sacrilege to a Chicagoan like Adam, but Jean had already been to the restaurant and said the meal I was about to eat would forever change the way I felt about the dish. And when I bit into a slice with a crisp, thin crust, a rich and almost floral tomato sauce, and dots of creamy mozzarella, I was indeed a changed woman.

Now we were staring up at Trajan's Column, the stone monument that had been built to commemorate Emperor Trajan's victory in the Dacian War.

"It's amazing that a flourishing modern city rose around ancient ruins," I mused to Jean.

"Isn't it just the darnedest thing?" she said. The column towered over a hundred feet, and every inch of it had been intricately carved with men and women fighting, working, and seducing each other. "That level of detail must have taken years to create! To think I get antsy if a painting takes more than a few weeks."

"That's the human condition," I said, moving out of the column's shadow to warm myself in the afternoon sun.

"Or maybe I'm just impatient," said Jean as she nudged me in the side.

I laughed. "Touché."

Trajan's Column was nestled in ruins near the center of the city, and after walking around the area for a while, we headed west to the Tiber River. "How are you holding up, Maggie?" Jean asked when we had reached one of the arched bridges over the river. Like many other things in the city, the bridge was at once deteriorating and spectacular. "Managing to enjoy yourself in spite of what's on the other side of the Atlantic?"

I ran my fingers along the bridge's stone rail. Below us, the Tiber's taupe water rushed wildly. "Oh, you know."

"Don't sugarcoat it, my friend," said Jean.

"I just keep wishing Adam had never told me the truth about Jillian. Now it's like he and his fake lover are haunting my vacation."

Jean nodded. "I'm not the type to say everything happens for a reason. Oftentimes that's just plain nonsense." She had a faraway look on her face and didn't speak again for a few minutes. "Sam and I—we had a daughter named Norah. She died of leukemia when she was three," she finally said.

I put my hand on her shoulder. "Jean, I'm so sorry."

"Me too. Sometimes I wonder if her death was what broke Sam's heart in the first place. We went on to have two more children." She fished her phone out of her purse and found a picture. "This is Sammy, our son," she said, pointing to a tall man with Jean's eyes. "And this is Hannah, our other daughter," she said, pointing to a petite Asian woman. "We adopted her when Sammy was eight because Sam and I couldn't manage to have a third child ourselves. Love 'em both like crazy, but I pray there's an afterlife so I can see Norah again. Anyway," she said, shaking her head as she slipped her phone back in her bag, "her passing is why I don't believe in that whole 'everything for a reason' line."

I was about to respond when Jean bent to pick up a euro someone had dropped on the bridge. She stood, rubbed the two-toned coin between her fingers, and chucked it into the Tiber. "But if there's one thing I do believe in, it's wiping the crap off your shoes and finding a fresh patch of grass to stand on. Let's get moving."

I would have to have a word with Barbara of Bridgewater Travel. She had been right: I was enjoying traveling on my own. I had already been living alone for the better part of a year, but vacationing by myself was something else entirely. It was freeing to decide what I wanted to see, when I wanted to eat, and if I had simply had enough of any given outing or experience without asking for another person's input.

But Barbara had failed to inform me that there would be loved-up couples at every turn, reminding me that my vacation was far from the romantic one I had originally planned.

The food tour I had signed up for was no exception. As we introduced ourselves at the tree-canopied public park where we were meeting, I discovered there were five pairs—and once again, markedly solo me. As I sat on the end of a park bench, waiting for our tour to officially commence, I felt like a teen who had been waiting too long to be asked to dance.

The tour guide, Benito, was a genial Italian man in his forties. He had beautiful black curls and wore a crisp blue shirt that fit impeccably, even at his stomach, which was the only part of his body that wasn't trim. He had grown up in Rome but attended college in New York, he told us in melodically accented English before turning to me and winking.

A wink? I was aghast. A younger man, and an attractive one at that, just winked at *me*? Maybe a wink didn't mean the same thing in Italian. I ordered myself to focus on food.

Testaccio, said Benito as we began to walk, had been a bustling trade center for meat, olive oil, and other foods for centuries. It was the culinary epicenter of the city, and since Rome was nothing if not its food, "some, myself included, would say this neighborhood is the authentic heart of Rome," he told us.

"This is Mount Testaccio," said Benito as we approached a hill. "Not much of a mountain, but surely a miracle: it is built on clay pots that held olive oil centuries ago."

As we drew closer, I saw that the hill's shrubs and greenery grew on thin dirt that was atop stacks of broken pieces of clay. "Olive oil makes anything porous rancid after a while, so the citizens could not reuse their amphorae, or clay jars. Instead, they were discarded here," said Benito, and if I wasn't mistaken, he was smiling right at me. "But as you can see, this garbage heap is not haphazard at all. The jars were arranged carefully and topped with a limestone mix that keeps them from crumbling. From the wreckage, a landmark was born."

I smiled back at Benito. I was a heap of wreckage myself. What did I have to lose by engaging in a little harmless flirting, if that was indeed what was happening?

Our first stop on the tour was a *salumeria* where cured meat, cheese, olive oil, and truffle products were sold. "If you have ever had truffle salt or truffle oil, what you've had was not the fungi at all, but an organic compound with an aroma similar to the truffle. This," said Benito with pride, passing out thin crackers topped with a fluffy white cheese that contained small gray bits, "is what truffle *really* tastes like."

I actually moaned as the cheese melted on my tongue. Benito laughed and sidled up to me. "Good, good! That is the intended reaction," he said. Then he lowered his voice. "I always hope for one true food lover on each tour, but I am rarely so lucky as I am today."

The playful gleam in his eye said he was definitely flirting, but it had been so long since anyone had flirted with me that I wasn't sure what to do about that. Italian men were legendary for their womanizing ways, I reminded myself, even as my cheeks reddened because no amount of rationalizing could dull the pleasure of being noticed.

After the truffles, Benito served us several cuts of meat that the owner of the *salumeria* had chosen for us: prosciutto, *coppa*, and a savory rustic sausage called *cacciatorini*. "Remember, we have several more stops, so go slow and loosen your belts," Benito cautioned.

Our pack headed to the Mercato Testaccio, a bustling food market composed of stalls beneath a metal-framed structure. The market itself was only a few years old, but many of the families manning the stalls were fourth-, fifth-, and even sixth-generation carryovers from the previous market that had once stood in the same place. There, we visited a cheesemonger who rose at three each morning to make mozzarella from scratch, and snacked on bruschetta, whose oil-drizzled tomatoes, basil, and crusty bread had all come from the vendors. Then we washed it down with small glasses of garnet-hued Montepulciano.

Yes, absolutely, please, thank you, I said to every single thing that was offered to me, including the wine, even though I was growing uncomfortably full. Each sip and bite seemed to signify that for as much as Adam had taken from me, he had not managed to sap all the pleasure from my life.

After the market, we moved on to a trattoria that specialized in classic Roman *fritti*: fried artichokes, fried peppers and eggplant, and my favorite, fried squash blossoms. Just when I thought I couldn't possibly eat another thing, Benito told us it was time for a late lunch. We headed to a restaurant that had been built into the side of Mount Testaccio. The aerated clay provided its own heating and cooling system, which kept the restaurant temperate all year round, Benito said.

We were seated at a long table at the rear of the restaurant, near a glass wall that showcased the cracked clay mountainside that made up the back of the building. "This is *cacio e pepe*," said Benito as a waiter placed before us platters of pale yellow pasta tubes speckled with black pepper. "Take a bite," he instructed after we had served ourselves. "What do you think the sauce is made of?" He smiled devilishly, and I felt my lips turn upward, too.

"Eggs?" asked one-half of a newlywed couple, and Benito shook his head.

"A bit of cream?" ventured a young British woman.

"That's precisely what it tastes like, but true *cacio e pepe* is made only with pecorino cheese and black pepper," he said, catching my eye. "The chef adds a bit of the water used to boil the pasta to mix it just before it's served, and that gives it its creamy texture."

Benito paired our pasta with a local Italian wine called *cesanese*, which he described as having hints of mulberry, juniper, and a forest floor. To me, it tasted like being an ocean away from my troubles. When he offered seconds, I held out my glass.

"Have you enjoyed yourself?" asked Benito. We had just wrapped up our last stop, for espresso at a bustling café, and the group had begun to scatter.

I put my hand on my stomach, which was threatening to break the zipper of my pants. "Maybe a bit too much."

Benito gave me a wide, almost wolfish grin. "Then I have done my job. I assume you won't want to eat tonight, but—" He slipped his hand into the front pocket of his shirt and retrieved a business card, which he handed to me. "If you are interested in joining me for a cocktail or a glass of wine, I would be pleased to show you more of Rome."

This sent a shiver of satisfaction through me. An attractive, interesting man had not only seen me, he had decided he wanted to see more. Of course, I had been alive long enough to know that his interest in me made him even more appealing than he would have been otherwise. But it didn't matter. Being attracted to someone other than Adam felt like a revelation. Maybe it was not the autumn of my romantic life. Maybe there was some spring left in me after all.

But what if he was crawling with crabs, or a psychopath—or *married*? My eyes traveled from his face to his left hand. I hadn't noticed a wedding ring, but I had heard that many Europeans didn't wear them.

My visual inquiry did not escape Benito. "I am not married," he said pleasantly. "I am a man who would be happy for the company of a beautiful woman and fellow food lover. But"—he bowed his head slightly, which made me laugh—"there is no pressure. Only an offer."

I felt a small flutter. Maybe Benito could be a new adventure on my Roman vacation. After all, what did I have left to lose?

Nothing. Not a damn thing.

"Yes," I said to Benito, whose face lit up at my response. "I would like to have a drink with you." *Possibly two,* I thought as I accepted his outstretched arm. A date with Benito sounded like just the thing to help me forget about Adam—and find out if the signs of life stirring within me meant I was ready to make contact.

ELEVEN

"Buongiorno, tesora mia!" sang a man's voice.

I'm still dreaming, I thought as a man's voice sang through the air. I threw my arm over my eyes to block the light. Just ten more minutes of sleep. Five, even. Three might almost be enough.

A shadow settled over my body, and I cracked my eyes open just enough to realize Benito was standing over me.

"Mary and Joseph!" I exclaimed. This was not a dream. I was awake, wretchedly awake, and I had just woken up in a strange man's bed.

"Hello again. Would you like *un cappuccino*?" said Benito, smiling down at me with big white teeth. He was wearing an undershirt, linen pants, and a gold watch. "I would be happy to make you one."

"Um," I mumbled, pulling the sheet to my chest as I attempted to sit up. It was then that I realized that I wasn't actually naked. But . . . I never wore a bra to bed, even though this was said to be the only way to avoid cleavage wrinkles, of which I had plenty. Had Benito put it back on me in an attempt to make me feel less exposed? The thought of him strapping my boulder holder back on my unconscious body made me flush with confusion and shame. What on earth had I been thinking?

Who cared if my husband had left me? I was still married, if only by law. And I didn't know Benito from—well, from Adam.

But I had gotten here on purpose, hadn't I? I couldn't actually remember. I knew Benito and I had sat at an outdoor patio on the edge of Testaccio and sipped negronis (delicious at the time; now the thought of the bitter drink made me want to regurgitate the previous day's food tour all over Benito's bed—this *was* Benito's bed, wasn't it?) as I made small talk and he made eyes at me.

When the sun slipped beneath the horizon, it had become quite chilly. We had still been too full to eat; I did remember that. To warm up, Benito and I had sipped sambuca and then walked for a while—where, I couldn't say, as it had looked an awful lot like everywhere else I had been. I recalled him telling me about how he had started the food-tour company, and about his daughter, who lived with her mother, and . . . I had no idea what else we had talked about. At some point we had hopped into a taxi to go to a wine bar in Aventino, where he lived; I remembered him leaning across the seat to kiss me, and thinking that he was a good kisser.

Everything after the taxi was a blank.

My stomach turned again as I realized I couldn't recall what had happened during my first sexual encounter with someone other than Adam in thirty-two years. "Bathroom?" I asked Benito, who was still standing beside the bed.

"Right over here, past the kitchen, on the left," he said agreeably, pointing through the door of the small bedroom.

I glanced around and saw that my clothes were folded on a chair in the corner. Either the night had not been too raucous, or Benito was a neatnik. Both thoughts managed to be mildly comforting.

"I will be in the kitchen," said Benito before closing the door behind himself.

I tossed on my clothes and ran past him into the bathroom. As I sat on the tiny toilet (why were European bathrooms designed for elves?), taking deep breaths and willing myself not to vomit, I felt as low as I ever had, which was saying a lot. I had cheated on my husband, even if he wouldn't be my husband for long, and I hadn't even been fully conscious to enjoy it.

In the mirror, I examined myself for bruises, though I doubted Benito had hurt me. What exactly had happened? The truth would probably be only seventy percent as awful as whatever I could imagine. But how could I find out? Ask my apparent Italian lover for a detailed play-by-play of the night before and pray he told me the truth?

When I reemerged, Benito was standing at his kitchen counter. He was dressed in a button-down and a pair of crisp slacks.

"Here you go," he said, handing me a small white mug. "I think you might want this."

What I wanted was a tranquilizer to slip into my cappuccino. "Thank you," I mumbled.

Benito sat at the small round table in his kitchen, drinking coffee, and I decided to join him. The table was in front of a large set of windows overlooking a public square of some sort; beyond that was the crest of a steep hill, and farther still, what looked to be much of Rome. "About last night," I began.

Benito smiled. Then his smile became a grin, which quickly turned into a chuckle.

So I *had* thoroughly humiliated myself. "What?" I asked crossly. "Didn't your mother ever tell you it wasn't polite to laugh at someone you slept with?"

Benito stopped laughing. "I slept on the sofa," he said solemnly.

"I meant in the biblical sense." It occurred to me that he might not be familiar with the expression. "Someone you had sex with," I clarified.

He continued to look at me quizzically.

"Intercourse," I said with exasperation, hoping that I would not have to resort to hand gestures to bridge what was turning out to be a sizable language gap. "Or, I don't know. Something like that."

Benito began to laugh again, and I was tempted to slap the table like I sometimes used to when Zoe and Jack wouldn't stop fooling around. "Maggie," he said, wiping tears from his eyes, "we did not have relations of any sort."

I could have fainted with relief. "Really?"

Benito smiled again, this time gently, and I realized he wasn't being unkind. "Of course, I wish that were not the case, but it is. You do not remember?"

I shook my head. "I'm afraid not."

"Then I am now very glad we did not go any further. I should have known to take you home after our cocktails, but you said you were so happy to not be thinking of this Alan—"

"Adam," I corrected. My cheeks were on fire.

"That's right," Benito said, nodding. "Anyway, you seemed happy, and we were having a nice time. In the taxi . . ." Now it was his turn to flush. "What can I say? I am attracted to you, Maggie. I was happy when you kissed me."

I kissed *him*? At this point it was splitting hairs to figure out who had made the first move, but this still astonished me. "Thank you," I said, managing a small smile. "I'm attracted to you, too, Benito. But clearly I'm a mess. At another point in life, maybe this would have worked out differently." I sighed. "If it's not too much trouble, would you mind telling me the rest of what happened last night? I don't remember much beyond getting out of the taxi."

"We ordered a bottle of wine at the wine bar. We split it, but—" He held both hands palms up. "You seemed fine. I am sorry I did not realize that wasn't the case."

I had to know the rest, however mortifying. "Then what?"

Benito took a sip of his coffee. "You asked to see my apartment. I agreed." His face grew serious. "When we got here, you became quiet. I told you I would take you home, but you asked to use my phone first."

I looked at him, appalled. "I did *what*?"

"You wanted to call Al—Adam."

"But you didn't let me, right?"

"Let you!" Benito laughed again. "You insisted! I could not have stopped you if I had thrown my phone out the window."

I ran some quick math in my head. It had probably been ten or so at night in Italy when I had called, which meant it had been five in the morning in Chicago. "He didn't pick up, right?"

"He picked up," said Benito cheerfully.

My gut was in knots. "Oh my word."

His eyes met mine, and only then did I realize they were such a dark blue that they were almost navy. "You were taking off your clothes as you talked to him. You told him you were about to make love to a handsome Italian man." Benito gave me another grin. "You can imagine that I was pleased to hear myself described in such a way. I did not hear the rest, because you disappeared into the bathroom. You were not gone long."

I put my head on the table. What else had I said? It was true that I had wanted Adam to feel terrible for hurting me the way he had. But I didn't want to utterly humiliate myself in the process. Now Adam probably knew what I was only beginning to realize: the bottom of my life had just given out, and I was now in free fall to somewhere even darker and more despairing.

"Do not worry, Maggie," said Benito, who hadn't gathered that my torment no longer had anything to do with whether he and I had played naked Twister. He touched the top of my head lightly. "My mother raised me to fear God and respect women. I could not convince you to put your shirt back on, but you accepted tea and toast. Then I put you to bed."

~

I finished my coffee and thanked Benito for his kindness. He flagged down a taxi for me and kissed me goodbye on both cheeks, and we parted ways. How strange to have shared such a moment with a person I would never see again, I thought on the ride back. How fortunate that said person had been Benito and not a different man, who might have taken advantage of my idiocy. How humiliating that I had drunkenly called my husband after knowing he truly did not want to be my husband anymore.

Even more than a shower, I needed a disinfectant for my soul. When I approached Piazza Navona, I asked the taxi driver to drop me in front of a church I had walked past several times. It was open to the public all day, and I ducked inside.

While I suspected there might be a higher power at play in the universe, religion itself held no lure; I would never understand how so many vastly different faiths could claim to have a patent on the afterlife. But after taking a seat on one of the pews, I bowed my head. My limited understanding of Catholicism did not keep me from feeling the presence of every weeping wife who had ever knelt before God beneath the opulently imagined heavens on the church's ceiling. I didn't yet know how, but just as many a woman before me had managed to, I would have to pull myself out of this.

~

"Jean, I'm a disaster," I said a few days later. We were at a busy restaurant in Trastevere, arguably Rome's best-known food destination and something of a tourist trap, albeit a delightful one. The neighborhood's bustling blocks were lined with restaurants, cafés, and shops; Jean and I had chosen a trattoria on the corner, not for its menu but for the red-and-white checked tablecloths and the twinkle lights strung inside and out. Now we were seated on the heated patio beneath a canopy of glowing strands.

Jean leaned toward me and narrowed her eyes. After she had examined me, she said, "You don't look like a disaster to me, dearie. Tired, maybe, but far from disastrous. But tell me more."

"I messed up," I said morosely. "I thought I was pulling my way out of my funk, but come to find out, I've slipped even farther down than I realized." I told her about what had happened with Benito. "I mean, I drank so much I don't remember half the night. What's wrong with me?"

"What's wrong with you is that you're beating yourself up too much," she said matter-of-factly. "You're going through a rough patch, but you're certainly not the first person to handle it in a way that's not ideal. When I realized I'd rather be alone than stay married to Sam, I drank my face off for half a year."

I stared at her. "Really?"

"Sure did. Instead of telling Sam the truth straight away, I drank too much. Finally a friend of mine pointed out that instead of making things better, I was heading in the exact opposite direction. So I stopped boozing and got honest with Sam. There were some tough months after that, and more still after he passed. But now I'm back to having an occasional glass of wine or jigger of whiskey without worrying about whether it will lead to six more," she said, pointing toward the glass in front of her. "There's no doubt it would serve you well to dry out for a while. But you're going to have to work through what's making you want to drink in the first place."

I took a bite of my caprese salad. "Thank you," I said after I had swallowed. "And you're right. I've got to work on not flogging myself all the time."

"Don't we all, my dear. Don't we all." She lifted her wineglass, and I lifted my sparkling water. "Cheers to shedding old habits and making new friends."

"Cheers," I said, clinking my glass against hers. "Let's hope my old habits don't follow me back to Chicago."

Jean was staring at me with a serious expression on her face.

"What is it?" I asked, instinctively wiping my mouth. "Is there something on me?"

"You've got basil between your front teeth."

I started reaching for my mouth when she swatted at me.

"I'm joshin' you. But do you really have to go back to Chicago? I mean, you already quit your job."

Although Gita had asked me this, too, I had not yet given serious thought to the question. Where else would I go? "Maybe? I don't know. It's the most likely scenario, I suppose."

Her cheeks folded like an accordion as she smiled at me. I wondered if I would look like that when I was her age. Jean made me think it wouldn't be so bad if I did. "I'm about to throw an offer at you that changes your most likely scenario—but before I do, keep in mind that you're not obligated to take it. My house in Ann Arbor is sitting open until I get back from Florence. It's a cute little place, in a private spot but not too far from downtown. Now, I know you and Adam went to school there, but that was decades ago, and there's a whole other city aside from the university that's pretty darn great. Course, it's not Rome."

I was so stunned that I said nothing. Me? Living in a town that had not been on my radar for a good thirty years? Because I had the good fortune to meet this lovely stranger who was now a friend?

Jean's eyes followed a gaggle of tourists for a moment. "If you wanted to take a break from Chicago, though, you could do that there. Six months would probably be time enough for you to figure out what you wanted to do next. Here." She slid her phone across the table at me. "Flip through. There are a couple pictures. Bought it not long after Sam died, and did most of the handwork myself. I'm proud of it."

The house was set on a wooded lot. It was barn shaped and painted slate gray, with a cherry-red door. The interior was white with colorful paintings on nearly every wall, and worn Persian rugs on the ground.

"This is amazing," I said as I gave the phone back. And it was. But this was not a one-week jaunt to Italy; it was a half-year commitment to live somewhere else. As much as I wanted to leave Oak Valley, was I really ready to start over? "It's incredibly generous of you to offer, but I don't know if I can accept. I mean, I just told you what a mess I am. How do you know I won't trash the place?"

Jean gave me a look that was a lot like the one I gave Zoe and Jack when they were being ridiculous. "A worrywart like you who's managed to raise two fine children? I'll believe it when I see it."

I laughed. "I see your point. But how could I ever pay you back?"

"That's exactly what I said to my friend when she helped me through the worst part of my divorce from Sam. Forget paying it back—this is me paying it forward. I think you've already gathered that I'm not the type to offer what I don't intend to deliver. You'd need to cover utilities, but I wouldn't charge you rent. You'd be saving me money, in fact, because I wouldn't have to keep paying my neighbor to make sure no one's stealing my paintings."

I bit my lip. If I didn't have to pay rent, and I rented out our home, I might actually come out ahead—provided my alimony went through. It was all sounding . . . doable. Except once again, I found myself wondering what was happening to me. Two days earlier, I had nearly been intimate with a man who was not my husband, then walked into a church and had something of a moment in spite of my spiritual skepticism. Now I was considering throwing caution—and my home—to the wind and moving to a new state. It was as though I had inadvertently opened a portal to a part of myself that I had not known existed.

Jean continued. "If you decide to go for it, I'll have my lawyer draw up some sort of agreement to keep things on the up-and-up and make it clear to anyone who stops by that you're not a grifter. Suppose I could run a background check on you, too, but if there's anything I've learned in sixty-eight years of living, it's to trust my gut about people—and my gut says I can trust you. Course, if I'm wrong and you light the place on fire, which I know you won't, I'm also old enough to know how to start over. Now let me tell you what's weird about my home before you make up your mind."

Dozens of reasons why not paraded through my head, and not one of them had anything to do with Jean's warning about the backward hot- and cold-water handles and a bedroom that was never quite warm. What would Gita say when she found out she was right about me moving, even temporarily? The kids would probably think I was having a bad reaction to the divorce. Rose—well, Rose did give me pause. If I left Chicago for half a year, who would she become while I was gone? And Adam—

Who cared what Adam thought? Or anyone? Like Zoe had said, it was time for me to start focusing on what I wanted for a change. And while wanting Adam may have been disastrous, this desire, at least, did not involve anyone other than me.

Yes, something—dear God, *something*—had to give if I was going to make it out of this divorce with a shred of my identity and confidence intact. I walked around the table to hug Jean. "Okay," I said. "It's probably nuts to make a change right now, but this feels right. Thank you."

Jean patted me on the back. "Maggie, I have a feeling this is one change that's going to do you good."

TWELVE

After dinner Jean and I said goodbye, though it no longer felt like a goodbye now that we knew we would see each other again later that year. The next day I packed my suitcase, had one last cappuccino, and flew back to Chicago, again in a first-class seat. This time I didn't ask if there had been a mix-up.

"Well, well, well!" declared Gita two days later. I was at her salon to have my roots touched up and had just sat down at her workstation. "Look who's glowing."

"Am I? It won't last with this weather," I said, brushing snow off the top of my head. I swallowed hard, knowing I was about to deliver news that Gita would not be happy to hear. "It was an incredible trip."

Our eyes met in her mirror. "But?" she pressed.

"You know me so well," I said. Then I told her everything: about my flight upgrades, Jean, Benito and my drunken mistake, and how I was heading to Ann Arbor for a while.

"I won't say I told you so, but I told you so," she said with a sad smile. "I have to ask: What about your support network? What about your house and—everything else?"

"Unless the court forces me to do otherwise, I'm not going to sell the house. I'm going to see if I can rent it. It's not forever." I would leave at the beginning of January. In an unfortunate twist, the court date for the formal dissolution of my marriage was on the sixth—two days before what would have been Adam's and my twenty-eighth wedding anniversary.

Gita retrieved a comb from a pocket of her apron and began pulling it through my hair. "I can't say I blame you," she said, peering at my roots. "I know Adam and I have been friends for years, but he acted like a real bastard. Are you sure you're not punishing yourself instead of him, though? I mean, what are you going to *do* in Ann Arbor?"

"There's plenty happening there," I said, even though I had not been to visit since Zoe was touring colleges ten years earlier. I bit my lip, thinking of how painful it had been to see Adam at Thanksgiving—and that was even before he revealed his terrible lie. "I just think it would be good to put some distance between me and Adam. The incident with Benito made me realize I'm not coping like I should."

"Well, who would?" said Gita.

"I know it's within the range of normal. But I'm drinking too much. Or at least I was," I corrected myself. "I haven't had anything since then." I had hated turning down free wine on the flight back, but not nearly as much as I had hated the feeling I'd had when I woke up in Benito's bed.

"No way," she said, putting her hands on my shoulders. "I know plenty of alcoholics. You're not one of them."

"I didn't say I'm an alcoholic. I've developed a bad habit. There's got to be a better way to get through this."

"Well, some of us, myself included, think you're doing great," Gita said quietly.

I was pretty sure I knew what Gita was thinking. If I gave up alcohol, would I have to skip the wine-tasting parties she and Reddy threw? Wouldn't I be a total snooze, sipping soda water when we went out for drinks—if you could even call an evening outing "drinks" when you were no longer imbibing? What would happen to us facing the worst with gin and tonics, a ritual that had turned many a rotten day into something sparkling and sidesplittingly hilarious? Drinking was part of our friendship. It was what we did.

And this one was more reason why leaving Oak Valley for a while was a good idea. I knew Gita would never push me to drink, but it would be easier not to if joining her to wash down the day's troubles with wine wasn't an option.

"You know I support you no matter what," she concluded.

"Thank you."

"You're most welcome. So, let's talk about your hair." She squinted at me over the top of her glasses. "I'd say you're at about forty percent gray, which means you're probably going to have to sit in my chair more often. Maybe even go a tiny bit blond."

"Blond? Oh no, no, no. I'll pull an Ophelia in your shampooing sink before I become a blonde," I said. My natural color was chestnut brown—or at least it was until I entered perimenopause and much of my hair's melanin decided to vacate the premises.

"I'm not talking Marilyn Monroe here. Just some golden highlights, maybe a lighter base." I must have winced, because Gita added, "I hope this isn't about money, because you know it's not an issue. You get the too-much-dirt-on-the-salon-owner special. I'm going to charge you the same thing no matter what you get. Of course, you'll have to come home to get the discount." She gave me a devilish grin, and I knew we were okay.

"Thank you."

"Don't mention it. And in case you're wondering, I think a new look would be good for you. But I'm happy to stick to the same old for now." She poked at my head one last time and excused herself to go mix my color.

Gita had just wheeled a cart loaded with foul-smelling dye back to where I was sitting when the doorbell jingled and a tall, immaculately dressed woman came striding into the salon.

"Who's *that*?" I whispered.

"Oh, her? That's Vivian," said Gita under her breath. "Isn't she fabulous?"

Indeed she was. The woman was wearing a red tweed cape—the type of contraption that would have made me look like a budget Sherlock Holmes impersonator but that painted Vivian as the picture of grace. She slid the cape off and hung it on the coatrack, revealing a crisp white button-down shirt, slim black pants, and a pair of knee-high leather boots. The main attraction, though, was her hair. Though her face was barely lined—she probably had half the wrinkles I did—her long waves were a bright, crystalline silver. I had never thought of gray as an attractive color before, but Vivian's hair paid no heed to the idea that sexy only came in shades of yellow, red, and brown. It was hair that was not to be ignored.

"She sees Sophie," said Gita, referring to a colorist at the salon.

"Is that her real color?" I asked.

"It is now," said Gita, and reached for the applicator stuck in the bowl of dye. She was a second from slathering the light brown paste on my head when I said, "Wait!"

She jerked her hand back, alarmed. "Did I hurt you?"

"No, no, I'm fine," I said. "I just—don't know that I want to cover up the gray. I want to grow it out so it's natural."

Gita looked at me like I had suggested a buzz cut. "If you aren't proof that heartbreak can make a person crazy, I don't know what is. I thought you wanted to stay dark?"

"I do—sort of. Isn't there a way to weave in the existing gray while I grow it out?"

"There's a way to do everything," she said, shaking her head at me. "But I'm sorry to report this does involve highlights, which means a little more maintenance, at least in the short term. It'll look good—but it will be different than what you're used to."

"I'm ready," I told her, and it almost felt true.

~

Later that day I stood in front of the mirror in my master bathroom. Beneath the bright, revealing light of the bathroom where Adam had once brushed his teeth as I slathered on antiaging cream that never did make me appear even one day younger, I saw that I did look different.

But it was not my golden highlights or pink cheeks that were a surprise. It was the absence of the innocence I had casually worn all those years when Adam was still mine. The shell-shocked expression I had adopted after his departure was gone, too, and that was almost as strange.

Now there was a new woman staring back at me. And she wore the weary expression of a traveler who had lost sight of her destination.

THIRTEEN

When I was a child, my mother did all she could to make Christmas joyful. She would put toys and clothes on layaway in the spring and summer so she would have gifts to put under our tabletop tree in December. Meals became increasingly creative as we approached the holidays, because she was setting aside part of our budget to buy a honey-glazed ham, chocolate, and oranges—foods that still suggest Christmas to me in a way that eggnog and peppermint sticks never will. On Christmas morning she would watch me closely, desperate for proof that she had not failed to deliver some version of a childhood fantasy she must have longed for when she was young. And in response, I put on a jubilant performance, because anything less would have crushed her.

As an adult, no performance had been necessary. I had all I had ever wanted: a permanent roof over my head, a delicious meal and gifts whose cost did not evoke a secret sadness in me, and above all, my husband and children.

But when I returned from Italy and began to prepare for Jack and Zoe to come home, it occurred to me that I would have to pull my old mask back out.

Just push through until you leave town, I told myself. *You made it through the past nine months; you can hold out two more weeks.*

It's not that I thought Ann Arbor would be Shangri-la. But I had begun to see it as a symbol of finished business. When I moved there, the divorce would be final. I would have received my last paycheck and begun receiving alimony. The house in Oak Valley—which Linnea, in a true feat, had rented to a pair of grandparents who wanted to spend six months in the same town as their new grandchild—would be off of my hands, if only temporarily.

True, I had a hard time visualizing what my life would look like in Michigan. But maybe, I thought—just maybe—in a place where I was not reminded of Adam and the life we had shared at every turn, I could find a way to begin again.

~

"You know you didn't have to put up a tree, Mom," said Zoe on Christmas Eve. The kids were dividing the holiday between Adam's loft and our house, which was now a maze of boxes. The three of us had spent the evening together; they would go to Adam's brother's house for Christmas Day, then spend the night at Adam's. I hated that we were now on a split schedule. Had Adam thought about that—really thought about it—when he left? If so, had he actually decided his own happiness was worth the cost of severing our family unit? It seemed so unlike him.

Then again, I didn't know who he was anymore—if I ever had at all.

Zoe and I were standing in the kitchen; Jack had fallen asleep on the sofa after dinner, and we had left him there. I looked from the Christmas tree in the living room to my daughter. "Well, this year was strange enough as it is. I wanted to preserve some sort of tradition."

"Tradition's overrated. Remember Thanksgiving?" she said, raising her perfectly manicured eyebrows. (How my daughter managed to master personal grooming with a seventy-hour workweek was the eighth wonder of the world.)

"I do, and it was fine," I lied.

She wrapped her slender arms around me and hugged me tight. "Oh, Mom. It's okay to not have things be perfect."

I cringed as I recalled my Italian almost affair and my drunken phone call to Adam. "Honey, if you knew how far I was from perfect, I don't know if you'd let me be your mother anymore."

Zoe let me go and poured the rest of the tea she had made into her mug. "Come on. You know that's not true." She cupped the mug between her hands and blew on it to cool it. "But humor me: What if your friend's house is actually a dump, or there's a serial killer waiting for you when you get there?"

Naturally, a string of ugly what-ifs had already paraded through my mind. I had decided that if Jean's place was unsafe or awful (which it very well might be), I would return to Oak Valley and seek temporary shelter in the mother-in-law suite above Gita's garage—this, provided the serial killer Zoe had alluded to didn't get to me first. "I don't know, sweetheart," I told her. "I guess I'll try to stab him back? As for what I'll do, I guess I'll figure that out as I go."

"It's okay if you change your mind, you know."

"Well," I said, trying to sound chipper, "maybe I will. Life is nothing if not full of twists and turns."

Zoe looked at me for what seemed like an eternity.

"What?" I finally said.

"Nothing."

"No, what is it? You can tell me."

She had set down her mug, and now she pulled at a piece of skin on her lip. I resisted the urge to tell her to stop. Finally she said, "I just know Dad's going to regret this one day. And I was wondering what will happen then."

"Nothing," I said quickly. "Nothing will happen then. Everything will be like it is now, only I'll be in a better mental place." I had envisioned so many scenarios by that point that I understood it was not in my best interest to entertain the one Zoe had just posed. I was finally starting to get on board with the idea that Adam would never have a change of heart. I could not go back to treading water in my sea of grief.

~

Yet Zoe's comment stayed with me as I spent a teary Christmas afternoon at Gita's and made it through the next couple of days with Jack and Zoe before driving them to the airport, kissing them goodbye, and collapsing into a puddle after they disappeared from sight.

Well, I hope he does regret it, I thought angrily as I sat in a corner, sipping seltzer while dozens of my closest acquaintances rang in the new year. Gita had convinced me to join her at a friend's party so I wouldn't spend the night alone, but it turned out that the only thing worse than being by yourself on New Year's Eve is being surrounded by inebriated couples.

Two minutes after the ball dropped, I said goodnight to Gita and our host, grabbed my coat, and walked the ten blocks home. I was not one for resolutions, but as I trudged through the snow, I vowed to send Adam away if he actually returned to me (which, given his confession on Thanksgiving and my foolish phone call from Rome, seemed highly unlikely).

Because even after everything, I wasn't sure I could summon the strength to tell him no. And that uncertainty made me feel like I had already failed a mission that I had not yet begun.

~

Just after the new year, a moving company arrived to deliver my boxes to a storage unit. The house would be rented out from February until the end of July; through our lawyers, Adam had agreed to take care of maintenance during that time and revisit the idea of a sale when I returned from Ann Arbor.

On the sixth of January—just two days before what was to be Adam's and my twenty-eighth anniversary—I arrived at the courthouse to finalize what my husband had set in motion almost a year earlier.

I expected it to hurt. To be honest, I expected to be racked with pain and maybe even weep quietly into my lawyer's blazer before throwing a shoe at Adam. But when I saw Adam standing beside his lawyer in the courtroom, I felt an almost clinical detachment toward him. Then I turned and stared straight ahead, saying yes to the judge each time I was asked to confirm that I agreed with the terms of our divorce. Adam's responses were identical to mine, but I refused to look at him again.

Eleven minutes later, we were legally unwed.

Therein lay the trickery of it all. Divorce was a legal guarantee that you were a free agent—but where were the guarantees for marriage? One day your husband would claim you were the love of his life; the next, he could decide he was done with said life, and you as his wife.

My lawyer led me out of the hall ahead of Adam and his lawyer—apparently there was some sort of etiquette to these things. I thanked her for her time and effort, which had cost a tenth of our savings. Then I fled to the bathroom, where I sat in a stall, trying to stanch the thoughts rushing through my mind.

Nine months had passed since Adam had left me. That was longer than I had gestated Zoe, who was born two weeks early; it was time enough for three seasons to pass, and roughly three hundred days in which to wrap my mind around life sans spouse. But now I had the paperwork to officially declare me the very thing I had spent my whole life trying not to be: alone.

I don't know how long I sat there; it must have been a while before I decided to find somewhere other than a courthouse lavatory to ruminate. I had almost reached the front of the building when Adam called my name. I spun around and saw that he and his lawyer were standing against a marble-paneled wall.

I shook my head vigorously, but Adam began walking over anyway. "Maggie," he said again.

I gave him a chilly stare.

"Hi," he said, slipping his hands into his pockets. When he first left me, he looked younger than he had in years. But beneath the unforgiving fluorescent lights, the years were etched on his face, and he looked exhausted.

Not your circus, not your clown, I reminded myself. *Just because your instinct is to care doesn't mean you have to.*

"Did you mean what you said?" he asked quietly.

My face grew warm.

"When you called from Italy," he added, like my flaming cheeks weren't indication that I knew exactly what he was talking about.

I could neither confirm nor deny that I had meant what I had said, as I had no memory of our conversation. But I was not about to further humiliate myself by telling him this. I tilted my chin up. "Of course I did."

"I see," he said. He rubbed his forehead for a minute. Then he looked back up at me. "Maggie? I'm sorry."

Yeah, well, that made two of us. But I could not—would not—slip back into the role of someone who grasped for what was long gone. "Save it for someone who cares," I said, sounding more tired than unkind.

His eyes searched my face. "What are you going to do in Ann Arbor?"

Learn how to go through life without you, I thought. But I owed him nothing—not my plans, not my motivation, not a single thought in my head. So I turned and walked away.

~

"I wasn't expecting you!" said Rose when she opened the door to her apartment the next day.

Her skin was like rice paper as I kissed her cheek. "I'm sorry, Rose," I said, trying not to let my spirits sink. I had called again that morning to remind her I would be stopping by on my way to Ann Arbor. "If it's a bad time—"

"Don't be ridiculous," she said. "It's always a good time for you. I was wondering if you'd visit sometime this century."

"I'm sorry," I said again, even though I had been to see her just before leaving for Rome. "Things have been . . . hectic."

"You don't say." She motioned for me to follow her to the living room and then sat across from me on one of the identical velvet sofas.

"Did Adam tell you our divorce was finalized?" I asked her, staring at the bowl of white Jordan almonds on the coffee table between us.

"Goodness, no!" she said.

"Yes, yesterday. I figured he would have told you . . ."

"Well, he didn't." Her hands looked like tiny bird claws as she wrung them in her lap, and I wondered if mentioning the divorce had been a mistake. "I begged him not to do this to our family. Where are you going?" she said woefully.

I had already told her about going to Ann Arbor, but I told her again. "I'm really sorry to be leaving. You'll still have Adam and Rick, of course, and we'll talk on the phone like we always do. Six months will pass before you know it." I wanted to promise I would return to Chicago or at least visit, but I wasn't sure if either was true. Adam had said he was done planning—but for the first time since perhaps high school, I also had no plans and had seemingly lost the ability to make them.

I asked Rose if she would be okay.

"I'm always okay. You and I are alike that way, Maggie." She sighed and looked out the window. "I do miss Richard, though," she said. "It's very hard to be alone sometimes."

"Yes, it is," I agreed.

"We fought like cats and dogs, you know."

I nodded; Adam had told me as much, and I had witnessed it on several occasions before Richard's death.

"Yet he and I stayed together," she continued, "and in the last ten to fifteen years, we were very happy, your father and I." She had begun speaking to me as though I were one of her sons, and I couldn't bring myself to correct her.

Nor was I about to point out that as long as I had known them, Rose had regarded Richard like a bothersome man-child, and he had treated her as someone who was constantly in need of correction. This dynamic had not changed during the last years of their marriage. But the only people who can truly understand a marriage are the ones in it, and perhaps this had fit Rose's definition of *happy*.

"Sometimes it's easier to be alone, not having to explain yourself to another person," she added. "Most of the time the pain is worth it if you love each other. You and Adam could still work things out."

I had a divorce decree and a broken heart that said otherwise, but at least she was no longer addressing me as though I were Adam or Rick. "I think it's a little late for that," I said quietly.

She gave me an incredulous look. "Oh, dear, that's not true at all. It's only too late if one of you is dead."

I had no response to her remark, so I gave her a sanitized recollection of my trip to Rome. This triggered Rose's memory, and she told me about her parents, Polish immigrants who had met after settling in Chicago and had found success in a series of small businesses. They were loyal to their roots, attending the Polish service at their Catholic church, making sausage, sauerkraut, and pierogies for meals, and dutifully sending money back to the old country every month. But they never returned to Poland, even for a visit. "I always meant to go there myself, but it was such a long trip and it simply never happened," Rose said, staring at her hands. "I wish I would have."

Her resignation seemed like proof that sometimes it really was too late, even if you were still alive. But when we said goodbye, Rose clutched my arms so hard I wasn't sure she would let me go. "I'll miss you, dear girl," she said. Then she whispered, "Remember—there's still time."

FOURTEEN

After having so many decisions foisted upon me, I was finally taking my destiny into my own hands—or so I told myself as I drove past the gray, half-frozen expanse of Lake Michigan, toward the industrial graveyards of Indiana, and through the snow-covered fields of southwest Michigan. No matter how ill-advised my previous decisions may have been, moving was something I could be proud of.

By the time I reached Ann Arbor, my optimism had been out too long and had begun to curdle. What had I been thinking? I didn't want to find new friends and new places to shop and eat. I didn't want to have to adjust to a whole new life—again.

The city was more charming than I remembered, but surely its allure owed much to the fresh layer of snow that had fallen, I decided as I drove through downtown. Even if its charm was authentic, I was obviously in the wrong age bracket to enjoy it, because everyone was young. Twentysomethings beeped their horns at me for driving too slowly on the icy roads. Trendy young professionals rushed into restaurants and coffee shops to escape the cold. A coed was throwing up into a snowy bush after what must have been a night of one too many cocktails. It didn't matter if Jean was a full fifteen years older than me, because she was young at heart. I was a crotchety old woman who belonged in a retirement community in Florida. This midwestern college town was the wrong place for me.

Jean lived in an eclectic, vaguely bohemian neighborhood on the city's west side; her house was on the last lot on a quiet street a few blocks from a river. After I pulled into the driveway, I called the number of the woman who had been tending Jean's home while she was away. A minute later she met me at the front door. I was expecting someone more artistic, à la Jean, but the neighbor's hair was clipped in a sharp bob, and she wore a long camel overcoat. She appeared to be roughly my age and introduced herself as Cathy.

"Well, here it is," she said, unlocking the front door for me. "What brings you to this neck of the woods? Are you going to be working at the university?"

"No. I just got divorced," I said, following her inside.

She frowned. "Oh."

I frowned back. I had already learned the hard way that many married people viewed divorce as a communicable disease. *But why?* pushed one woman at the New Year's party I had attended with Gita. Like I could offer an antidote made of one part less nagging and two parts not neglecting to wax my bikini line ever since the elder Bush was president.

I was ready to yell *Thanks!* at Cathy as the door hit her backside when she said, "I'm sorry. I got divorced two years ago."

"Really," I said, eyeing the diamond-encrusted band circling her ring finger as she handed me the keys she was holding.

Cathy nodded, wearing a new expression that was impossible to read. "It was awful. Let me know if you ever want to grab a drink."

I wanted to grab a drink. Three, in fact. Why did eighty-five percent of all social invitations involve alcohol?

"I'm not sure I would have made it through that first year without talking to people who had been there," said Cathy. "It's true what they say, you know."

"And what's that?"

"Divorce is worse than death," she said grimly.

"Hmm," I said, because I wasn't so sure I bought that. Losing Adam had made me feel like I had been broken in two. Yet even this was not the same as the empty, irreplaceable loss I had experienced after my mother passed.

"Don't go it alone," added Cathy.

This was lousy advice for someone who had just moved to a new town by herself. But I was pretty sure Cathy meant well, so I thanked her and promised I would keep her offer in mind. Then I closed the door behind her and went to explore the place that would be my home for the next six months.

While small, the house was bright and airy, and smelled of a surprisingly pleasant mix of paint and cinnamon. The ceiling above the living room was vaulted and had a large skylight on the southern side. Fractured rays of sun were streaming onto one of Jean's paintings, and as I took a step forward, what seemed to be an abstract riverfront from afar revealed a stunning level of detail up close.

Jean had hung paintings like this in most rooms. As I examined them, I found myself wondering why I had not checked county records to make sure this home was really hers to rent out, nor combed through various Internet databases to confirm that my friend and her neighbors were not murderers or sex offenders.

But these worries were dwarfed by a larger, more looming thought.

And that was that I didn't belong there.

This house was suited for someone with a sense of adventure who was content enjoying all that tranquil beauty by herself. But save a few moments of joy in Rome, I no longer seemed to be able to enjoy myself.

No, I thought suddenly as I looked at a small painting of a dark forest with a glowing red light coming from deep within the trees. The problem was not that I had lost the ability to enjoy things.

It was that I had lost myself.

~

My first few days in Ann Arbor were busy enough to seem pleasant, and I tried to view this as evidence that my initial despair had been nothing but a spike in anxiety. I unpacked. I walked around the neighborhood and got reacquainted with the city. I found a grocery store and a café, and when the coffee at that café turned out to be brown water, I found another, Maizie's, where the cappuccinos were nearly on par with the ones I'd had in Italy. I called Rose, Jack, and Zoe, and assured them all that I was fine.

Then I hung up and cried.

In Oak Valley, I could hear cars zip past on the nearby highway, and the wail of sirens in the distance; even though my kids had left home, someone else's were usually hollering down the street. But at Jean's, deer bounded inaudibly through the yard into the woods. The air above seemed impervious to the roar of planes. The neighbors existed—I had seen them dashing in and out—but the houses were far apart, and I couldn't hear anyone in the distance.

The quiet was a constant reminder that I was completely alone. I could clearly remember my children screaming as they ran through the house, attempting to tear limb from torso, and Adam turning up the television so he could hear the Cubs' score over their clamoring. *I would kill for a day of silence,* I used to think to myself, even though I knew every word to "Big Yellow Taxi" and was presumably intelligent enough to understand that the paved paradise Joni Mitchell sang of could very well be a metaphor for an empty nest. Now I had all the silence I ever could have wanted—and far more. As I stood at the sink one day, my lips pressed together as my shoulders shook because I didn't want to fill the house with the sound of my crying, I was forced to admit that perhaps Cathy had a point.

~

"I'm having a hard time," I confessed to Gita one night. We chatted most days, if only for a few minutes. I quickly added, "That's not to say I'm turning around and heading back to Oak Valley."

"I would never suggest that you would—at least not yet," said Gita. In the background, I could hear Reddy talking to Amy. "Have you met anyone? Anyone you could go grab coffee with?"

"Not really." I stared at a water lily in the painting over the bed, wishing I were wherever that place was, rather than huddling in front of a space heater in thirteen-degree weather. If I had half a brain, I would have joined Jean in Florence rather than moving into her Michigan home.

"What have you been up to then?"

"Grocery shopping. Unpacking. Reading a lot." I fell back onto the futon mattress. It was like a pile of rocks covered with cotton, but I had been sleeping deeply for a change. "Jean has shelves full of apocalyptic-type novels. Some of them are strangely good, though the main takeaway is that if you manage to survive the beginning of the end of time, your reward is prolonged misery, and maybe the occasional roll in the hay with some survivor who's even more screwed up than you are. Might as well let the zombies or aliens or whatever just have their way with you at the get-go."

"You know when you talk like that it really worries me," said Gita, and I laughed.

"I worry enough for both of us. But if you hear that a giant meteor is heading for earth, please show up at my front door with some nightshade."

"If that happens, I'll be there in a flash," she quipped. "In all seriousness, you need to stay busy if you're going to get through this. Look for a job. Join a dating website. Just do *something*, preferably something that doesn't involve rattling around in that house all day. Loneliness can kill you. There's actually research to prove it."

"Great. So in addition to the honor of being a freshly minted divorcée, I get the bonus gift of a shortened life span."

"I'm trying to be encouraging, Maggie."

"Oh, I'm encouraged, all right," I said. But I didn't want to leave things on a bad note, so I promised Gita I would find a constructive social activity to occupy my time and increase my longevity.

I would slowly pry my nails from their ragged beds before purposefully looking for love, but I *was* searching for a job. I had already applied for four bookkeeping positions and had received a callback on one. The hiring manager informed me I could start as soon as the following day. The catch: I would be making minimum wage for the first three months as I "trained" for a position I was overqualified for. The manager was in the middle of yammering about what a fantastic growth opportunity it was when I hung up on her. I was having a hot flash, it's true, but that wasn't the impetus for my behavior. I was simply tired of being lied to.

As I stood at the stove frying an egg the next morning, I wondered if maybe it was finally time for me to go back to social work or something in that vein. Leaving the field after my client attacked me had seemed the right thing to do at the time. Twenty-four years later, I wondered if I would have been better served by taking a long maternity leave or a sabbatical. Now I would have to start over at the bottom, as Zoe once pointed out when questioning why I had not kept my "real" career.

When I looked online later that day, the social work positions listed were far more appealing than the bookkeeping jobs I had inquired about, which seemed like confirmation it was the right path to take.

But should I really look for a long-term position when I was only here for a limited time? Anyway, how did one craft a résumé in a field one had not worked in since the dawn of the World Wide Web? Mothering was nothing if not fieldwork, but I could not exactly list it under "experience." And the paperwork—the paperwork! If I decided to apply for a job that required licensure, I would have to submit a dozen forms to begin the recertification process. I would have to perform thousands of hours of supervised work in order to prove my competency. Then and only then would I be permitted to take a test that could send the most stoic professional into a fit of spontaneous sobbing.

I closed my computer, feeling confused and weary. If I were still drinking, I would have thrown myself a one-woman wine party. I suppose there are all sorts of ways one can feel when imbibing; personally, I was more sanguine and self-assured with each sip. I would have used liquid courage to decide if I truly wanted to return to social work, and if so, to begin the application process.

It was so tempting to run back to my old ways—to give myself a boost, if only to make it to the next day. I could hop in my car and run to the market for a flavorful Rioja or crisp Sancerre, knowing that even half a glass would have made the world more welcoming.

But as I turned away from Jean's desk and walked to her bookshelves to find something to read, I reminded myself that the last time I had marinated my misery, I had ended up in a stranger's bed. Like so many other things I had once enjoyed, divorce had eliminated casual drinking for me, at least for the time being.

And just as well. I may have lost myself, but if I had learned one thing since Adam had left, it was that I wasn't going to turn up in a bottle of wine.

FIFTEEN

I had been in Ann Arbor for two weeks when I drove past a church on the way back from a grocery run. The sign out front read:

NONDENOMINATIONAL DIVORCE SUPPORT GROUP, TONIGHT AND EVERY TUESDAY, 7 PM. ALL WELCOME!

Support group, pshaw, I thought. I had facilitated a few support groups when I was a social worker, and I hadn't enjoyed them all that much. One-on-one counseling had been far more rewarding, or at least it had been until someone had taken a knife to my neck.

Except now I was the one who needed support, I realized as I put my groceries away. And aside from Cathy and the baristas at Maizie's, the coffee shop I went to most days to get my caffeine and conversation fix, I had not met a single person in town.

Still, a group wasn't for me; I wasn't going to go. That's what I told myself. But after I had eaten dinner, washed my lone plate and cup, and checked email only to realize it was just six forty-five at night, I stood up from Jean's worn farmhouse table. Maybe the support group would be a bust, but that was still better than moping around the house and wondering if I should just cry uncle and drive back to Oak Valley. I gathered my things and got in the car.

The scene at the church seemed less like life and more like a movie set. Linoleum-floored basement with circle of metal folding chairs: check. Burnt coffee and day-old doughnuts: check. Affable facilitator: check.

Upon closer inspection, the people attending the group, at least, weren't typecast. There was a woman so young I thought surely she could not have secured a marriage license, let alone gone through a divorce. An older man in athletic apparel sat across from another even older man, who was wearing a suit. Another woman looked like the best-case scenario of me—also in her early fifties, but beautiful and impeccably groomed. A handsome man with warm brown skin sat across from me.

"So!" said the group leader, bringing his hands together. He was thin and pale, and ninety percent of his body hair had congregated in the inch of space between his nose and upper lip. "I'm Bob. As most of you know, I'm a licensed social worker as well as a divorcé, and I've been running this support group for the past three years." His mustache wiggled up and down as he spoke. As I stifled a grin, the man across from me, who looked to be in his forties, caught my eye and smiled. I smiled back, which prompted Bob to home in on me. "I'm happy to see we have a new face joining us today. Welcome, welcome!"

"Thank you," I mumbled, grateful he hadn't asked me to introduce myself. I was pretty sure this wasn't for me, so what was the point?

"We're happy to have you here. Now, would anyone like to talk about the past week?"

The very young woman raised her hand and told us how disappointed her mother was about her divorce. Then one of the two older men shared how his recent wedding anniversary had left him feeling empty and alone, which prompted another man to talk about how he had gotten through a similar situation. When no one else volunteered to speak, Bob redirected the conversation. "Today I was hoping to spend a little time discussing loving kindness—that is, the idea of compassion for your ex-spouse. The Buddhist monk Jinpa Min says that loving kindness is the path to all healing. In divorce, it's easy to get trapped in a cycle of anger and regret. But those feelings make it impossible to remember that the person you were once married to is actually a human being, rather than an archetypal villain. Only once you learn to wish your ex-spouse well will you break the cycle and begin the next step of your journey."

"No offense to you or Buddhism, Bob, but that's some serious bull right there," announced the man who had smiled at me earlier.

Someone to my right gasped.

"Sorry, but it's true." He glanced around the circle. "I've got a hundred bucks that says most of us here—just by being the kind of people who show up to a divorce support group—spent years, and maybe our entire marriages and divorces, wishing our ex-spouses well, even when they didn't deserve it." His voice was low and measured as he said this. "Maybe I'm just speaking for me, of course. But if anything, I need help wishing *myself* well. Because even more than a year and a half after my split, I'm still feeling like it's all my fault. And you know what's really screwed up?"

"Tell it," said the elderly man in the suit.

"When I think about my ex-wife, I am almost *always* wishing her well." His voice began to rise. "It's New Year's; poor Lucinda, she hates this day! It's raining! Does Lu have an umbrella? I mean, I would like to get to the point where I'm worried about how *I'll* handle the holidays and whether *I* have weather-appropriate gear. I would like to stop wishing my ex-wife well and actually get angry with her."

Yes, maybe anger was the key. The only real fury I had managed to exhibit toward Adam was when I had kicked him out on Thanksgiving night. (And possibly when I had called him from Benito's—though it was unlikely I would ever find out what I had said, and that was probably for the best.) Maybe if I had torn into him when he was first leaving, he would have told me then and there that Jillian was not the problem. Then instead of sitting in a church basement, waiting for my turn to talk about how horrible I felt, I would have already healed and been—

Doing what? I thought suddenly. I didn't even know what to wish my future would look like, and that was even more depressing than going to a divorce support group.

"Yeah," said the young woman. "I feel the same way about my ex. I hate him, but I still somehow want good things for him."

"Hmm," said Bob, nodding. "That's certainly an interesting way of perceiving it. And you're both right. Getting through divorce is a process. It's important to practice self-love as you work through it."

The older man in athletic gear snickered, which sent another man in his thirties into a fit of laughter. "Self-love," he mouthed. I found myself smiling again, and soon the entire circle was giggling like a bunch of kids.

"Let's pause for a moment, okay?" said Bob, whose broad forehead was beginning to bead with sweat. "Please help yourself to the refreshments along the wall. We'll reconvene in five."

Did Styrofoam contain toxic chemicals? If so, did piping hot coffee unleash them? Would dipping a two-day-old doughnut into a small bit of coffee put me at risk? These were the pressing questions on my mind as the fortysomething man came up beside me at the coffee station, filling the air between us with the scent of cedar and citrus. "Hello," he said.

"Hi," I said.

"Don't worry, you don't have to introduce yourself," he said, pouring coffee into a cup.

"I'm Maggie Halfmoon," I whispered, "but don't tell Bob."

He laughed, and I decided he was all right. "Maggie Halfmoon. That's a great name. I'm Charlie Ellery," he said.

"Nice to meet you, Charlie. I liked what you had to say back there."

"It wasn't too much?"

"Not at all."

"Thanks," he said, almost shyly, looking down at his cup. "I don't usually talk about my ex, so when I do it just kind of comes out like, blarg!" he said, mimicking an explosion with his free hand.

Now I laughed. "That's why I try to refrain from discussing my—" I grimaced. "See, I almost just said *husband*. This is all pretty new for me, and I'm not finding it particularly fun, if you know what I mean."

"Do I ever," said Charlie.

"Ah, the power of connection!" said Bob, coming up behind the two of us. "Hope you two bring this same spirit of conversation to the group when we return!"

Charlie turned to me and subtly rolled his eyes, and I had to cough to cover my laughter.

~

The rest of the meeting was uneventful. There were no revelations or epiphanies, but listening to other people's experiences did make my own seem more bearable.

Still, when the hour was up, I was questioning whether I would return the following week. What I needed most was friendship, and I wasn't convinced a support group was the place to find it. I was still thinking about this when Charlie fell into step with me in the church parking lot.

"Brr," he said. "This weather makes me want to die."

It was bitterly cold, and I tucked my gloved hands into my underarms and shivered. "Or you could just move south. I hear Texas is ten percent more pleasant than death."

I stopped in front of my car, and Charlie, who had paused in front of me, grinned. His was the bright, open face of a person with nothing to hide. Maybe mine was, too. Maybe we had the faces of people who were left behind. "You're smarter than me, Maggie," he said.

"Such a genius that I didn't believe my ex-husband when he said he was leaving."

"Come on now. That's not your fault." Charlie touched my upper arm lightly as he said this, and even though his gloved hand only made contact with my down-filled jacket, a wave of confusion washed over me. How could I possibly be attracted to anyone at a time like this? But attraction didn't mean anything, I quickly reminded myself. It was how you acted on that feeling that mattered.

"Thanks. So. Um. How long have you been going to this group?" I asked him.

Snow had begun to fall, and he brushed a few flakes off his nose, which was crooked yet sculpted, like a work of art. He had crinkly eyes, with the perfect amount of webbing at the corners, and I decided he was probably closer to my age than I had originally guessed. "Two months?" he said. "Maybe three? Yeah, I guess I first started going around Thanksgiving. It's not great, but I've looked and there doesn't really seem to be that much else around." Sadness, as unmistakable as it was brief, surfaced in his expression. Then he righted himself and smiled at me. "Maggie, I don't think I can keep dealing with Bob by myself. Will I see you next Tuesday?"

Funny, disruptive Charlie with the great nose, who knew a thing or two about divorce: maybe he could be a friend. I smiled back at him. "I wasn't planning to, but I think I'm going to go out on a limb and say yes."

SIXTEEN

Dear Maggie,

Florence continues to amaze me. The air is sweet, there's so much beauty that this old gal's heart may just give out, and the colors—oh, the colors. Even at the tail end of what passes for winter here, the light paints everything so darn vivid and unfiltered that I wonder why I'm bothering to attempt to re-create any of it. My tubes of paint and I just can't compete.

MH, I hope you're still holding down the ol' fort, and more important, that you're enjoying yourself. I trust you're finding good company to keep; just don't invite the coyotes in. Italy and I miss you already.

Most sincerely,
Jean

Jean and I had emailed back and forth a bit after I arrived, but I was pleased when her postcard fell out from between a grocery circular and the electric bill. I read it while standing in the doorway, the wind whipping my hair around my face and sending icy air blasting into the house. Only after I had gone over the card a second time did I close the door.

Was it wrong to be envious of Jean? At the very least, she was living proof that a person's best years could still be up ahead.

But she had a purpose; I did not. She had wanted to leave her marriage; I had not. Maybe this was why I could not envision a future even a fraction as good as my past.

I had been in Ann Arbor for nearly a month, and I *had* mostly stopped crying at home—though I still allowed myself to openly weep in the car when, say, "Total Eclipse of the Heart" came on the radio. I had become friendly with Walter, the owner at Maizie's. I turned down Cathy's offer to grab a glass of wine but had joined her for a shift at a local food pantry. I had returned to the support group the following Tuesday night and had stayed even after Charlie didn't show (so much for my new friend).

I was keeping busy as best I could. But try as I might, I could not stop thinking about why Adam had not told me the truth in the first place.

"Only cross-eyed folks keep looking behind them," my mother liked to say if I launched into one of my could-have, should-haves. Getting to the bottom of things would not improve my circumstances, as I constantly reminded myself. But then I would be in the middle of a conversation with Rose or plucking an errant hair from my chin and suddenly think, *I was too clingy.*

Or *I was not clingy enough.*

Or *He* wanted *to hurt me, even if he didn't realize it. Why?*

That was the problem with attempting to hew yourself from another person: the work was never done. Just when you thought you were through, your past pulled you back for another round.

~

"I'm obsessing about why my ex left," I announced at support group. It was my third week in a row attending, and Charlie was back this time, wearing a ratty t-shirt and a pair of jeans that looked like they were ready to walk off without him. I sensed him watching me and chided myself for caring. The last thing I needed was to have a stupid crush on someone from my divorce group. I kept my eyes trained on Laurie, the woman who was my age but well preserved, as I spoke. "More specifically, I don't actually know exactly *why* he left, and I'm obsessing about that."

"You'd be weird if you didn't obsess," said Laurie. She had a New York accent, and I reminded myself to ask her how she had landed in the Midwest. "I can't say it goes away, but it gets better."

I attempted to smile. "I hope so. He lied to me. He said he had a girlfriend and he was leaving me for her, but turns out they were never serious. He just . . . well, I don't even know what he was thinking."

"That's messed up," said Laurie.

"How are you feeling about all this?" said Bob.

I considered his question for a moment. "Honestly? It hurts like hell, but I think that's better than being numb." I thought about the bar a few blocks from the church, which advertised three-dollar glasses of wine on Tuesdays. "I'm not always great about dealing with my feelings the way I'd like to, but at least I'm not pushing them back below the surface."

"I can't deal with mine," said one of the older men, whose name was George. "It's been four years since me and Elise split, and hearing her name still makes me angry. When I ran into her at Costco last year, I told her to stay the hell away from me."

This was not reassuring. But that was the thing about support groups: sometimes people said the exact thing you needed to hear, and other times they accidentally shot you with a poison-tipped arrow.

After the session let out, I skipped refreshments. I was tired, and George's remarks about not recovering years after his divorce had left me feeling sunken. What if I couldn't rebound from Adam, either?

I had just reached the parking lot when Charlie came jogging up behind me. "Maggie!" he said. "Hey. I'm sorry I wasn't here last week."

"Hi, Charlie." My mood instantly lifted because he had sought me out, but I felt silly about that, too. "No need to apologize."

He frowned, and I realized that his eyes were a bit bloodshot. "Well, I said I was going to be here, and I wasn't, so I'm sorry about that. I had a bad cold. I still kind of do," he said, motioning to his face. "Anyway, I would have texted you to let you know, but I don't have your number."

I took a deep breath. There was no need for this to be fraught. Unlike Benito, he wasn't coming on to me. "That's okay," I said.

"But maybe I could get it from you? Maybe we could go out for a drink sometime."

Oh. So maybe he *was* coming on to me. That was as unnerving as it was thrilling. On the one hand, an attractive man was attracted to me. On the other, asking a tattoo artist to ink a design of his choosing across my lower back sounded slightly more intelligent than dating at this juncture in my life.

But maybe the best way to rebound from Adam was with a rebound lover, I thought suddenly. I could rip the Band-Aid off—and unlike my time with Benito, I would be able to remember it the next day.

There was one small problem. "I'm not really drinking right now," I told Charlie.

His face broke into a smile, and I braced myself for his laughter while frantically scouring my mind for an explanation that didn't make me sound like I had to use a Breathalyzer in order to start my car. But instead of cracking a joke, he said, "Well, that's fantastic, because I don't drink."

"So . . . why ask me to get a drink?"

He shoved his hands in his coat. "Because that's what people usually do, I guess? I guess there's always coffee . . ."

"Or we could do something that doesn't involve food." My cheeks burned, because the only nonfood activity that immediately sprang to mind was sex.

But Charlie just laughed again. "Yes, we could. You free next Monday? This bug I'm fighting should be gone by then."

"That sounds great."

"Great," he repeated.

"Great," I said, and we both started laughing. Even though I was still nervous, Charlie was so easygoing that I doubted there was much I could say or do that would rub him the wrong way.

"At least we're working with the same limited vocabulary," he said.

I unlocked my car and opened the door. "Thank God. Anyway, I'm looking forward to Monday. I haven't met a lot of people in town yet."

"I'm looking forward to it, too," he said, walking backward away from my car.

I had just started the engine when Charlie knocked on the window, startling me. I rolled the window down and stuck my head out.

"Uh, we're back to the same problem we had before—I don't have your number. Wanna give it to me?" he said.

I flushed again. "Oh yeah. Sorry."

"Don't be," he said, pulling his phone out of his pocket. I rattled off my phone number, which he punched into his screen. "I just texted you, so you have my number, too," he said.

"Great," I said, and we smiled at each other. "We'll figure out details this weekend."

I smiled like a fool the whole way home, overcome by the unexpected delight of having something to look forward to.

~

An hour before I was supposed to go out with Charlie, Adam called. I was so shocked that it did not occur to me to not pick up. "Adam? Are the kids okay?"

"Hi, Maggie," he said. "And no, it's not about the kids. Is this a bad time?"

I immediately sensed that there was no emergency at hand, nor was he going to refresh my nonexistent memory of whatever I had said when I drunk-dialed him from Europe. "Why are you calling?"

"Listen, Maggie—"

"I no longer go by 'Listen, Maggie,'" I said, bristling. "You may call me Maggie. Or even better, just don't call."

"List—um. It's about my mother."

I instantly softened. "Rose? Is she okay?" She and I still spoke every few days, but our calls were often far shorter than they used to be, and Rose could not seem to wrap her mind around the fact that I was no longer in Oak Valley.

"No."

I was not used to hearing Adam at a loss for words, so I tried to fill the space for him. "Did she fall? Did she hurt herself?"

"It's not that," he said, his voice faltering. "It's her Alzheimer's. It's getting worse. She saw her specialist the other day—it's bad."

This was not news. Rose was diagnosed the year before Adam left me, and every few months had brought more changes. Adam and I had gone with her to most of her early neurology and gerontology appointments, and each doctor had repeatedly stressed that Alzheimer's was a progressive disease. Her dementia would likely develop in fits and starts, but there was no possibility of recovery.

"It's really serious, Maggie," said Adam. "And Mom's refusing to take the medication her neurologist prescribed her. That's going to mean she'll have to move out of her apartment a lot faster than she was planning to. She's going to land herself in the other side of the building within a year," he said, referring to the section of Mountainview Manor that was a traditional nursing home.

Rose was the kind of person who would refuse Tylenol for a broken leg. That she didn't want to take a medication known to provide temporary and potentially nominal benefits without ultimately changing her prognosis was not surprising. "I'm really sorry to hear this, but I'm not sure what you want me to do about it."

"You're a daughter to her, Maggie. She listens to you. She won't listen to me or Rick, and you know she can't stand Heather," he said, referring to Rick's wife. "I need your help. *Mom* needs your help."

I leaned against the counter and stared out the kitchen window. Not a hundred feet away, a fawn-colored bird of prey landed on the branch of a large evergreen at the edge of the yard. Its eyes darted around for a moment before it took flight and disappeared into the sky. "I'll give her a call tomorrow," I said.

I suppose I was expecting gratitude, maybe even an actual "thank you." Instead Adam said, "I was hoping you would go see the specialist with her. Maybe together we could talk her into taking the medication."

Anger rose like bile from my gut. I knew he was right—if anyone could talk Rose into it, it would be me. But I had barely left town; we had just divorced. I was trying to establish a new life without him, and coming home was at odds with my ability to do so. Surely he knew this.

"Please," he added. "Mom needs you."

"Adam," I said sternly. "I love your mother. But any responsibility I have toward her is mine to determine."

"I need help," he said softly.

He should have thought about that back when he started meeting Jillian Smith for coffee. "Don't we all. I'm trying to move on, and you calling me—"

"I know, I'm sorry," he said.

"I wasn't finished speaking."

"Sorry."

"I appreciate your apology, but now I can't remember what I was saying."

"Something about moving on."

"Right," I said, pacing the kitchen. I glanced at the clock over the sink; I was supposed to meet Charlie in twenty minutes. "I have an appointment. So you'll have to excuse me, as I need to go."

"Okay." He sounded resigned. "Can we talk again sometime soon? Only about Mom—I promise. I could really use your input."

The correct answer was no. "Maybe," I said.

He exhaled audibly, like I had agreed. Which was probably how it sounded to him. "Thank you."

Those two little words were all it took to throw off any civility I had been clinging to. *Now* Adam thanked me? Preemptively, when I hadn't done anything yet? Where were his thanks for the years I put in caring for our home and raising our family and supporting his career? Where was his gratitude for how stupidly graceful I had been after he had failed to hold up his end of our deal?

"Adam," I said sharply, "please don't call again. I'll reach out to you if and when I'm ready."

~

Charlie suggested we meet at the conservatory at the local botanic garden, which was only open until five. I agreed, though I wondered what he did for a living that he was free at three in the afternoon. Perhaps he was a chef or a high school teacher or a psychopath who got off on murdering hapless singles in broad daylight.

Or maybe he was just like me: unemployed.

I found him standing in front of a basin of water brimming with lily pads. He was wearing a pair of jeans and a pale blue cashmere sweater. The sweater had a hole in one elbow and another near the collar, but the color was perfect against his skin.

Charlie broke into a smile when he saw me. "Maggie, hi! I wasn't sure you would come."

"I could say the same for you. Except I was also wondering if you might be a serial killer who cruises divorce support groups to find your next victim."

He twisted his face into a mock grimace. "You're with the FBI, aren't you?"

There was something about his banter that pulled me out of my thoughts, and my phone call with Adam moved to the periphery of my mind. "Now why would I actually tell you about my top-secret spy career?" I said.

"You probably shouldn't, because I don't really like talking about work."

"No one *likes* talking about work, but we all do it anyway. You know, the old 'So what do *you* do?'"

He shrugged. "I try never to answer that question unless I'm being threatened."

So he probably was unemployed. "Noted. I'll bring a sharp object next time."

"I'd like to see you try," he said with a laugh.

We began on the path down the center of the garden. It was a gray, soggy day, but as we emerged from the canopy of palms and vines at the path's entrance, the glass ceiling intensified the sun's rays, rendering the greenhouse bright and tropically warm. "This is nice," I told Charlie.

"It's one of my favorite places. I come here a lot, especially during the eight months out of the year that it's cold."

"It feels like that, doesn't it? But I live . . . I used to live in Chicago," I said, catching myself. "Which was even worse, with all the wind and lake-effect snow."

"Chicago, huh? How did you end up here?"

As we wandered, I gave him the short version, taking care not to get into too much detail about Adam, whom he had already heard about at the support group; I didn't want our get-together to turn into another session. In turn, Charlie told me that he had lived in Ann Arbor for four years, having moved to the city from Atlanta for his ex-wife's job at the university. Before Atlanta, he had lived in Boston; New Orleans; Twin Falls, Idaho; and even Ottawa, for a spell. He had grown up in Kansas, he said, in a town I had never heard of, and had left as soon as he was able.

"You've moved around a lot," I said.

He turned and our eyes met. "I like change."

"Weird," I said, and we both laughed. "Do you have children?" I asked.

"No kids. It wasn't in the cards."

There it was again: that same sadness I had noticed in the parking lot the night we met. I didn't want to make him uncomfortable, so I peered at a tree with bright yellow orchids hanging from its gnarled branches. A carpet of impossibly small leaves was nestled at the tree's base.

"Baby's tears," said Charlie.

"Pardon?"

"That's what that's called," he said, pointing to the swath of green. "Baby's tears."

"Better than adult tears," I said, and we smiled at each other.

There was another pond at the opposite end of the greenhouse. When we reached it, we sat on its wide stone rim and watched the large koi swimming about in the shallow water. The fishes' eyes were bulging, and their mouths gaped at the water's surface. But their scaled skin, which was orange, white, and black, was brilliant and beautiful, and they were hypnotic as they circled each other.

After spending a few minutes in a comfortable silence, we stood and circled the gardens again. As we walked, I told Charlie about Zoe and Jack, and he told me about his sister, who had just left a job at a pharmaceutical company a lot like the ones Zoe's law firm represented. Then I told him about Jean and my trip to Rome, and he offered to take me to a café downtown that had what he described as the best coffee in town.

It all felt easy and right. But when it was time to go, Charlie went to hug me, and we both lunged in the same direction and ended up bumping shoulders. He pulled back and grinned, which sent a zing through my core.

"Well, thanks for getting together," I said, sounding like I had a mouth full of marbles.

If he noticed my awkwardness, he didn't let on. "My pleasure," he said. "See you at group tomorrow?"

I nodded.

"Good," he said. "I'm looking forward to it."

I was, too. And as I waved goodbye to him from my car, I realized that I would need to be careful with Charlie.

SEVENTEEN

Many a time in life I had longed for the luxury of nothing to do. Now I found myself wishing for the opposite. While I was filling the hours as best I could—deep cleaning Jean's house, dealing with mountains of postdivorce paperwork, and making the mile-long walk to Maizie's for coffee daily—a job increasingly sounded like a good idea.

Fortunately, I wasn't broke; in addition to alimony and half of the savings and retirement Adam and I had accrued over twenty-seven years of marriage, Jean's generosity meant my overhead was low. But the lessons of my childhood were never far behind me; I knew all too well that cash in hand today could well be lost to the wind tomorrow. Working would give me purpose while upping the odds I would not run out of money.

I began applying for anything even remotely in my wheelhouse, and my canvassing paid off: at the end of February I received a callback for a community services coordinator position at a local nonprofit called CenterPoint.

CenterPoint billed itself as a stewardship collaborative that was dedicated to community outreach and pairing donors with family-oriented causes. I had no clue what most of that meant, but the position was a temporary gig with the potential for permanent hire, and they had actually found my résumé promising enough to offer me an interview. I was ecstatic.

When I arrived at the CenterPoint offices, a man named Adrian Fromm greeted me at the door. Adrian guided me through the lobby, which contained a foosball table and an elaborate coffee station, into a conference room. Though he was barely pushing thirty, he introduced himself as the executive vice president of the foundation, which was only a few years old.

"So tell me what attracts you to this position, Margaret," said Adrian, who had taken a seat at the head of the table and indicated I was to sit to his left.

I perched myself on the edge of the swiveling ergonomic chair he had pointed to. "Please—call me Maggie," I said, just as I had in the lobby.

He leaned back. As he crossed his legs, one of his feet emerged from beneath the conference table, clad in a leather loafer that probably cost four times as much as my entire outfit. "Right," he said. "So. Tell me about you, Maggie."

I took a deep breath. I was well aware that having not practiced social work for more than twenty years made me a tough sell, but I reminded myself that this was barely above an entry-level position. Anyway, being called in for an interview meant I had already won half the battle . . . didn't it? "I worked for Illinois' Department of Child and Family Services as a caseworker for children across greater Chicago. After DCFS, I worked at Chicago Safety Zone, counseling hundreds of men and women while I was there. It's my understanding that your foundation directly supports women and families in crisis, which makes it seem an especially good fit for me."

He peered at the paper he was holding, which I assumed was a copy of my résumé. "You've been out of the field for quite some time."

"Yes, I was working with another family—my own," I said, smiling in what I hoped was a winning way. "Chicago Safety Zone had an extremely high turnover; most of my colleagues came and left in under a year. I was there for four. I bring that level of commitment to everything I do." It was unfortunate that said commitment was not a guarantee of success (see also: my marriage), but it seemed like the right thing to say.

Adrian pursed his lips as he frowned, and I wondered if he had anyone in his life who loved him enough to tell him that expression made him look like he needed to use the bathroom. "Interesting. Would you need to brush up on modern practices?"

"Do you mean social work?" I asked. "Because if so, I'm up to date on current counseling and outreach methods. And as my bookkeeping experience indicates, I'm extremely well organized and able to juggle a number of projects at one time. I believe I would enjoy and excel at coordinating effective programs for CenterPoint."

Adrian's expression had begun to glaze over. "I would love to hear more about what the position entails," I said in an effort to engage him. "Would I be working exclusively with outside organizations to coordinate programs for CenterPoint, or would I begin facilitating them at some point? Because if the latter, I would be happy to apply for state licensure."

He sat up, as if he were making an effort to look awake, and began rambling off buzzy phrases about fostering community connections and looking at every endeavor through the lens of the foundation's mission. None of this was a legitimate explanation of what I would actually be doing. He must have seen the cynicism on my face, because he added, "We'd talk more about what the actual position entails later down the line."

Neither of us spoke for at least five seconds longer than was comfortable. "I'm looking forward to hearing more," I finally said. "I'm passionate about helping others, and it sounds like you and your colleagues are, too." *Liar,* I thought as soon as I heard myself say this. As far as I could tell, Adrian Fromm's primary passion was the sound of his own voice as he recited jargon.

"Great," he said. Then he began telling me about CenterPoint's "donor communities" and the "shepherding process" for each donation they received.

By the time he finished, I was ready to wallop him, so it was probably for the best that he stood, indicating that in less than ten minutes' time, he had deduced that I was not the right person to fulfill the foundation's mission—or more likely, to work in an office containing a foosball table. The entire reason I had been called in was probably so the company's hiring manager could claim to have interviewed a broad range of candidates before hiring the person they had intended to choose all along.

"Thanks so much for meeting with us, Mary," Adrian said, gripping my hand so forcefully that I felt one metacarpal bone crunch against another. I cringed, but his eyes were on his phone, which was faceup on the conference table. "I have a meeting in another minute. You remember the way to the door?"

"I do, and it's Maggie," I said. Based on the length of our interview, it was safe to assume that he wouldn't be calling me for a follow-up. Even so, I did not want to walk out the door being called another woman's name.

Adrian's head lifted and he looked at me—actually looked at me, perhaps for the first time since I had walked into the office—and compassion flickered in his eyes. Perhaps I reminded him of his mother, or one of the women his foundation purported to support. "Absolutely," he said. "Thank you for your time, Maggie."

~

I was retrieving my coat from the coatrack after support group when Charlie shimmied up next to me. I startled, as my mind was still on Laurie, who had just revealed her ex-husband was a sex addict. This had got me wondering how often intimacy was the root of separation. For the past several years before we divorced, Adam regularly had trouble achieving an erection, and when I had encouraged him to see a urologist, he had informed me that the problem was not mechanical but the result of my approaching sex as another task on my to-do list. (Which I suppose I sometimes did.) If I had come on to him more often, would he actually have found it easier to get aroused? If he had come on to *me* more often, would I have been able to feel desire at a moment's notice—or even after many long minutes of what was supposed to be foreplay? In the final years of our marriage, at least, he had clearly struggled to relate to me as a sexual being. In turn, this had switched my libido off, which had probably exacerbated his arousal issues. It was like one big downward spiral of sexual dysfunction. (And to think we had once been able to spend an entire day in bed, finding new ways to delight each other.)

Charlie's presence brought me back to the present. "Didn't mean to surprise you," he said. He was leaning against the wall. "I was just wondering if you were interested in going out with me again sometime."

Why yes, yes I was—but wasn't dating a fellow support-grouper against some sort of rule? I glanced around nervously, but no one else was in earshot.

As I turned back to Charlie, it occurred to me that the real issue at hand was not support-group politics. It was that the last man I had been so immediately drawn to was Ian, my college boyfriend. Could I really attempt a casual relationship with someone who made my body hum?

I was going to have to try, I realized as I leaned in toward him without thinking about what I was doing. "When?"

He gave me a big grin. "Now?"

I zipped my down coat and looked at Charlie's worn leather jacket. It was the kind of jacket few men could pull off, but he was one of them. "I was going to head home."

"I could go with you." Charlie laughed at himself. "Listen to me, inviting myself over. Sorry, I'll—"

"No, that's perfect." The minute the words tumbled from my mouth, I wanted to shove them back in. So much for being careful.

"Okay," said Charlie shyly. "If you're sure."

I wasn't, but it was too late for that. Charlie drove behind me, which was just as well; I didn't want him to see me clutching my steering wheel for dear life. Had I applied deodorant earlier? What if he thought I was inviting him over for sex? (Because I wasn't. Was I?) This could end in a mess that made my night with Benito look like a tidy package tied with a bow, and that would be my fault.

In the rearview mirror, I watched Charlie pull up behind me in the driveway. Unless I was imagining it, he looked anxious, too.

"This is nice," he said after he got out of the car. "Rustic for a spot so close to town."

The porch was lit with twinkle lights, but my nerves were blinding me and I couldn't seem to find the right key on my keychain. "Thanks. I can't really take credit, though. It's all Jean."

"She's your friend, so I'm going to call this an extension of your good taste." His words soothed me, and I located the key and unlocked the door, which Charlie held open for me, motioning that I should go in first.

"This is really something," he said as we entered, but his eyes were on me, not the house, and desire shot through me.

I understood then what an insane idea this had been. Benito was good looking in an abstract, unthreatening way, sort of like a catalog model. But Charlie's full lips, his muscular arms, and even the deep timbre of his voice created the sort of visceral experience that overpowers your senses before you have time to back away.

"I'm nervous," I blurted. "I'm attracted to you, and I don't know if I'm ready for that."

He chuckled. "Sorry, I think?"

"Don't be. I know I'm overanalyzing it, but that's kind of what I do."

"That's not necessarily a bad thing." He took my jacket from my hands and hung it on a hook next to the door. "But you should know that this doesn't have to be anything you don't want it to be."

I wasn't sure if I believed him, but I said, "I think I can handle that."

He slid his jacket off and hung it on top of mine. "Well, if that changes, tell me."

"I'll do my best. Would you like some tea?"

"Tea sounds like just the thing."

When I was done in the kitchen, we sat on opposite ends of the sofa, each holding a mug. Things between us had again normalized, and we talked about Laurie's dilemma and whether sexual addiction was real (we both presumed it was, but couldn't say for certain). This led to a discussion about why neither of us drank. I explained that I had relied on alcohol too heavily during the separation and wanted a fresh start. Charlie, in turn, told me that his father had been a drunk. "Not the fun-loving, functional kind," he said. "The kind who drinks away the grocery money and belts whoever he can reach before passing out. I didn't want to be anything like him as an adult, and not drinking seemed like a good place to start."

His voice was measured, but his face was full of pain as he told me this. I put down my tea and moved closer to him without thinking. "I'm so sorry. I had a rough childhood, too, but not like that. That must have been terrible for you."

"Thank you," he said quietly. Then he inched toward me, so that our knees were touching. "This is off topic, but I like the color of your hair."

"Oh." His compliment was unexpected, and I felt shy again. "Thank you. It used to be darker, but I'm trying to incorporate the gray, so . . ."

"You'd look great gray, too," he said, so sincerely that I wanted to reach into the space-time vortex, find his father and this Lucinda character he had been married to, and give them both a piece of my mind.

"Charlie," I said, "you never did tell me what you do for a living."

He leaned back. "Oh, this, that, and the other thing. I've had a lot of different gigs over the years."

His reticence to discuss work when we had just delved into far deeper issues struck me as odd. The leather-strapped watch on his wrist and the black sedan he drove told me that he was not hurting for cash. Did he, say, run errands for a mobster or work for a company that manufactured chemical weapons?

Before I could keep speculating, he added, "I worked in tech for a long time, usually at start-ups. I owned the last one I was at, and got burned out and sold it. That's one of the seven hundred reasons Lucinda divorced me—because I didn't like settling down with one company. She said it made her feel insecure about our future. So I guess I don't really like talking about it."

At least he didn't make a living dissolving bodies in lye. "We can talk about something else," I said.

"Thank you," he said. His eyes were deep pools of black as he looked at me, and longing spread in me like heat. "I'm going to be honest with you right now."

"Anything."

"I'm thinking about kissing you, Maggie," he said. "What are your thoughts on that?"

Thoughts? If I had a single one, I could not locate it in my head. I was an animal running on the pure, biological instinct to mate. But after I panted at him for a moment, some semblance of self-protection kicked in, and I managed to say, "I'd like that, but only if we can keep this casual."

"Absolutely," he said, and I willed myself not to concentrate on the fact that his voice had just lowered an octave. "You probably won't even like kissing me anyway."

I could feel my hands trembling. "Probably not," I said.

"Then I apologize in advance," he said, and put his hand on my neck and brought his lips to mine. His kiss was soft but hungry, and—dear God—he was kissing me as if I were delicious. As I kissed him back, it occurred to me that maybe I was delicious, and somewhere along the way I had forgotten that.

But after a few minutes, I started to think about Adam, and how little we had kissed at the end of our marriage. When we bothered to be intimate, there had been at most a perfunctory tongue touching before we moved on to the act itself. Had that been part of the reason our marriage had fallen apart? Or was our lack of kissing a symptom of the larger disease that had destroyed us?

I pulled away from Charlie. "I need a breather."

He sat up and cleared his throat. "Of course. Obviously I don't want to do anything you're not comfortable with."

See? I thought. There were brakes, and I was not afraid to use them. "Thank you. That was . . ." I blushed. "Wonderful. But like I said, this is really new for me."

"Think it will be okay to see me at the support group next week?" Charlie's face was flushed, too, but his voice was back to its usual register.

I nodded.

"Great." He stood and bent to kiss me on the cheek. "I'm going to get going, but feel free to call or text if you want to get together before Tuesday. It was nice to spend some time with you, Maggie Halfmoon."

Charlie Ellery was ninety percent more complicated than I had been aiming for. But when I was with him, I felt good. Not like my old self, necessarily—but nonetheless better than I had in a long time. Maybe that's why, as I watched him walk to the front door, slip on his jacket, and turn to say goodbye one more time, I gave myself permission to see where this might lead.

EIGHTEEN

Adrian Fromm called the following Monday. "Maggie, hello!"

"Hello, Adrian," I said, stretching the two words out as if he were new to the English language. I had just pulled eggs from the fridge to begin making an omelet for lunch, and I tapped one on the counter and broke it into a bowl with my free hand. Adam used to call this one of my secret ninja moves. "I wasn't expecting to hear from you."

"Why's that? I really enjoyed our chat," he said.

Is that what they were calling eight-minute interviews these days? At least he had not called me Mary or Margaret. I cracked a second egg into the bowl. "I'm glad," I told him, because I was not going to fib and say I had, too.

"Unfortunately, we did go with another candidate."

"Then may I ask why you're calling?" I said, wedging the phone between my ear and shoulder. A year ago, I would have danced around this question or waited for Adrian to volunteer information, but in addition to ripping my bleeding heart from my chest, divorce seemed to have removed my social-niceties filter.

"I'm reaching out to see if perhaps you would like to come intern for us."

I pulled a whisk from the drawer. "Pardon?"

"It's a paid position, of course; you'd be making thirteen dollars an hour." That was a dollar more than I had made as a bookkeeper. "There's plenty of room for growth," he added.

"But you filled the community services coordinator spot, yes? And you said there was only one at the foundation, so it's safe to say I wouldn't move up into that position as a result of interning."

"All true!" he enthused. "But we have many other career paths. In particular, we're always in need of development professionals."

"Development . . . you mean fund-raising?"

"Yes. Specifically finding and interfacing with donors. I apologize if I'm being forward, but you have the sort of gravitas that could really take you far in the development arena. And the ability to raise capital is arguably the most charitable endeavor a person can undertake."

Arguably indeed. And I would sooner call myself Mary than use the term *interfacing*. But I was mostly stuck on *gravitas*. I was pretty sure Adrian's definition of this word was *old*. "What would I be doing as an intern, exactly?" I asked.

"A bit of everything. We would want you to understand all the nuts and bolts of how the foundation works."

Translation: sorting mail and running errands. I did need a job, however, and given how long I had been out of the field, I already knew I'd need to start at the bottom. Adrian Fromm's foundation could be that bottom. "Who would I be working with?"

"Oh, nearly everyone here. We have three C-level executives, myself included, though we don't call ourselves chiefs. And you'd work with Ned, the new community services coordinator. This is his first position out of graduate school."

I had a strong suspicion that my duty as an intern would center on supervising this Ned character. I said nothing.

"Hello?" said Adrian. "Mar—Maggie? Are you still there?"

"Oh, I'm here."

"So? Would you like to come work with us?"

I poured the eggs into the cast-iron pan on the stove. My mother used to say all work was good work, and I did need a job. One that could be a potential path to a career was even better. And yet I couldn't bring myself to say yes then and there. "Adrian, I'm flattered by your offer, but I'd like to sleep on it. Let me get back to you."

~

"What do you think?" I asked Charlie the following evening. Like the week before, he had approached me after support group to see if I wanted to get together. "No pressure," he had said, all dimples and innocence. Now we were standing across from each other in my kitchen, waiting for the teakettle to boil, and I had just finished telling him about Adrian's proposition.

Charlie scratched his head. "Well, I'm glad you want my opinion, but I think the more important question is what do you think?"

"It's not the worst offer, and I need to find something to do with myself."

"But do you *want* it?" he asked.

I thought for a moment. "No," I confessed. "I don't really like the guy, and I don't feel legitimately excited about the possibility of working for him or his organization. I guess I'm just worried that this will be my only opportunity, and I don't want to live on alimony alone."

"I get that. But I don't think fear is a good reason to take a job, especially if you'll be okay financially for the next few months. I think you could find a dozen other ways to tide yourself over until you figure out what it is you really want to do next."

"Hmm. Like what?"

"Well, I took a job at a bike shop a few years ago after leaving a start-up. They paid peanuts, but I was interested in seeing how bikes were put together and I needed a change. It was the most fun I'd had in a long time."

The kettle began to whistle, and Charlie walked to the stove and turned the burner off. Then he reached into the cupboard for mugs and tea bags.

"Watch out, or I'm going to start asking you to make me dinner," I teased.

Charlie had just begun to pour water into the mugs, but he set the kettle aside and placed his hands on my thighs.

Without thinking, I leaned forward and kissed him. After a moment, his lips moved from my own to my neck, and then to my collarbone, and down to the V of my blouse. "Is this okay?" he asked quietly, his lips still on my skin.

"I'm not sure," I said softly. I wanted him to tear my shirt off when I should have been telling him to stop. "I don't know how to do this."

"It's like riding a bike."

"I don't actually know how to ride a bike. I never learned."

"I'll teach you," he murmured.

"That's not what I mean—" I couldn't finish my sentence, so I found his mouth and kissed him again. Then I pulled back.

Our faces were inches apart, and we were staring at each other, almost cross-eyed. If we took things further, this could be incredibly awkward, I thought. Or cheap and meaningless—or just plain terrible. Then one of us would have to quit support group, and if we saw each other around town, we would turn our heads and pretend to be strangers.

"Maggie," Charlie said softly. "If you don't want to—"

My worries were a Greek chorus in my head, but desire roared over them. I wanted to. I wanted to so much so that I had to pull Charlie to me and show him because I could not speak.

~

Afterward, as we lay there panting, he kissed me again with the same sort of hunger he had shown before he had seen me hit a high note. Then he said, "Was that okay?"

"Are you kidding? That was amazing," I told him. And it had been. I could not remember when intimacy had pulled me out of my mind like that, and my body was still buzzing with residual pleasure.

"I'm glad," he said, wiping his brow with the t-shirt I had tossed on the counter just before we had taken to the floor like a couple of teenagers. "I thought so, too."

I stood up, still naked. It was chilly and I would need to get dressed soon, but the fact that I had not rushed to cover myself was yet another surprise. Adam had seen me nude at every stage of my adult life, and yet I had always preferred to be partially clothed, or to at least have the lights dimmed, when we made love. Now here I was, every one of my imperfections revealed beneath the glare of the bright kitchen lighting, and I felt fine. Charlie had only ever seen this version of me, and it was the one he had chosen; there seemed to be no need to hide any sagging or bagging.

"Oh, Maggie," he said, rising from the floor. "You're really something."

I smiled. He was, too. And I wanted . . .

More.

You're infatuated, I told myself, half chiding, half gleeful, as I tugged my clothing back on. Instead of ruining things between us, being intimate had just transformed my crush into something more potent and intoxicating.

I wondered if this was how Adam had felt when he started flirting with Jillian. Not that I was excusing him, but there was something enlivening about the affection of someone who hadn't known you for most of your life.

"Hey, Maggie?" said Charlie as he pulled his t-shirt back over his head.

"Yes?"

"You want to go hang out on the sofa for a little bit?" he asked with an uncertain smile.

It's funny how a grown man can glance at you a certain way and reveal exactly what he had looked like as a child. While I had felt exposed earlier, Charlie was now the vulnerable one. I had hoped the night would end with a kiss, maybe a bit of spirited groping, and then we could enjoy an encore performance sometime soon. But I didn't want to hurt Charlie or push him out the door, so I smiled and said I would love to hang out.

On the sofa, I leaned back into the broad expanse of his chest as he wrapped his arms around me.

It was only then that panic began to set in.

In addition to the magnetic physical connection I felt with Charlie, I happened to like him an awful lot. But I was in uncharted territory with a rebound relationship. When the time came, would I know to jump ship—or would I end up wrecking myself again?

NINETEEN

I was on the back porch, surveying Jean's yard, when Zoe called. Late March had mistaken itself for May, and what had been a foot of snow the day before was now a small lake littered with dead leaves and floating twigs.

"Honey? Is everything okay?" I immediately asked.

"Yep. I was just calling to see how you were."

I almost fell right off the porch. "My daughter is reaching out in the middle of her workday—to check on *me*? Surely something's wrong."

"Ha ha, Mom. I ran out to lunch and had a second, so I thought I'd try you." The horns bleating in the background confirmed as much. "What have you been up to?"

"Still looking for a job." I told her about my interview at CenterPoint and Adrian Fromm's follow-up offer.

"Yeah, don't take that," said Zoe after I had finished.

"Really? I thought you'd be all over it. Career path, new opportunities, blah blah blah."

"Blah blah blah, huh?"

"You know what I mean."

"Sure I do. And that guy you interviewed with sounds like every guy I dated in college. He's only out for himself."

"You never told me about any of the guys you dated in college."

"Basically, picture that jerk with six different haircuts."

I laughed.

"Whoa!" said Zoe, and I heard something whiz past her.

"Sweetheart, please tell me you didn't almost get run over."

"It was just a bike messenger, Mom. I'm fine. So, are you dating anyone?"

My heart did a little skip when I thought of Charlie, who had been over again the night before. We'd had frenetic sex in the shower, then spent more than an hour talking on the sofa with our limbs intertwined. I wanted a no-strings relationship, but cuddling seemed like . . . a string, albeit a thin one. As such, I wasn't sure what to call what it was that Charlie and I were doing. "Not necessarily. I made a friend, though."

"A *male* friend?"

"Yes."

"Very on-trend of you to not call him your boyfriend. I mean, do or do not—there is no try, right?"

"Zoe!" I sputtered.

"So you are!" she said, laughing. "Good for you. A fling is probably just the thing you need right now."

That was exactly what I had been thinking, but it was strange to talk to my daughter about a relationship I was having with someone other than her father.

Zoe continued. "No need to be embarrassed about it. I mean, after years of Dad neglecting you, you deserve some attention."

"I was not *neglected*," I said sharply. "Your father worked a lot. I always knew that, and that's not what ended our marriage."

"Okay. But let's just say there's a reason I'm not in a relationship with anyone, and that's because, unlike some people who will remain unnamed, I know I'm married to my job."

I stared at a mud puddle a few feet from where I was standing. "Ouch."

"I'm not trying to be mean. I just think maybe now you have a chance to really be happy."

"I *was* happy."

"A different kind of happy."

A better kind of happy—I knew that's what she meant. Zoe hung up soon after so she could order her salad and get back to the office, but I stood on the porch for a while, thinking about what she had said.

Had Adam neglected me? I had not felt unloved, or at least I hadn't until he had announced he was leaving. But yes, I supposed I would have liked more time with him. Quality time—as opposed to sitting in front of the TV together while Adam combed over a legal brief. He would inevitably look up in time to catch the show's conclusion, which meant I then had to summarize the whole plot for him. He did make it home for dinner several times a week . . . but if I was honest with myself, a significant number of our conversations over the past few years had revolved around whatever case he was working on. Afterward, he would escape to his home office and work until he came to bed. "I'm doing this for us, Maggie," he would say. "Social Security will go extinct any day now, and God only knows what will happen with Medicare. I'm trying to squirrel away as much cash as I can while I'm still able."

As I let myself back in the house, I wondered if I should have taken the same approach with Adam: asking for more, more, more; storing up my husband's love for the long, lean winter that I had believed would never arrive.

~

"So, do you want to come to my house sometime?" asked Charlie, peering at me through an opening in the bookshelf we were standing on either side of. He had asked me on a "real date," as he had described it: brunch, followed by a trip to the bookstore.

"Your house?" I said through the shelves.

"Why not? We always end up at your place. Though I have to warn you—my house is a lot messier than yours. But maybe I could attempt to clean it, and you could come over for dinner sometime?"

"Sure. When?"

His head disappeared. Then he snuck up behind me and whispered into my neck, "A couple days from now, maybe?"

His breath tickled my skin, and I laughed and spun around. As I looked at him, it occurred to me that if I went to his house in a couple of days, I would have seen him three times in a single week, not including the divorce support group. "Or maybe next week?" I suggested.

He began to frown, but he fixed his face so fast that I almost wondered if I had imagined it. "Whenever you want. I thought maybe I could show you what I used to do for a living."

"I'm going to warn you, if you show me a bunch of code on a computer screen, my brain might explode. I'm a bit of a Luddite."

"No code—promise," he said, holding his hands up. "I was going to show you one of my sensors. Remember I told you I owned a company?"

I nodded.

"I made crop-monitoring sensors that help farmers make better decisions about irrigation, harvest, and whatnot, which improves their yields. The company sold a year and a half ago, but I still have one of the sensors, if you want to see it." For someone who didn't like talking work, he looked awfully proud of himself.

"That sounds neat. Why did you sell?"

He shrugged. "That's half the fun. Create something new, see how much it'll go for. Sometimes it works, sometimes it doesn't. I created a humidity sensor for vineyard owners and debuted it three weeks after a competitor put out an identical product that now owns that market. Lost a boatload of cash on that one."

"Oof."

"It's all part of the game."

"Are you working on anything new now?"

"Sort of. I'm poking around with a soil monitor, which might work for organic farmers. But it's in the early stages, and I'm trying not to spend all my time on it."

"So . . . you're basically okay with being uncertain about what's next for you."

"Pretty much." His smile faded. "Lu hated it. Now she's married to a doctor. Set salary, safe life."

I took this as a sign that I shouldn't tell him that his whimsical approach to the world gave me hives. Of course, I myself was living on a "for now" basis—but as soon as I figured out what I was aiming for, I planned to point myself in that direction and shoot.

Charlie pulled a book from the shelf, flipped it over to read the back, and tucked it under his arm.

"That's it?" I said, raising my eyebrows. "You look at one book and decide to buy it?"

"You missed the other four I looked at on the other side of the bookshelf. But yeah, I know what I want when I see it." He winked. "So, dinner next week, my place? *Puhleasse?*"

"Just for the record, I *can* say no to you," I said, bumping my hip against his. "But lucky for you, I don't want to."

~

The next morning in the shower I thought about Charlie. It was so strange to be intimate with someone other than Adam. Not bad, but markedly different.

It was not just a new body and new ways to communicate needs and desires, though there was certainly that. But it was that we were not hindered by the memory of the people we used to be. Charlie's current self, physically and emotionally, was all I had ever known of him—and vice versa. You could not say, "But you used to" or "Why do you always" to someone you had just met.

But if we continued on this path, however meandering it might be, all of that would eventually change. Soon boredom, lack of passion, and the countless other irritations that were part and parcel of familiarity would surface. Then what?

I had just rinsed the shampoo from my hair when my phone, which I had left on the sink, rang. I let the water continue to run over me as I recalled Charlie laughing heartily after I had told him the only joke I could ever remember was about two melons who can't elope.

"You're adorable," he had said when he'd finished laughing.

I didn't mind adorable one bit. Irresistible was more problematic, and this happened to be the best way to describe Charlie. When I had told him that I could say no to him in the bookstore, it wasn't entirely true; to be around him was to have my guard down. The last person who had made me feel that way was Ian, and that had turned out to be a spectacular disaster.

And yet I had fallen in love with Adam slowly, rather than all at once, and that had ended in ruin, too. It seemed there was no way to be in a relationship without getting maimed.

The phone rang again, and I let it go to voicemail. Only after it rang a third time did I turn off the faucet, throw a towel around myself, and flip the phone over to see who it was. I assumed it would be Rose, who now often called repeatedly when I didn't pick up. But the lit-up screen revealed that it was Adam, and I was so aggravated to see his name on my caller ID that I actually answered.

"How is it we're talking more now than we did when we were separated?" I asked sharply. "Wasn't the whole point of you finalizing the divorce to not deal with me anymore?"

"Maggie," said Adam. He sounded kind of froggy.

"Unless this is about one of our children, I need to go."

"It's not."

"Good—"

"There's something wrong with my heart."

I gripped my towel tighter around my body. "That's for damn sure." His last call, about Rose's dementia, had seemed like a paltry excuse for reaching out, and I had a strong suspicion this was more of the same. He probably had high cholesterol or a heart murmur or some other minor problem that was his alone to fix. After all, he was the one who had broken the vow of "in sickness and in health."

He cleared his throat. "I had a heart attack."

My own heart nearly stopped. "What? When?"

"Last night."

My irritation immediately evaporated. "Are you all right? What happened? Were you at work? At the gym?"

"I was at an improv class."

In spite of—or maybe because of—my tense mental state, I actually started to laugh. Straitlaced Adam, whose hobbies included work, more work, and the occasional game of tennis with a colleague, had gone to an *improv* class? "Are you serious?"

"I'm serious," he said gruffly. "And thank God, because at first I thought it was heartburn. I threw up and wanted to go home to sleep. One of the guys there had a heart attack last year and realized what was happening. If he hadn't . . ."

If he hadn't, he might be dead right now. I sat on the edge of my bed, breathing shallowly. Not so long ago, I had wished Adam dead. Only now did I realize just how terrible that wish was.

"You're sure it was a heart attack?" I said.

"Positive. I'm at the cardiac unit at Northwestern. I got to the ER right away, so my heart muscle didn't sustain any major damage. But . . ."

I could feel my pulse thumping in my neck. "But?"

"I have to have double bypass surgery."

"*Double?* Oh dear God. Why?"

"Two of my arteries are clogged. One is almost a hundred percent blocked. I have to stay at the hospital for monitoring, and I'm having surgery tomorrow at noon."

Guilt flooded my chest as I thought of how satisfying it had been to see Adam looking exhausted at the courthouse in January. If I'd had any idea his heart wasn't pumping blood like it should have been, I would have felt differently. "Is Rick there with you?"

Adam didn't answer.

"Adam?"

He coughed. "Rick and Heather are in Bermuda right now for his annual conference. He's the keynote speaker, so he can't get home in time—I already asked. But they're flying back in three days."

"And the kids? Did you call them?"

"Yes. They're getting on a flight tomorrow morning."

"Good." Even after everything, I didn't want Adam sitting by himself after surgery.

"Maggie," said Adam.

The minute he said my name I knew what he was going to ask.

"I can't," I said plainly.

"There's no one else."

"But the kids are coming in."

"Yes, but that's just it." He paused. "You know my father died during heart surgery."

He had, and it had been horrible. But Richard had been eighty-one years old at the time. "You're fifty-three and in great health," I said to Adam.

"Except my arteries, which are apparently blocked like the Hoover Dam. It's bad, Maggie. Really bad."

I forgot that I was not dressed, and when I rose from the edge of the bed, my towel fell to the floor. I stood there, cold and naked but too paralyzed to move. "Adam . . ."

"Maggie, please," he said. "I don't know if I'm going to make it through surgery. To be honest, something deep within me tells me I won't. And I want you to be here for Zoe and Jack if I die."

TWENTY

One night over a pitcher of gin and tonics, Gita and I had gotten into a lengthy discussion about whether we loved our children or our spouses more. Of course, there was no reason to actually choose, but these were the sorts of conversations we liked to have. Gita had said she loved Reddy most, if only because she had loved him first and longer, and after further thought, she had added that without him, there would have been no Amy.

I, on the other hand, loved my children more than Adam—no question. It was a different sort of love, but I would have given my life for them without hesitation. Whereas if Adam had offered me the only piece of driftwood in the ocean as the *Titanic* sank in the distance, I probably would have accepted it so that I could have more time with my son and daughter, whom I loved not just more than my husband, but also myself.

And yet as I made the drive back to Chicago, I acknowledged that supporting my children was not the only reason I had agreed to come in for Adam's surgery.

"You're a miracle worker, Maggie," he had said to me as he placed Zoe in my arms moments after I had given birth to her. His tears fell on my breast even as Zoe put her mouth to it, and I gazed up at him with more love than I ever had, because he had just handed me my world.

Adam had given me both his DNA and his blessing to make mothering my life's work. I suppose in a way, I felt I owed it to him to be there for the kids as he had asked.

But even beyond that sense of obligation, something else was plaguing me.

When I tried to imagine the future—not the far-off future, but even a few days or weeks after Adam's surgery—I could not come up with a single scene in which Adam was present. While I was no soothsayer, this suggested to me that there was a distinct possibility that he was right, and he would not make it through the surgery. If that were the case, then our parting at the courthouse would be our final goodbye.

In spite of the many ways he had hurt me, I did not want us to end that way. And so I would honor his request and be there when he went into surgery. Not just for our children and Adam—but also for myself.

~

"Maggie. Is that actually you?"

Adam was lying back on a hospital bed with an IV running into his arm. He was not tall and had always been on the slight side, but he looked like a shriveled version of himself beneath the thin sheet, and I wanted to weep. I had slipped down a WebMD rabbit hole for nearly two hours the day before. Though double bypass was minimally invasive and would only require a small incision through Adam's ribs, an irregular heartbeat, memory problems, and stroke were a small sampling of complications that might befall Adam after surgery. Even patients who received a clean bill of health could drop dead for no apparent reason.

I lingered near the curtains partitioning Adam from the rest of the surgical prep area. "Don't get up," I said, trying to sound normal. "The last thing we need is for you to have another heart attack."

He managed a smile, and I wondered if my being here for his surgery was the start of a healthy new relationship between us. Maybe we could be loving, respectful co-parents, like . . . well, not like anyone I personally knew, but I heard it happened all the time. Of course, this was only an option if he survived. "I know the kids said you were coming, but I didn't believe it until I saw your face," he said.

"Well, here I am," I said in what I hoped was a chipper tone. "Jack and Zoe are on their way from the airport now. I just wanted to let you know I was here. So good luck today. You'll be fine."

His eyes went cold at the mention of surgery. "They say there's a five to seven percent chance I won't survive this," he said.

The air was sterile and suffocating, and medical monitors beeped in the background. "I'd say those are pretty good odds," I lied. They were good odds for a stranger. For Adam, even a one percent risk was too high.

He shook his head. "Maybe. I still can't shake the feeling I'm not going to beat them."

"Don't catastrophize, Adam. That's my job."

"My father, though."

"You've got your mother's genes going for you," I insisted. "Dementia might actually be the first health problem she's had in eighty years."

The lines in his forehead softened. Despite my own high anxiety levels, I had always been the one to talk Adam down from the ledge, and there I was, performing my wifely rescue routine once again. I wanted to hate him—he had given up the right to count on me when he first served me divorce papers—but I couldn't actually fault him for reverting to old comforts hours before major surgery. There was almost something comforting about it for me, too. "I hope you're right," he said.

A nurse pushed past the curtain into the partitioned area. "How are we feeling?" she asked as she fiddled with Adam's IV bag.

"Never better," he said with false bravado.

"Glad to hear it. The anesthesiologist is going to swing by to speak with you in just a few."

"Listen, I should go," I said to Adam. "Good luck in there. You're going to do great."

"I hope so." His expression landed somewhere between a smile and a grimace. "Thank you for being here, Maggie. I'm sure it wasn't easy for you, but it means a lot to me."

I had been working so hard to get over him, and in a sick way his confession about Jillian had probably sped the process. But now that he was teetering on the precipice of life itself, it was all I could do to try to remember why we were no longer husband and wife. I found myself wondering whether I had been right to move so far away from him, to rule out all possibility of our having a future together. For the first time since Rome, I didn't know. "It's nothing," I said.

"It's a lot," he said.

The word *Love* had been woven into the blue-and-beige curtains partitioning Adam from the rest of the room. I pulled my eyes from it as I responded to him. "You're welcome," I said. "Don't die."

~

Zoe rushed into the waiting room, where I had been nervously flipping through a tattered *Redbook*. Her eyes were bloodshot, and her chin was wobbling like it had when she was a small girl on the verge of a meltdown.

"Oh, love, I'm sorry. I know this is hard," I murmured as she sat beside me.

"So hard," she warbled, burying her face in my shoulder. When she caught her breath, she added, "It's just—hasn't the past year been enough already? I don't want Daddy to die."

I put one of my arms around her and the other around Jack, who had squeezed next to me on the other side of the love seat. "It's going to be fine," I said, because I could not get my mouth to say the words, "He won't die." "We have each other, and your father is heading into surgery knowing he has his family's support. I know that means a lot to him."

"He's happy you're here, Mom," said Jack. For all of my son's tough talk about how his father had treated me, he still wanted us to be together. I understood. Adam's heart condition was nothing if not a reminder that life can turn on a dime. Now more than ever, it was impossible not to want everything to be like it used to be.

"I know," I said, squeezing Jack's hand. "I am, too."

The hours crawled by. The three of us stared at our phones and paced the halls and made multiple trips to the cafeteria. Jack eventually fell asleep on a recliner, and Zoe toiled over a brief on her laptop. I retrieved a novel from my bag, but it was no use; even Laurie Colwin could not pull my mind away from my worries.

Finally, a surgeon appeared and asked us to follow her into a small room off the lobby. There, she introduced herself as Dr. Chen. She and her team had removed a blood vessel from Adam's left leg, she said, and another from his chest wall. They had reattached both grafts from his aorta to arteries beneath the two that were blocked. It was like rerouting traffic after an accident, she explained; if all went as planned, the new arteries would allow his blood to flow freely again.

"So is he okay?" said Zoe.

"For now," said Dr. Chen. "The big risks right now are infection and atrial fibrillation—that's a condition that causes an irregular heartbeat, which can lead to stroke and other issues. He's on a breathing tube until at least tomorrow, so he won't be able to talk. And he needs to rest, so for today, keep your visit brief."

The minute she was done, we raced to Adam's room in the intensive care unit. He was lying on an incline with his chest heavily bandaged; a ventilator covered his mouth and nose.

"Dad," said Jack softly, and Adam's eyes shot open.

Zoe and Jack rushed to the bed and took his hands. He looked at them both, and I realized he was crying.

This hurts in more ways than one—and let it, I thought as I walked to his bed. *At least you're alive to feel the pain.*

Our eyes locked as I touched Adam's arm. I had met so few people in life with eyes like his—not hazel or green gray or a murky blue, but clear, bright green. "See? You made it," I said. "I'm going to give the kids some time with you, but I'll be back tomorrow to check in. I'm glad you're okay." I took his hand and squeezed it lightly. Then I turned and left the room before I could start thinking about what I had lost.

~

"Oh, Mags," said Gita that evening. The kids were spending the night at Adam's apartment and would meet me back at the hospital in the morning. "You're a saint for coming back."

"Or a martyr," I remarked.

"One and the same, no?" Gita stuck her head in the fridge. "What do you want? I have plain and passion-fruit seltzer, grapefruit juice . . ."

"Seltzer, any flavor," I called to her.

She emerged with a can of water in one hand and a bottle of sauvignon blanc in the other. "You don't mind if I have a pour while I cook, do you?"

"Of course not." I eyed the green glass bottle as she uncorked it. Four months had passed since I had had a drink, and much had changed during that time. I no longer had a pang while driving past vineyard-touting billboards on the highway. I instantly declined happy hour specials when I was out to eat, even if sangria was less expensive than a latte. Rather than chardonnay, I now sipped chamomile before bed and was rewarded with the deep sleep of a child. I had kicked my bad habit. At some point, I might be ready to see if I could have a glass of wine without it turning into several. But not when I was stressed the way I was today, and certainly not when the cause of my stress was my ex-husband.

She looked at me over her shoulder. "You sure?"

"Positive. But you can pour my sparkling water in a wine glass."

Gita did and set my glass in front of me before raising her own. I lifted mine in response. "Here's to us—"

"And the ones that we love—"

"And if the ones that we love don't love us—"

"Screw 'em. Here's to us," Gita finished and broke into a smile as I brought the edge of my glass to hers. She had taught me this toast twenty-plus years earlier, not long after Adam and I had moved into the neighborhood. A couple that had lived a few doors down, whose names had since gone missing in my mind, had invited us to a barbecue. It had been perfectly pleasant, but I had spent the first hour struggling to make conversation. Enter Gita stage left. She liked to say she took one look at me huddled next to our neighbor's garage and knew we would be friends, but the truth is, I had spotted her in her flowing yellow dress beside the pool and was already walking toward her when she flagged me down. Like me, Gita was an only child; in each other, we had found the sister we had always wanted.

"So," she said. "What does Charlie think about you being here?"

I shrugged. "I don't think he's thrilled." ("Of course, do what you think is right," he had said when I called him before I left. "I'll be thinking about you and your family.") "But we're not serious, so what he thinks is really beside the point."

Gita raised an eyebrow. "Charlie makes you happy, though. I can tell that even over the phone."

"Happy and serious aren't the same thing. In this case, I think us being not serious is why I'm happy."

"Okay."

I picked up a cashew from the bowl on the counter and threw it at her. She laughed as it hit her shirt. "What was that for?"

"That was for you being a big fat skeptic."

"Maybe I am, but I know you." She perched herself on a stool, folded her arms, and regarded me. "This past year has been a doozy."

Had it already been a full year since Adam had walked out the door on me? It had, I concluded with surprise, even though at times each month had felt like a decade. "Yes, it has."

"And yet you're doing better than ever."

"Better?" I scoffed. "I could hand you thirteen articles on why women's financial status takes a nosedive after divorce, even if their alimony is decent. Everything's cheaper when it's split between two people. And don't get me started on the emotional trauma." On the car ride from Ann Arbor, Ella Fitzgerald's "Our Love Is Here to Stay" had come on the radio. It had been the first song Adam and I had danced to at our wedding, and when I heard it again, I had almost collided with the semi in front of me because I could not see through my tears.

Gita popped a cashew in her mouth. When she was done chewing, she said, "I understand that. At least, I understand that as well as someone who isn't in your shoes is able to. But Maggie, there's a light in you that wasn't there those last years of your marriage to Adam." She gave me a look that was at once fierce and kind. "Maybe you haven't noticed it yet, but it's there. Don't blow it out before you've had a chance to see it."

TWENTY-ONE

When I returned to the hospital the next morning, Zoe and Jack were rolling dice on a laminated tray a few feet from Adam's bed. Adam, who was tethered to multiple monitors, was fast asleep.

"Greedy?" I whispered, referring to the game that my mother had taught me, which I had taught them. Zoe nodded, but Jack, who had just thrown down a hand, exclaimed, "A thousand. Taking it!"

Adam groaned, then opened his eyes. "Oh," he rasped, his voice bearing the effects of being intubated.

Jack was sheepish. "Sorry, Dad. I didn't mean to wake you."

"It's okay. I want to be awake." His gaze shifted to me. "Maggie. You came back."

"Yes." I swallowed the lump in my throat. "I'm glad you're looking better today."

He struggled to look down at himself and grimaced. "I feel like someone ran a lawn mower over my chest. It hurts like hell."

I gave him a small smile. "They said the first few days would be pretty awful."

"This makes *awful* sound like a cakewalk. I need more painkillers."

Like Rose, Adam acted as if he were allergic to all forms of medicine; if he was requesting it now, he was in a bad way. "Do you want me to see if I can get a nurse?" I asked, and he nodded.

As I pressed the red call button to page the nurses' station, Zoe touched Adam's foot beneath the sheet. "Dad, you up for playing a round? Might be good to distract yourself until the nurse gets here."

"We can move up," said Jack, who was already pulling his plastic chair toward the front of the bed. "Can you roll, Dad?"

Adam smiled weakly. "I suppose I can try, though you might have to help me with the score. My head's still fuzzy."

Zoe made four new columns on a piece of paper and told Adam to roll the first hand. He didn't get the six hundred points required to enter the game, so he passed the dice to me. As his fingers met my skin, I didn't dare look at him; I was too afraid I would begin to feel the stirrings of affection that I had the day before. Instead, I squeezed the melamine cubes for luck, as my mother used to, and tossed them onto the bed, pretending I cared deeply that my lousy hand meant I would stay out of the game until the next round.

We had been playing a few minutes when a nurse came in. Adam told her his pain had gone from a six to an eight or nine, and she disappeared again. Soon after a doctor came in to check Adam's vitals and scans, and a nurse anesthetist showed up and added something stronger, as he put it, to the IV drip.

Within minutes, Adam's lids fell to half-mast, and the game was abandoned. "It's so nice to be here with you guys," he murmured.

"Dad, you sound cooked," Jack said.

"I mean it," said Adam, slurring slightly. "Love you three."

I turned toward the window so the kids wouldn't see the grief that was ripping through me. As a young boy, Jack had once said, "Love you three!" after hearing Adam say, "Love you, too" to me. We had laughed our heads off and adopted it as a family joke, but I had not heard Adam say it in years—maybe because it had stopped being true. Had he said it now because he had finally come to understand what a fool he had been? I found myself wishing it were nothing but a medicated blunder, because I had just begun getting used to life without him.

"We love you, too, Dad," said Zoe. "Get some rest. We'll be here when you wake up."

With Adam passed out, the three of us moved our chairs to the foot of the bed and talked quietly for a while. When Zoe and Jack decided to go to the cafeteria for coffee and some food, I told them I would stay behind.

I watched Adam, whose sleep was fitful; his face kept twisting as though he were running through a field of brambles. With his furrowed brow and pink skin, he looked like the oldest child who had ever been born.

I must have been staring at him for a while when I found myself thinking of our wedding day. Adam had walked me down the aisle himself, in spite of his mother's protests and his father's offer to stand in for the father I had never known. We had conceded on every other point of tradition that they had requested—church, minister, bridal parties, lengthy procession, and lengthier guest list—but on this one, Adam would not budge.

And so we made our way to the front of the church, two people who were unable to believe their luck at finding the exact right person with whom to spend the rest of forever. Just before the minister began to speak, Adam took my hands in his own and said, so quietly that only I could hear, "Maggie, I promise to be the best husband I can for you."

I remember staring at him, overcome with love. And then—I don't remember why—I turned to look at my mother, who was in the front pew, weeping into a tissue. I knew that she, unlike Rose, was not crying because she felt she was losing me. She was weeping with joy because I was about to embark on the safe, stable, loving life she had always wanted me to have.

Maybe Adam had kept his promise, I thought as I watched his bandaged chest rise and fall, then shudder frighteningly only to return to a normal rhythm. Maybe he had been the best husband he could be, and in the end, that had not been enough.

~

After Jack and Zoe returned, the three of us sat sipping burnt hospital coffee and whispering among ourselves about nothing much. We must have been like that for some time when Adam's eyes sprang open. His face immediately relaxed at the sight of us. Then he smiled, which made us smile back. For a second—only a second, but a lovely one—it seemed we were an intact family of four again.

"Maggie," he rasped. "How was Rome?"

I startled. Was he making a veiled comment about my phone call from Benito's, or was he actually interested in whether I had enjoyed the trip we were supposed to take together? "It was wonderful, actually. Thanks." I wasn't sure if I was thanking him for asking or for not putting up a fuss about the bill. Both or neither, it didn't matter.

"Good. I'm happy you went," he said earnestly.

I looked at him. "Adam," I said slowly, "did you pay for a flight upgrade for me?"

A new smile formed on his lips. So he *had* paid for my first-class ticket. And though that ticket had been lovely and landed me next to Jean, who of course had led me to Ann Arbor—and yes, Charlie—learning that he had done this for me made me inexplicably angry.

"You always said you wanted to fly first class at some point," he said. "I just thought . . ."

He just thought it was the least he could do, given what he had put me through. He might have fallen out of love with me, but he cared. He might even still love me. But most likely, he had been looking for a way to ease his guilt.

And with that realization, the spell was broken. We were not an intact family of four, because the man before me had decided to stop being my husband.

It was time for me to go home.

I stood from my seat. "Adam," I said, "I'm relieved you made it through surgery. I'll be sure to let your mom know you're doing great, and I'll call Rick to ask him to bring her to visit you once you're out of the hospital. But I need to get back to Michigan."

"Now?" he croaked.

I nodded. "Now."

"What about—" Zoe began, but I held up my hand. She, Jack, and I were supposed to have dinner that night. I would call later to apologize and arrange another time for the three of us to get together.

"I'm so sorry to dash, but I must. I love you two," I said to Zoe and Jack, and kissed them both quickly. "Be well, Adam," I said.

He waved weakly, looking so helpless that I almost changed my mind. As Dr. Chen told us, it would be days before Adam was out of the woods. Even if his recovery went as planned, hard times were up ahead, both for Adam and for the kids. By leaving, I was letting them down.

But if I stayed, the glimmer of affection I was feeling for Adam might turn into something more—something that threatened to blow out the light I was still waiting to see.

TWENTY-TWO

The problem with not having dated since the Berlin Wall was intact was that I did not know the rules, particularly for a casual relationship. I had not asked for Charlie's blessing to go to Chicago, and that had seemed fine at the time. Upon returning, however, I felt uneasy, like I had done something wrong.

If Charlie felt the same way, he didn't show it. "I'm glad you're back," he said. We were standing on the deck at the back of his house, which was a midcentury ranch overlooking the river. "And I'm glad your ex-husband is okay."

"Me too," I said. "It was good to be there for my kids." That morning I had spoken with Zoe, who had said Adam was still doing well. If his recovery continued to go smoothly, he would be released from the hospital in a few days. Zoe and Jack would stay with him for the rest of the week, and Rick would step in if Adam still needed help after that point.

Charlie leaned his elbows on the deck railing. Before us, the river rushed wildly. "How was it? When I saw Lucinda six months ago at a funeral, it was really strange."

I thought of Adam lying in his hospital bed. In a way, he had seemed more relaxed than I had seen him in a good long time. "Strange as in you missed her?" I asked.

He shook his head. "It was more like seeing an actor from a television show in real life, but she's dressed differently and she doesn't behave like the character you're used to."

"That sounds unsettling," I said.

"It was. Was it like that with Adam?"

"No, it was . . ." I had paraded around in front of Charlie in broad daylight with my various varicosities on display. But talking to him about Adam felt even more intimate. It was like I feared he would uncover some secret feeling that I didn't even know I was having. "For a moment it was almost like old times, and that was more disturbing than anything. That's why I ended up coming back sooner than I'd planned."

"I think that was smart." His mouth turned up in a lopsided grin. "Anyways, I'm happy to see you."

"Me too."

"Good." Charlie straightened himself and pulled me to him. "I like us, Maggie. I know it's early, and I understand why you have reservations about dating so soon after your divorce."

"And you don't?"

"I've been divorced almost two years already. And I believe that if something between us is off, I'll know it. Right now, this feels right."

This was a good theory. However, I was not sure I was able to put such intuition into practice.

"You hungry?" Charlie asked.

"Starving," I said, grateful he had changed the subject.

"That makes two of us. Let's see what's in the fridge."

His house was spacious, well lit—and as he had warned, messy. Laundry here, dirty dishes there, piles of paper everywhere. Charlie was thinking of selling; it was the kind of place he had dreamed about as a kid, he said, but now it mostly reminded him of his arguments with Lucinda, and he barely kept up with it.

The kitchen was mostly clean, though, and it had beautiful cherry wood cabinets, slate floors, and a six-burner stove. I was happy to find the fridge well stocked, and Charlie and I put together sandwiches made with prosciutto, thin slices of manchego cheese, and a layer of tapenade on slices of crusty baguette. Then we returned to the deck to eat.

"So," said Charlie as we finished the last of our meal, "is now a good time to tell you I have a surprise for you?"

I made a face. "Like a herpes kind of surprise?"

He laughed heartily. "You're a nut. No, it's a good surprise. Come with me."

I followed him through a door off the foyer into the garage. He flipped a switch. The garage door inched up, and afternoon sunlight flooded into the space.

I squinted. "It's a . . . lawn mower?"

He pretended to frown, and I laughed. "It's a *bike*," he said, pointing past the mower.

It was indeed: a shiny mint-green bike with a brown leather seat and a wicker basket affixed to the wide handles. It was quite possibly the most charming bicycle I had ever seen; I could easily imagine Audrey Hepburn—or myself—riding around Rome on it.

But a bike was not a casual gift. It was the kind of thing a person got for their significant other.

"I know you don't know how to ride it," said Charlie, who had misinterpreted my hesitation. "But you can't learn to bike without a bicycle. I saw this one when I was at the shop I used to work at, and it just screamed *Maggie* to me." He looked at me bashfully. "I hope it's not too much."

It was. It was way too much.

My throat caught. "It's really nice. Thank you." I had always wanted a bicycle when I was a young girl. But I knew my mother could not afford it, and that if I asked for one, she would sacrifice too much in order to get me one. I suppose I could have bought a bike after college, but by then it seemed too late. But maybe it wasn't too late, after all. "I might end up maiming myself," I said to Charlie as I ran my hand along the painted chrome.

"That's what this is for." He handed me a large white helmet.

"Ground control to Major Mom," I droned as I stuck it on my head.

"Take your protein pills and put your helmet on," said Charlie. I smiled, slightly more relaxed; here was a man who actually caught my David Bowie reference. (Adam was more a Chet Baker kind of guy.)

"Let's give her a whirl, yeah?" he said, wheeling the bike out of the garage. "Come on. I'll help you."

"I hope you know I'm doing this for you," I said as I swung a leg over the seat.

"Nope. You're doing it for you," said Charlie as we made our way to the flat part of his driveway. "So, butt on the seat, feet on the pedals."

The moment my feet were in place, the bike and I began to wobble. But Charlie put his hands on my waist. "I've got you," he said in a low voice. "Let's go."

I was not graceful, but each time I tipped, Charlie kept me from crashing. Within half an hour, I was riding on my own. "This is fantastic," I called as I wheeled past him.

"You're a quick study," he said after I had stopped in front of the garage. "Won't be long before we can go on rides together."

When I didn't say anything, he said, "Or not."

Just a moment earlier he had looked so hopeful and happy, and I had just undone that without even trying. "No, I'd like that," I said quickly. "I'm just nervous about falling."

He looked at me for a moment. Then he put his hand on my back. "Don't be," he said. "You might fall, but you'll be okay."

~

I awoke several days later to a bright and temperate late April morning, and decided to take advantage of the weather and walk to Maizie's. I strolled slowly, enjoying the warmth of the sun and the fact that I had no loose ends to tie up. Jack had decided to stay in Chicago for another week to help Adam, and through him I knew that Adam was home and on the mend.

Maizie's was on a corner, with floor-to-ceiling windows that looked out toward the street. As I approached the front door, a sign taped to the glass caught my eye.

VOLUNTEERS NEEDED—HELP GIVE WOMEN LEAVING PRISON A SECOND CHANCE

There were pull tabs with a phone number and website at the bottom of the sign. I hesitated and then took one. If I was going to take a volunteer gig, I might as well have taken the internship with Adrian Fromm. But May was just around the corner, which meant my stay in Ann Arbor was almost halfway over; unless I intended to stay in town past August, there was no point in trying to find a job. Mostly, though, I was thinking about what Jean had said to me in Italy, about paying it forward. Maybe this would be a way to begin doing that.

"Hi there, Maggie," said Walter as I approached the bar. "The usual?"

"Hey, Walter," I said. "Yes, please."

A few people lined up behind me, but Walter worked fast, steaming the milk as espresso streamed into two small shot glasses, which he then poured into a to-go cup and topped with a generous dollop of foamed milk. "Cappuccino with an extra shot," he said as he handed me the cup.

"You're the best."

"That's what they say. Can I get you anything to eat?"

I eyed the pile of pillowy croissants nestled beside an array of scones. "Tempting, but not today. Do you know anything about the volunteer sign on your door?"

Walter nodded. He had a big belly, and white hair that levitated a few inches from his scalp; I often imagined him in a Santa costume. "Indeed I do. One of our regulars, Felicia, runs the organization. It's great, but they're on a shoestring budget, and they have a hard time finding good volunteers. You interested?"

"I might be. But I still haven't decided if I'm sticking around town when my lease is up."

"Well, I hope that you do," he said. "But I have a feeling Felicia would be thrilled for whatever help she can get for as long as she can get it."

"You know, Walter," I said, "I think I'll give her a call."

I left a message for Felicia when I got home, and she called back almost immediately. Any friend of Walter's was a friend of hers, she said after I explained how I had heard about Second Chance; did I want to come in for an interview?

I did, and so the following day I met her in her office in Ypsilanti, Ann Arbor's sister city. Second Chance, Felicia explained, helped women leaving prison transition to everyday life. She and two other social workers served as counselors and helped the women sort through the emotional burden of returning to society, but they relied on volunteers to find job opportunities for the women they served.

I told Felicia that I had been hunting for a job myself and had not been successful. "It's for the best, I think, since I'm not actually sure where I'm going to live after my sublet is up in August," I told her. "Because of that, I can't make a long-term commitment right now. Would that be a problem?"

"Not at all," said Felicia. She was short and curvy, and had a kind face that reminded me of Gita's. "If you'd be willing to give me five hours a week for the next three months, I'd be thrilled to have you on board. What do you think?"

What I thought was that an unpaid position would not help my long-term bottom line. But while I waited to figure out what was next, this would be a meaningful way to spend the short term. "I'd like to give it a try, if you'll have me."

"Then welcome to Second Chance," said Felicia, shaking my hand. "Conditionally, of course," she added. "You have to pass your background check first. But your social work experience will help an awful lot. You're not supposed to be counseling the women, technically." She raised an eyebrow. "But you will anyway, if you know what I mean."

"I've been out of the field for years, though," I said. "I'm rusty."

"You don't unlearn what you know. And I know from past hires that your life experience will be as useful as any degree." Her smile was nearly as wide as her face. "You're going to do just fine."

~

"That sounds terrific," said Charlie when I told him about Second Chance the following night. "But does this mean you're going to stay for a while? Because if you are, I might have to, too." He popped a tortilla chip into his mouth. We were at a Mexican restaurant and had just disappointed the waiter by turning down half-price happy hour margaritas.

I looked at him with surprise. "I only committed for three months. But back up a second—you're thinking of leaving town?"

"I've been thinking of leaving since Lucinda moved out. I'm not saying I'm going to, but I was thinking of putting the house on the market next month to at least get that off my hands."

"And then what?"

He shrugged. "I'm not sure. I'll probably rent something in the short term."

What about the long term? I thought. I felt like someone had just tied a rope around my gut and pulled it tight. I was halfway through my stay in Ann Arbor; I was the one who had no real plans for the future. But Charlie's lack of planning sounded like an admission that this—that *we*—were meaningless.

But I had not been looking for something meaningful. So why was I bothered?

"Living on the edge," I said.

Charlie looked at me for a moment. "Is there any other way?"

"What does that mean?" I asked.

He leaned back in the booth. "The best-laid plans can change at any minute. That's just the way life is. So I try to enjoy whatever I have while I have it."

And then you move on to the next thing? I wondered, recalling what he had said about loving change when we were at the botanic gardens.

He continued. "By the way, I told Bob that I wasn't returning to the support group anymore."

"Really?"

"Yep." He took a sip of his water. "Felt like the right thing to do."

I had skipped the last meeting, and Charlie had skipped the one before that. It hadn't been intentional, but I had to admit I had found it easier to open up about Adam when Charlie wasn't making eyes at me from across the room. "It probably is. Thanks," I said.

Beneath the booth, Charlie rubbed my leg with his foot. "So . . . you want to sleep at my place tonight?"

I examined the basket of tortilla chips as if it were my life's mission to find just the right chip to chomp on. For all our lovemaking, we had not yet spent the whole night together. To hear the rhythm of another person's breath as he sleeps, to nestle against his body as you slip out of consciousness, to see his sleep-crumpled face in the stark light of morning: these were markers of a different sort of relationship than the one Charlie and I had been having.

"Can I get a rain check?" I said, looking up from the basket. "I'm not feeling all that great tonight."

"Sure," he said evenly, but the subtle line in his forehead betrayed his disappointment.

"Sorry. I just need a good night's sleep," I said, barely able to avoid cringing at the sound of my own hollow excuses.

Instead of looking at me, Charlie retrieved his phone from his pocket and ran his finger over the screen as he scrolled. He never used his phone when we were together; most of the time he forgot it at home. I had hurt him. And in doing so, I had hurt myself, too.

But as I had told my children when they went in for their shots, a little preventive pain was far better than the alternative. After all, who knew better than I the dangers of failing to inoculate against heartache?

TWENTY-THREE

Dear Maggie,

I was as pleased as punch to get your last email. Of course, I'm sorry to hear about Adam's health problems, but it was good of you to be there for your children, even if (thank the good Lord) his prediction didn't come to pass. But worry most about your own heart, you hear?

Lucky you, the best part of the year has just arrived. There's nothing like May, after the students leave and return the city to us townies. I'll miss it, just as I miss the feel of my rough kitchen floor beneath my feet. There is something about the familiar that is just so darn appealing.

I met a lovely painter named Al, and we're getting on like two hogs in a mud puddle. Course, that's probably because I know it's just for now. Ever since Sam, I've found that the life of a lone wolf mostly suits me. At any rate, I'm painting my heart out, and I've learned enough Italian to ask for thirds on the mozzarella and to call out if I've fallen on the cobblestones and can't get up. Familiar is good, but maybe sometimes unfamiliar is even better.

This Charlie fellow sounds like a catch. And I'm awfully happy to hear about your volunteering gig, too. Which leads me to: Any plans for August? You can't fault me for hoping you'll fall in love with Ann Arbor and stay on longer—but neither could I fault you for moving on. The world is your oyster now!

Much love,

Jean

I wasn't one for oysters, and I still had no idea what I was going to do when Jean returned. Would I put the house in Oak Valley up for sale, as Linnea had been encouraging me to? Was I expecting a burning bush to declare my next move? Or waiting for a stable option to present itself to me instead of going out and creating it?

I was still staring blankly at my computer when there was a knock at the front door. I jumped up; delivery drivers left packages on the porch, so I immediately wondered if it was Charlie. A week had passed since I had turned down his offer to sleep over. We had gotten together for coffee a few days earlier, and though we had spoken like everything was normal, neither of us had suggested going to the other person's house afterward, and we had parted with tepid promises to be in touch later that week. Already the space I had wedged between us seemed like a vast distance, and I was having withdrawal pangs that suggested I had become too dependent on him.

But maybe he was here to say he missed me. Maybe we could draw new boundaries and close the gap without completely merging. I smoothed my hair and went to the front of the house.

The window atop the door was low enough that I could see that whoever was standing there was not Charlie, but rather a white man with close-cut salt-and-pepper hair. As I opened the door, however, it took several seconds for my eyes to inform my brain that the person to whom this hair and skin belonged was Adam.

"What on earth are you doing here?" I said, stunned. I looked past him and saw an unfamiliar car in the driveway. "You *drove* here? You're not supposed to be driving."

There were bags under his eyes; he looked like he hadn't slept in days. "It's been more than a month since my surgery. I was cleared to drive last week. Though technically I only drove from the airport. I took a flight to be on the safe side."

Hours of travel following heart surgery sounded like the opposite of safe to me. Moreover, it did not sound like a risk Adam would take. WebMD had said postbypass personality changes weren't unheard of. Still.

"I wanted to talk to you," he added.

I crossed my arms over my chest. "You came all the way from Chicago to do that? Without calling first? What if I wasn't here? And where did you even get my address?"

"Jack," he said, embarrassed.

I was going to have to have a word with my child.

"I didn't call, because I knew you would tell me not to come," he added.

"Quite prescient of you."

"Maggie, please. I just want to have a conversation."

The uncertainty I had felt after Adam's surgery immediately resurfaced. To allow him into my life—or even into my borrowed house—was to knowingly step in emotional quicksand. I slipped on my shoes, which were beside the door, and joined him on the porch.

It was a warm day, but Adam appeared to be shivering in his thin cotton trench coat. "Are you all right?" I asked.

"Yes." He sighed. "I'm just tired."

"I can only imagine. In the interest of my time and your health, you want to give me the CliffsNotes version of why you're here?" I had started at Second Chance at the end of the previous week and was due back for another training session in a few hours. "Please tell me you're not going to ask me to get in the car with you so we can drive to your mother's to convince her to take her pills," I added. I had spoken with Rose about the Alzheimer's medication several times since Adam's initial request. As I had anticipated, she was determined to march toward her fate without chemical intervention.

Adam looked sheepish. "No, you were right about that. I'm here to apologize."

I cocked my head. "You already did that in court. And with first-class airfare."

He stood there blinking in the sunlight. "I don't think I made myself clear, though."

"And you traveled two hundred and forty miles to clarify."

He nodded.

"When I saw you in the hospital, things seemed normal as they could be, given your taking a hammer to our marriage last year. I thought we were on the same page. But that assumption was why we ended up divorced, isn't it?"

He shoved his hands deeper in his pockets. "Maggie, please. I'm trying to make things right. I lie awake at night thinking of how I hurt you and destroyed us. The guilt is eating me alive."

I couldn't tell if his confession pleased me or made me pity him. A bit of both, I supposed. "Yes, well, I spent many a night imagining all the ways that you and Jillian Smith made love."

His eyes clouded over. He had probably assumed that I would be moved by his pain and plea for absolution. And to be honest, I was moved—at least a little. I didn't know how to *not* care about him.

"I've changed," he said quietly. "A lot. Give me a chance to show you that."

I stared at him. A chance? Did that mean what I thought it meant? I felt as if I were at the top of a roller coaster ride, waiting to plummet. "Well, I've changed, too. I've moved on," I said, and I was content to hear that I sounded more resolute than I felt. "You showing up at my door unannounced isn't helpful."

"I'm sorry." He kicked at some nonexistent dirt on the ground, just like Jack had sometimes done when he was a child. "Can we go get coffee, maybe talk things through?"

A sob rose in my throat. Even after everything, the idea of going to have coffee with him sounded so damn lovely. I could tell him about my life in Ann Arbor! He could tell me about his pro bono work! We could commiserate about our children and kvetch about Chicago's latest political scandal the way we used to! Not that we had been in the habit of doing this in the final stretch of our marriage. We probably hadn't been on a proper date with just the two of us for a full year before he left me.

I swallowed hard, readying myself to say no.

"It doesn't have to be right now," he said. "I rented a hotel room, so I'll be here until tomorrow night. I could even stay on longer, if there's another day that would work better for you."

The man with the watertight calendar had open-ended plans? Maybe he *had* changed. I hated that this idea excited me. "No, I'm not going to go to coffee with you."

His head dropped. He stood there for a moment, allowing my rejection to sink in. Then he began to walk away.

"Wait," I called. It was lunacy, giving into my curiosity like that, but I just had to know what he had come all the way from Chicago to say. "Five minutes," I said as he practically trotted back to the porch.

"Thank you, Maggie," he said humbly.

"You're welcome, but seriously—make it quick." I sat on one of the two small metal café chairs on the porch and indicated that Adam could take the other one.

As soon as he sat down, he began rotating his shoulder. "Sorry," he said when he realized I was watching. "My shoulder has been worse than ever since the surgery. Back and shoulder pain are common side effects."

Adam had once said I was a natural-born caregiver, and I suppose he was right; I had to ignore my urge to push a painkiller on him. "So . . . are you healing okay?" I asked.

"I guess." He looked down, then back at me. "I—I almost died. I don't know if you know that."

"You didn't, thank God."

"I almost did, though," he said. "I passed out in the emergency room. It was as close to death as I'd ever been. I saw *white lights*, Maggie."

I would have laughed—this was the least Adam-like thing I had ever heard him say—but his hands were clamped on either side of his chair, and he was staring at me intensely. "Everything was black, but then it was suddenly bright white. And somewhere deep in my mind, I was conscious enough to understand I was dying."

I thought of my mother, whose death I had always described as peaceful because she had not been awake for it. I wasn't sure I would ever say that again. "I . . . I'm sorry. I had no idea."

"I wasn't ready to talk about it before now. When I woke, I saw everything so clearly. When I left you, I had felt so dead inside."

I winced. "Yeah, well, marriage isn't always roses."

He shook his head. "That's not what I mean. Every day of my life for the past thirty years was the same, Maggie. Give or take a few details, I'd basically been living out *Groundhog Day*."

I felt like I had been slapped. Here I thought having the same person at your side year after year was a good thing. "If that's true, then it was self-imposed."

The color in his face was starting to return. "If I had left my job, what would we have done? You wanted to be home with the kids, and I wanted that for you—for all of us—too. And we had to pay for college and save for retirement, and there's Jack . . ."

Without rising from my seat, I stomped my foot once, hard. "I've been telling you for ages that you should tell Jack no. Being broke is rotten, but maybe that's what it will take for him to grow up."

"I know," he said quietly. "I've been thinking about that."

While I was glad he had acquiesced so quickly, our son wasn't really the point. "If you had told me you were feeling trapped, I would have found a way to help. I could have gone back to work earlier or gotten a full-time position." Even as I said this, I found myself questioning my own choice not to return to work full-time. I must have been futilely wishing and waiting for life to return to the wonderfully chaotic mess it had been when the kids were still home. There were several occasions during my years as a bookkeeper—Zoe's bout of pneumonia during her first semester of law school, Adam's father's death, Rose's hip fracture—in which it almost seemed that secret wish might come true. "We could have downsized our life," I concluded.

Adam sighed. "You seemed content with the way things were, and I wanted at least one of us to be happy. But then . . ."

"But then Jillian," I supplied.

"Yes. I guess so." He looked miserable. "She made me feel like I had options. Like I could make a change anytime I wanted to."

"Great."

Adam stared at me. "If you met someone who made you feel alive again after your life had flatlined, can you honestly say you wouldn't have been tempted to go for it, even if you knew deep down it was a mistake?"

I instantly thought of Charlie, who made me feel alive. But I had not pursued him while I was still married. "That's some serious rationalization on your part, Adam."

"No, listen. I'm not trying to make excuses. I understand now that I picked the exact wrong way to go about it. It wasn't even just the heart attack—after I started doing pro bono work, I realized my job was even more soul sucking than I had ever admitted."

"So that's what the improv class was about? You trying to shake things up and learn how to live in the moment?"

He nodded. "I'm horrible at it, but it's the most fun I've had in a long time."

I crossed my arms over my chest. "Not counting your affair. I mean, that's the root of all this. Instead of starting with improv or a new job, you tried to find excitement with a new woman. And even after you had the good sense to end it before it got serious, you lied to me about that, knowing it was tearing me up inside."

"Yes," he said quietly. "I failed. I failed us, and I failed you. It really seemed to me that our marriage was over, and lying to you was the best way to make that clear. I knew if I only said I wanted to leave, you would do everything in your power to keep us together, and I—I needed a clean break," he said, looking down at his lap. "Saying I was in love with Jillian was my way of helping you move on sooner than later."

"Well, mission accomplished."

"I know now that it was incredibly stupid. Maggie . . ." He lifted his head. His eyes were welling with tears, and I had to remind myself not to reach out and give him my hand. "Seeing you in the hospital room after I woke up from surgery was probably the happiest and saddest moment of my entire life. It shouldn't have taken a heart attack for me to realize how incredibly lucky I was and how I had thrown that all away."

I had waited a full year to hear him admit this—that he had squandered his good fortune. Yet his words did not bring any relief.

"What did I ask you on the phone when I called from Italy?" I asked suddenly.

He pulled his head back with surprise. "You don't remember?"

"You couldn't tell I was drunk?"

"I mean, yes, but I didn't realize . . . it's not like you to get messed up like that."

"It's not like me to get dumped by my husband."

Adam grimaced, like he was afraid to tell me. Which he probably was. "You . . . you asked me what it would take for us to be together again. That's all you kept asking: What would it take?"

Shame rushed through me. No wonder I couldn't remember. Deep down, I didn't want to.

"That's why I came today, Maggie. I finally have an answer for you. All it would take is you forgiving me." He leaned toward me. Even in his fraught state and fragile health, he was still so handsome. "I am so sorry. I'm asking you to consider taking me back. Please."

I sucked in my breath.

"I know that's too much to ask for now, but maybe we could start talking again. I want to show you that I'm a different person." His eyes searched mine. "I'm planning to sell the firm to Michael," he said, referring to his junior partner. "I don't know what I'm going to do next, other than keep on with the pro bono work. But whatever it is, it won't involve sixty-hour workweeks. We could set up our own nonprofit, like we used to talk about before the kids came along. We can travel the world. We can even buy a condo someplace warm. Or in Ann Arbor if you want," he added hastily. "I'll move here if this is where you want to be. We can be a family again."

Maggie, you'd be God's own fool to lose that boy, I heard my mother say.

Another voice in me argued, *But what if he changes his mind?*

I looked at the cracks in Jean's wood porch for a while. One was curved like half a heart. Another looked like a dagger. "I don't know, Adam," I finally said. "I just don't know."

"I know I wasn't there for you before. You were right in front of me, but I didn't see that your needs had changed, too. I believe that's why our marriage fell apart."

My silence was my affirmation. We had both neglected each other in our own ways, but yes—if we were keeping score, then Adam's neglect far outweighed mine.

"I can't answer you today," I told him.

He stood from his chair. "I understand. I wasn't expecting an answer on the spot." I thought he was leaving, but instead he reached into his pocket and fished out something small, which he pressed into my palm. When I looked down at my hand, I saw that it was a rose-gold band that looked like my original wedding ring. I had lost it swimming at the community pool with the kids, and Adam had replaced it with a diamond-studded eternity band I had always felt was too flashy for me, but which I wore anyway. I was so taken aback by the replica that I almost dropped it. "What *is* this?"

Adam bent on one knee before me.

"Get up," I hissed, pulling him by the sleeves of his trench coat. I could just imagine what Cathy would say if she happened to look out her door and see a strange man proposing to me on Jean's porch. Or—a chill ran down my spine—what if Charlie showed up? "You just had heart surgery. Please, get up."

Reluctantly, and not without effort, Adam stood. "Maggie, I want to marry you again. I want what we had—but better. And I know it's possible, if only you'll take me back."

I wasn't sure whether to projectile vomit or kiss him. How many dozens, even hundreds, of times had I imagined this scene in my head? Except even in my fantasy version, I had not dared dream that my then husband had not actually carried through with his affair. Nor did I wish that he would give up his workaholic ways. And though we *had* talked about traveling and creating some sort of charitable organization earlier in our relationship, I had long since accepted that I would sooner hitch a ride to the moon than see these particular plans come to fruition. All I had permitted myself to fantasize about was his remorse and newfound devotion. Now he was offering me all that, and much more.

As I looked at Adam, I allowed myself to admit what I had spent months denying: I had loved him so long that my love for him had become a part of me. I could no sooner undo it than I could rewrite my own genetic code.

And there was so much about sharing a life with him that I missed. Talking about how our days had gone before falling asleep beside each other in bed. Watching him rise and dress in the morning—the sight of him slipping on his nice pants and buttoning a pressed shirt had always brought me a strange pleasure. Knowing that being alone was only ever a temporary state that Adam's presence would soon relieve.

The idea of having all of this back brought tears to my eyes. Yet I could not bring myself to say yes. I wanted a guarantee he would never again go back on his promises.

"What can I do? Just tell me what it will take," Adam said, searching my face.

The words tumbled out before I considered them. "Prove it," I said. "Find some way to show you'll never hurt me like that again."

TWENTY-FOUR

When Charlie called the next day and asked if I wanted to go on a bike ride that evening, I was still so mentally muddled by Adam's visit that I almost said no. But even that one word seemed duplicitous; I needed to tell him what had happened. We agreed to meet at a riverfront park near my house an hour before sunset.

"Hi," he said, and kissed me lightly after getting out of his car. Then he pulled his head back and looked at me. "You okay?"

"Me?" I squeaked, all too aware that I looked like someone had just taken a Super Soaker to my t-shirt. When Charlie's eyes met mine, I blurted, "I saw Adam yesterday."

"So . . . this isn't about me asking you to spend the night," he said, slipping his car keys into the pocket of his shorts.

My face crumpled. "Sort of? But not really?"

Charlie sighed and leaned against the side of his sedan. "Okay. Let's start with Adam."

There were dozens of semi-eloquent ways I could have described what had happened. Instead of choosing any one of them, I said, "He asked me to take him back."

He ran a hand over the top of his head. "Fantastic."

"I'm trying to be honest."

He glanced at his bike, which was on a rack fastened to the back of his car, looking as perturbed as I'd ever seen him. I wondered if he was debating whether to bother taking the bike off. He turned back to me. "I'm going to make a wild guess: you didn't say no."

"I didn't say *yes*," I said, gripping the handlebars of the bike he had given me.

"But again, you didn't say no. Am I allowed to ask how this went down?"

"What do you mean, 'Am I allowed'?" I said defensively. "You can ask me whatever you want."

"That may be true, but between this and the spending the night thing, you've been putting up some fences lately."

"Given what I've been through the past year, is that such a surprise? Anyway, you might be leaving. Good fences make for good goodbyes."

He snorted. "Funny, but I didn't say I was leaving. I said I was thinking about it, which isn't the same. And if you're so intent on keeping this," he said, gesturing between us, "casual, what does it matter to you?"

My eyes smarted. Like me, he was being honest, but it felt mean—maybe because his honesty highlighted the chasm between my words and my actions.

Charlie sighed. "So Adam shows up and says . . . what? 'I almost died, and it made me realize what a mistake I made'?"

I stared at the tread on my bike wheel. "Pretty much. But the man just had a brush with death. I needed to hear him out."

"No, you didn't," he said firmly. "You knew any conversation you had wasn't going to change the past. I mean, I've got to wonder if you've been waiting for him all along."

I could feel blood rushing to my cheeks. "That's not fair."

"Isn't it? If you're really done with him, then what's the point of talking through things?" His dark eyes were boring holes into me. "But you're not done, are you?"

"Charlie!"

He looked at me sadly.

I had only known Charlie for four months, and much of our relationship had played out between the sheets; how could I really consider him a factor in whether to remarry my husband of twenty-seven years? Okay, so he liked to stroke my hair after we made love. And maybe we had long, interesting conversations about crop circles and global warming and the many iterations of Fleetwood Mac. But just as I had with Ian many years ago, I was on the verge of mistaking lust for love. I mean, even with a muted scowl on his face, my instinct was to touch Charlie somewhere, anywhere—maybe his stomach, as he liked when I ran my fingers down the plane of it; or his arms, though to feel them beneath my fingers was to morph into the sex-crazed teen I had not actually been—and speak to him in the language in which we communicated best.

Charlie reached into his pocket again and retrieved his keys, and I understood that the only ride I would be taking this evening was back to my house. "I was okay with casual," he said in a low voice. "I was ready to get more serious, but I was also willing to go at your speed so you stayed comfortable. But I'm not okay with being someone's second choice."

"You're not my second choice!" I protested. How could he be second, if I didn't know who first was?

"The thing is, Maggie, I didn't make a big deal out of you going to be with Adam for his surgery. I tried to be understanding since it was a crisis and you needed to be with your kids. But I'm fifty years old, and I know where my line in the sand is." We were in the parking lot, and Charlie pointed to the asphalt we were standing on. "This is it."

"I share two children with Adam," I said lamely. "I can't just send him a cease and desist."

Instead of answering, he put his head in his hands. After a moment, he looked up. "What do you want to do, Maggie? Tell me what makes sense here."

The park was just in front of us, and fireflies were rising from the grass and lighting up the yard with their aerial mating dance. They were the first of the season, and I watched them for a moment. "I don't know," I finally said.

"I should go," Charlie said.

No, I thought.

"Fine," I said.

Our eyes met, and for a split second I thought maybe I did know what made sense. Charlie reached forward and touched my arm so quickly it was almost as though I had imagined it. Then he stepped back and said, "Bye, Maggie. I'll see you around."

I waited until he had driven away. Then I wheeled my bike through the grass toward the water. When I reached the shore, I laid my bike in the grass and sat on a boulder stationed at the water's edge.

I sat there until it was almost dark, even though the mosquitoes were making a meal of me and I would have to walk home because I didn't have a light for my bicycle. Charlie had said he was ready for something more serious. I, however, was not—otherwise I would have stopped him from leaving.

As the river rushed before me, I thought of the Tiber in Rome, which then made me think of Jean. She said she was happiest by herself. Maybe my indecision indicated I would be, too. Well, perhaps not happy. But I would be safe—and that was almost the same thing.

TWENTY-FIVE

I once read that the recipe for a good life had but three ingredients: something to do, someone to love, and something to look forward to.

I had my children, Gita, and Rose to love. And now that I was volunteering at Second Chance, I had something to do. Felicia had asked me to put in five hours a week, but there was enough work to fill forty, and I had already told her I would gladly double my shifts.

It seemed again, however, that I had nothing to look forward to. For a long time after Adam left, the only good thing I could anticipate was a glass of wine at the end of the day. That had begun to turn around for me in Ann Arbor, even though my future remained a murky cloud on the horizon. I had Charlie to thank for some of that; life was brighter when I was with him, and when I wasn't, I was always looking forward to the next time we would be together.

Beyond Charlie, though perhaps partially because of him, I had begun to recover from the divorce. Finally, I was able to get excited about what was around the corner—whether my morning coffee run or the kids' upcoming visit to Ann Arbor. It was like I had slowly begun to remember what it was like to be the old me, even if I had not reinhabited her.

But now I was starting to slide backward, away from myself and toward the unknown.

This time, however, I knew how to do this. I knew how to claw my way out of the dark.

~

The first thing I did was throw myself into work.

Felicia set me up in a brightly lit office in the small bungalow that was Second Chance's headquarters. "You're my only career counselor right now, so make yourself comfy," she told me, and though I wasn't sure why I was bothering sprucing up a space that I wouldn't spend more than a few months in, I brought in a few houseplants and a couple pictures of the kids.

The work itself was all-consuming, and maybe that's why I enjoyed it. As I had learned as a social worker decades earlier and was again reminded at Second Chance, it was impossible to focus on your own worries when those of the person in front of you were so much greater.

There was Elizabeth, who had shot her abusive husband in an attempt to save her own life and was rewarded with a prison sentence for firing an unregistered gun. Elizabeth did not trust anyone, but especially not men, she told me. If I could not help her find a job where she wouldn't have to be around them, then she wouldn't keep coming to see me. This sounded like an impossibly tall order, but I promised her I would do my best.

Another client, Tonya, had robbed a 7-Eleven, netting ninety-six dollars and a twelve-year prison sentence. She was lucky to get out two years early, she said, but now she felt hopeless. "My kids were practically babies when I went away. Now they're in high school, and I don't know what to say to them," she said, her voice void of affect.

I suspected Tonya was grappling with depression, but when I suggested she talk to Felicia, who was a certified counselor, or see a psychiatrist affiliated with Second Chance, Tonya told me she didn't believe in voodoo or witch doctors. And when I started talking about potential jobs that might be a good fit, she stood up and walked out on me. "I'll be back when I'm ready," she said.

Then there was Crystal. A wisp of a woman, she stomped into my office one afternoon and stared me down from across my desk. Her hair was bleached blond, and she was wearing a t-shirt so large it threatened to swallow her whole; her bra, which was the color of dishwater, was visible through the armholes. "Don't you have my record?" she retorted after I asked her why she had been in prison.

"Sure, but I want to hear your story from you," I said.

"Drugs," she said.

"And?"

"That's it." She was staring at me like I'd been the one to put her away in the first place. "What makes *you* think you can help *me*?"

I searched my mind for a reason that would not offend her and failed to find a single one.

"Exactly," she said, looking me up and down. "As far as I can tell, you can't."

My defenses were on their way up, so I took what Gita called a cleansing breath, which neither cleansed nor calmed me. I wanted to remind Crystal that I was not her parole officer; she was at Second Chance by choice, not obligation, and at no cost to her. But even more than I wanted to clarify, I wanted to help her. I pasted a smile on my face. "I don't know what you've been through. What I do know is that you need a job, and I have a list of leads for you." I pushed the paper in front of me across the desk toward her.

She peered down at the list I had printed out. "I don't know shit about baking. And I sure as shit am not cleaning toilets."

"It's up to you to decide what you want to pursue. Just keep in mind that the baking position provides on-the-job training; you don't have to know anything. The pay is decent, and you could work early mornings so you'd be home for your daughter in the afternoon. In your paperwork, you mentioned that was a top priority. Is that still true?"

"I guess," she said, and looked out the window.

I followed her gaze. It was a beautiful June day, clear and crisp and bright. The weather was perfect for a bike ride, or a picnic for two, I thought with a pang as I turned back to Crystal.

"I'll think about it," she said after a minute. "They're not going to want me, though."

"How do you know that?"

"'Cause I didn't get the last four gigs I applied for. Didn't the woman who worked here before you tell you that?"

I tugged at my ponytail, which suddenly felt far too tight. "No, she didn't. I just started volunteering here, and whoever was here before was already long gone. Would you like me to help you fill out the application?"

She crossed her arms over her chest. "Like I said, let me think about it."

I told her the job could be filled by next week, but if she wanted time, we could revisit it when she came in again. What I did not tell Crystal was that I was beginning to think waiting was often the worst idea. Sometimes the longer you thought about something, the harder it became to make a decision.

~

I had not spoken with Adam since he showed up at my door in May; the ring he had pressed into my hand was in a sealed envelope in my sock drawer. But he had been emailing what he must have thought of as the proof I had requested since the week after he left. His messages were brief missives that were addressed to me, but never signed:

> *Saved a client from a life sentence for a murder he didn't commit.*
>
> *Sold the firm to Michael; half the profits from the sale go to you. My lawyer will reach out.*
>
> *Was offered a full-time position at the Innocence Collaboration. Think I'm going to take it.*
>
> *Clean bill of health from my surgeon.*
>
> *Took the offer.*
>
> *Have started meditating.*

Each time one of these messages arrived, I thought, *Is this enough?* And each time, I didn't know.

It seemed to me that Adam was, as he had sworn, a changed man—and that he was still changing. Yet there was something about the situation with Jillian that didn't sit right with me. Sometimes I wondered if she existed at all; other times, I felt she had a key to my husband's secret heart.

She made me feel like I had options. Like I could make a change anytime I wanted to, he had said. But why? Was it her youth? Her adoration for him? If I figured out what it was about Jillian that had made Adam feel like he could change, could I take that knowledge and apply it to my new relationship with him in order to keep him from flip-flopping again?

~

One morning in mid-June, I stopped at Maizie's before heading into Second Chance. Leah, a barista I was friendly with, was making my coffee, and I stood to the side, waiting for her to finish. As I waited, a tall, thin man wearing a suit strolled up to the counter. I immediately recognized him as Adrian Fromm.

"Large latte, two extra shots, please," said Adrian, typing furiously on his phone. My mother, who had worked as a waitress off and on for years, had always said that you could tell who a person really was by watching the way he treated someone serving him. That Adrian had said "please" without actually looking at Walter seemed to sum him up perfectly.

"That'll be three fifty," said Walter agreeably.

Adrian reached into his back pocket and handed Walter a gold credit card without looking up. He signed the receipt Walter handed him, then shuffled to the side while typing—walking right into me in the process.

His fingers froze and he glanced up. "Sorry," he mumbled. Then he immediately began typing again, perhaps updating his vast social network on the middle-aged woman he had just looked through.

"You don't recognize me," I said.

His head rose. Still, for a moment there was nary a light behind his eyes. Finally he said, "Maggie! Hello. Funny seeing you here."

"Hi, Adrian. How are things at CenterPoint?"

He made the same duck face he had made during our interview. Then he said, "Good, good. Everything's right on track." Then he surprised me and said, "What about you, Maggie? Where did you land?"

"I'm working as a volunteer at Second Chance. It's an organization that helps women transition back to everyday life after leaving prison. Ever heard of it?"

"Can't say that I have, though it sounds like a great place. Volunteering, though? Wouldn't coming to work for CenterPoint have made more sense for your career?"

He was wearing tortoiseshell glasses, and even inches from my face, the lenses did not distort his eyes in the slightest, making me wonder if they were non-Rx frames intended to lend him the gravitas he thought was required in order to convince people to hand over their cash.

"In theory?" I said. "Definitely. But I'm in a somewhat transitory period in my life, and I wanted to do the thing that interested me most, rather than the one that offered the safest path." I smiled; I had not quite thought of it that way until I said it out loud.

"Maggie?" called Leah from over the bar. "Your cappuccino is up."

I thanked her and retrieved my coffee from the counter. Felicia had recently told me that Second Chance could offer far more programs if only they had additional funding. Adrian had said the ability to raise capital was arguably the most charitable endeavor a person could undertake. Well, I was about to undertake it.

I turned back to Adrian. "If I recall, one of CenterPoint's main missions is to secure financing for charitable organizations, yes?"

He nodded and took his coffee, which had just been called, from the counter.

"Would you mind if I gave you a call later this week about Second Chance? We have a literacy program and a housing initiative that we desperately need funding for, and I have a feeling our director would love to have a conversation with you about a possible partnership."

Adrian stared at me for a moment. Then he smiled. "Call me anytime, Maggie. We'll get a meeting on the books."

I told him I would. Then I went outside and sat on a bench, thinking that I might have just seen the faintest glimmer of the light Gita had spoken of.

TWENTY-SIX

At the end of June, Zoe and Jack flew in for a weekend to celebrate my birthday. I wasn't big on birthdays, at least not my own; it was really an excuse for me to spend time with my children, whom I missed as much as I ever had.

I cried when I spotted them waiting for me outside the airport. Zoe, who was wearing a sundress and a wide-brimmed hat, looked every bit as self-possessed as she had been as a girl. And there was Jack, who reminded me so much of my mother. It wasn't just his brown saucer eyes and high cheekbones; as she had, he took the world in stride, happy to be along for the ride. These were my people, and when they walked toward the car, I ran out and embraced them like we had been apart for years.

Zoe had instructed me to pick my favorite restaurant for dinner—and I would have, except it happened to be Charlie's favorite, too, and I didn't want to up the odds of bumping into him. I was desperate to see him, and yet I had not called, because what would I say? *Sorry I'm such an indecisive jerk? I wish I could watch the* Sliding Doors *version of my life to see if I would actually be happy with the alleged "new Adam," or if I'd be more content with a semiserious relationship with you?* Of course, by doing nothing, I was choosing the third option: solitude.

So the kids and I went to a restaurant that was rumored to have decent fried chicken and the best biscuits in town.

"Drinks?" asked the waitress after we had been seated at a booth.

"Sparkling water with lime, please."

"No champagne for your birthday, Mom?" asked Zoe.

"I'm not really drinking these days."

"Okay . . . I'll have sparkling water, too," she told the waitress.

"A Coke for me," Jack said.

"So you gave up wine? That's no fun," said Zoe after the waitress left.

I immediately thought of Charlie. "Turns out it can be fun. More fun, in a way; you miss a lot less of life as it's going by. That's been the biggest surprise of all this."

"Interesting," said Zoe. "Well, good for you."

"Thanks, love. It's been enlightening."

Over dinner, we talked about Zoe's unrelenting caseload. She claimed it was a prerequisite for making partner at a big firm one day. Just as she didn't understand why I had hopped off the career track early in my adult life, I questioned her desire to sign over her best years to a corporation. But it was her choice to make, and I had to trust that she would know if and when to make a change.

Then I told the kids about my work at Second Chance, and how I was close to securing a $20,000 grant through Adrian Fromm, whom I had met with the previous week.

"The jerk who offered you an internship?" said Zoe.

I laughed, thinking of the buzzy phrases Adrian had tossed around during our meeting. But he had also told me he would find funding for our new housing initiative. "The one and only. Maybe not quite as much of a jerk as I thought."

"Sounds like you and Dad are doing similar stuff," said Jack, and Zoe raised an eyebrow.

"How's that?" I asked.

"You're both working for charities and doing good things."

I watched the bubbles rising in my water. "Yes, I suppose we are."

"Is this what people do after divorce?" Jack added. His sandy hair, which had grown since I had last seen him, was tucked behind his ears.

"What do you mean?" I had not told Jack and Zoe about Adam's proposal, and from previous conversations with them, I gathered that Adam had not, either. Just as well, I decided: while they were adults and could handle the truth, there was no need to inform them that their parents were in a relationship purgatory of their own making.

"Like, you're both making big changes in your life."

I almost retorted that I had not changed by choice, but it was no longer true. I was again steering my own ship. "I suppose we are. What about you, Jack?" I asked. "We haven't heard a word about what you've been up to since you got back from helping your father."

His cheeks flushed. "Um. Yeah. So I don't know how to tell you this . . ."

It was amazing what could flash through my mind in two to three seconds. Jack had defaulted on the student loans we had required him to take out for his extra semester of college! He had been arrested for smoking weed on his apartment stoop! He had fathered a child and wanted me to meet my secret grandbaby!

"I'm planning to move back to Chicago," he blurted. "Like, in two weeks."

"You? Chicago?" I said with disbelief. "What about New York being the creative epicenter of the world?"

"It's kind of not anymore, Mom. Only rich cogs like Zoe can afford to live there."

She lobbed a piece of biscuit at him, and I tried not to laugh. "Well, that's unexpected."

"Yes and no," he said. "Dad cut me off. Financially, I mean."

I almost choked on the sip of water I had just taken. Adam firmly believed it was our duty as parents to support Jack until he found his wings—however long that took. It was what his father had done for him, Adam had always argued; no matter that unlike Jack, Adam had been an A student who had gone directly from college to law school to a good job. I had assumed that our financial help would stop when we negotiated alimony during our divorce, but Adam had opted to continue supporting Jack off the record, shelling out an unspecified amount of his own spending money.

"Is this because he sold his business?" I asked.

"How did you know about that?" said Zoe.

I held up a finger. "We'll come back to that."

"Nope. He just said it was time. He said I needed a flame under my—" Jack coughed. "Under my butt." He looked down guiltily. "I mean, he's not wrong. I called Miller and Nasir," he said, referring to his childhood friends, "and some other contacts, and got a couple of interviews lined up. Miller's dad works at an ad agency, and he arranged for me to come in and meet the human resources director. If they hired me, I'd start in the mail room, but like you always say, all work is good work."

Well, wasn't that something! I didn't even try to hide that I was pleased.

He grew serious, and I again steeled myself for bad news. "Don't take this the wrong way, but being there with Dad after surgery was good. His mind was wonky there for a while, but we ended up having some decent talks and . . . I don't know." He shrugged. "Seems like it would be really good for one of us to be around in Chicago for him. You know, just in case."

"Well," I said, blinking like I'd just walked into a sandstorm, "I really appreciate that, Jack. I'm sure your father does, too. Where will you live?"

"I might share a place with Miller in Pilsen. It's cheap, Mom. I could afford it even if I take a job at a convenience store." Jack, content to have told me his secret, leaned back and took a bite of his drumstick.

"So, Mom," said Zoe. "You know about Dad selling his firm. Have you guys been talking? He said he went to see you in May."

I frowned. Why would he tell them that? "Yes, he did. Very briefly. What else did he say?"

"Only that he had made a mistake and wanted to apologize." She shot me a knowing look. "I told you so."

"Well, you were right. And yes, he apologized."

"Did you forgive him?" Zoe asked.

"Of course I did." I thought of Adam sitting on Jean's front porch, looking so simultaneously pained and expectant. I wondered what he was doing now and what it would be like if he were sitting here at dinner with us.

"So are you guys considering getting back together?" Jack looked so hopeful that I wanted to cry. He was such a laid-back kid—he always had been—that I sometimes forgot that beneath his cool demeanor, he was as sensitive as I was.

"I hope you're not, Mom," said Zoe before I had a chance to answer. "I love Dad, but—" She made a face. "You know what I mean. You have a good life now."

I did, I realized at once. My day-to-day existence—my work at Second Chance, my newfound friendship with Felicia, and even little things, like planting tomatoes in a corner of Jean's yard—was joyful.

The big picture wasn't so bad, either. While I had gone through an unwanted divorce, I had also traveled to Rome by myself and moved to a new town and kicked a bad habit. Instead of merely surviving, I had managed to thrive. "You're right," I told Zoe. "And for right now, my focus is just to keep living it."

~

"Mom, Zoe, come out here!" The three of us had gone out for cupcakes after dinner, and we had just returned to the house. While Zoe and I were making lemonade, Jack had wandered into the yard. Now he was on his back in the grass, not far from the small vegetable garden I had planted a few months earlier. "Lie down," he called as we came running out the screen door at the back of the house. "You have to see this."

I lowered myself to the ground beside him, and Zoe got on the other side of me. It had been a scorcher of a June, but I had watered the grass liberally, and it was soft beneath my skin.

"Jack, humor me," I said from beside him. "You're not high, are you?"

"Mom, come on. I know it's not good for me."

"No, it's not," I agreed, thinking of Crystal and the two years she had spent in prison for passing a joint to a friend within view of an undercover cop. "I'm glad you know that, too."

"Anyways, that's not why I asked you to come out here. Look at all that!" he said, pointing over our heads. Above us, the sky was a deep navy, with a million twinkling lights. I had not looked at a sky like that—really looked at it—in quite some time, and it was magnificent.

"Happy birthday, Mom," said Zoe quietly.

I found her hand, and Jack's, and squeezed them both. Would they ever know what incredible joy they brought me? "Thank you, love. You and Jack being here is the best gift I ever could have asked for."

"We're happy to be here, Mom. Fifty-four, huh?"

"Fifty-four," I said. "Which sounds awfully old."

"No, it doesn't," said Zoe. "You still have your whole life ahead of you."

Yes—that was true whether I lived one more day or another thirty years. A lump formed in my throat as I thought of my mother. Even before she'd had the first imaging test, she had known that it was the end for her. "Now don't you cry, Maggie. I've had more years than many people will, and I've loved every minute," she had drawled after her diagnosis. Though I knew she had not literally enjoyed every minute, she had loved the life all those minutes had formed together, and that had been enough for her.

"You know, your grandmother died when she was fifty-four," I said.

"Really?" said Jack.

"You were just four then. Do you remember her at all?"

"A little. I remember thinking she was nice. She used to slip us pieces of candy."

I laughed. "That sounds about right."

"I remember her," said Zoe. "She was funny. And she always told me I was smart, like you."

I felt the tingle of tears forming behind my eyes. "She was my biggest fan. I wish she were still here."

"Sorry, Mom," said Zoe. "That's got to be really hard."

I was about to agree when a flash of white shot across the sky above us.

"Did you guys see that?" said Jack.

"I did," said Zoe.

"Me too. It's been decades since I've seen a shooting star," I said.

"It's your birthday star, Mom! What did you wish for?" said Zoe. She poked me in the side and added, "Don't you dare say 'good children.'"

I laughed; that had always been my response when she and Jack had asked me what I wanted for holidays. But then I thought for a moment, and an unexpected wish, like the star itself, surfaced seemingly out of midair.

"Well? What was it?" asked Jack.

I told him I didn't want to jinx my wish by saying it out loud, but that I could at least confirm that it wasn't a person or a material thing. Jack made a few guesses, and Zoe posed a handful of possibilities.

"How about I share it with you after it comes true?" I said. Then I closed my eyes and made another wish: that one day soon, I could tell my children I had inherited my mother's ability to fold life's bad moments into the good and believe it was enough.

TWENTY-SEVEN

As I was driving the kids back to the airport, Zoe asked me what I was going to do with the house in Oak Valley. I confessed I wasn't sure. Financially, selling it made the most sense; if I didn't have a full-time job come the following January, then I would at least have extra savings to cover the health insurance policy I would need to secure for myself at the start of the new year.

"Okay, but how do you *feel* about it?" pressed Zoe. "Not financially. Emotionally."

Emotionally? While it had been a place of love, the house no longer symbolized that or security for me, and I didn't want to move back there. Trouble was, I hadn't settled on staying in Ann Arbor—or anywhere else. With just over a month before Jean's return, the walls were closing in quick, but I kept standing there, a woman paralyzed by her own options.

"Ditch it, Mom," said Jack from the back seat. "We're not waiting to inherit it."

"It was your childhood home," I said as I switched lanes.

"And it always will be," said Zoe, reaching across from the passenger seat to pat my shoulder. "We're not going to forget the memories we had there just because we can't go back." She began to laugh and swiveled to face Jack. "Do you remember when you sledded down the stairs on your flamingo pool float?"

"You told me to!" he said indignantly, but then he started to laugh, too.

"I did not," said Zoe.

"Either way, it was a very bad idea," I said. "Jack, remember the two black eyes you had after you hit the wall headfirst? I was so worried people would think me or your father had hit you."

"You two? Yeah, right," he scoffed.

"Or what about the time you almost set fire to the kitchen trying to make muffins?" I said to Zoe. She had been maybe seven at the time and had been convinced that she could follow instructions out of a recipe book. I had come downstairs just in time to pull out the fire extinguisher and coat the oven and everything near it with white foam.

"I still owe you for that one," she conceded. "But sell the house, Mom. It's weighing you down."

~

What I needed, I decided after I returned from the airport, was clarity about whether I was going to stay in Ann Arbor after Jean's return. Though I would have preferred warmer weather, I had grown to like it there. The townies, as the year-round residents called themselves, were both nice and interesting. I liked my coffee shop and going to the farmers' market on Saturday mornings and the river that roped through the city. There were far worse places to live.

The next day I began looking at rentals to get a sense of what my options were. I checked out a quirky one-bedroom with cupboards customized for a professional basketball player, and a new-construction condo within walking distance of downtown. The latter piqued my interest, but the lease revealed dozens of hidden fees. The next half a dozen other places I saw were just as problematic for different reasons.

Then a rental agent showed me a small yellow craftsman on the west side of town, about a mile from Jean's place. It was not quite as charming as Jean's, and instead of a view of the woods, bungalows and backyards greeted me when I looked out the windows. The neighborhood, however, was a friendly mix of young families and those who had lived there for decades.

The house itself had two bedrooms, a spacious kitchen that opened into a dining nook, and a yard with a verdant vegetable garden and fresh lavender and rosemary bushes, whose scent filled the air.

"What do you think?" asked the agent eagerly as we were standing in the garden.

It was nearly ninety degrees, and I wiped sweat from my brow. "I think it's perfect," I said.

"Would you like to fill out a rental application?" he asked.

"No," I said.

The agent looked at me like I had sprouted a second head.

"I'm not ready to make a decision," I explained.

"It'll be gone by tomorrow," he said.

So be it, I thought. I wasn't sure where my indecision was coming from, but I had begun to realize it was having an unexpected effect. Rather than exacerbating my anxiety, embracing uncertainty was bringing me peace.

Crystal did not show up for our second meeting, but the following week she landed back in my office. Not at her scheduled meeting time—or even on Wednesday, her scheduled day. Instead, she showed up on a Monday afternoon. I had just sat down at my desk and was gearing up for a busy afternoon. "Can we talk?" she said, sticking her head in the door.

I had managed to raise two children without murdering them during their teen years, and that was largely because I had allowed them to learn the law of natural consequences. If it had worked for them, it could work for Crystal, too.

"You'll have to come back at six," I told her.

"Six?" Her eyes bulged. "I've got Jade then," she said, referring to her daughter.

"Bring her. I have a box full of toys and art supplies she can play with while we talk. But right now," I said, pointing toward the clock on the wall, "I have another client. And then another, and another, until six."

"Really?"

"I'm sorry." I shrugged. "But lucky for you, I don't have plans tonight, and I'll stay late. That's the best I can offer."

She eyed me suspiciously. "Thanks, I think."

I smiled at her. "You're welcome, I think."

Six came and went. Just when I started wondering if I had given Crystal too much credit, a small child with bright blue eyes stuck her head in my door. A second later, Crystal appeared behind her, red-faced and out of breath. "Bus trouble," she huffed. "Me and Jade got here as fast as we could. I'm sorry."

An apology? All was forgiven. "It's fine," I told her. "Come on in."

I pulled the box of toys out from under my desk and handed them to Jade. She looked at them solemnly, then back at me, then at my door. "Can I take them into the hallway?"

I had been accustomed to keeping to myself as a child, and I saw a glimpse of that girl in Jade. "Sure, love. But you're also welcome to come in here with us if the hallway gets boring."

Jade glanced at her mother, and Crystal nodded at her.

"You're trying to pull your life together for her," I said once Jade was settled in the hall. "I admire that."

"I'm out of work, and I'm doing a crap job," she said miserably. "Jade's jammed into a tiny room with me and my brother's girls. They don't like having us there, and we all know it." She lowered her voice. "Things were better for Jade when I was locked up. At least then she had a whole bed to herself."

"That can't possibly be how she really feels," I said. "You love her, don't you?"

"Of course."

"Yes, it's obvious to me. And it's obvious to Jade, too."

Crystal gnawed at a cuticle. When she realized what she was doing, she wedged her hands underneath her thin thighs. "Love won't undo the last two years. She's constantly worrying that I'm going to disappear. She cries when I put her to bed at night, and I don't even like taking her to school, because she makes a scene when I have to leave her at her locker. I can't blame her for feeling like I'll go missing, either. That's exactly what happened when I got put away."

I was almost afraid to open my mouth again for fear I would unintentionally silence her. "Maybe getting a steady job would show her that you're going to stick around."

"I never kept a job longer than a few months."

"I'm sure it sounds overwhelming, but let's find the right job for you and then make a goal. Maybe you can aim to stay for six months?"

"That sounds like a long time."

"Yes and no," I said, thinking of how my six months in Ann Arbor would soon be up.

Crystal looked toward the hallway, where Jade was playing, before turning back to me. "Okay. So you want to tell me what's available?"

"You know I do," I said, turning my computer monitor toward her so we could look together.

~

"You're good," said Felicia, appearing in the doorway shortly after Crystal left.

I had been working my way through a pile of paperwork. I lifted my head and smiled. "You eavesdropping?"

"Just a little." Felicia motioned to the chair in front of me. "Mind if I sit for a minute?"

"Please do."

She crossed her legs and leaned back in the plastic bucket chair. "You've been putting in at least twelve hours a week."

"I know," I said, looking at Crystal's file on the table in front of me. "Sorry. It's hard to get what needs to be done accomplished in ten. But I can cut back."

"Cut back?" She hooted. "Girl, please. I'm not asking you to do less if you want to do more. I love having you here."

"Thank you," I said. "I'm really enjoying it."

"I can tell. You put any thought into going back into social work? Officially, I mean." Felicia and I went to lunch often enough that she now knew how up in the air my life was at the moment.

I bit my lip, considering this. "I mean, I'd have to pick someplace to live, then go through the certification process and land a position where they'd be willing to supervise me until I had the hours I needed in order to be licensed . . ." Then I stopped myself. When I helped Elizabeth get a job at a mission run by nuns and she cried, I was so happy you would think I had just found the answer to world peace. I awoke in the middle of the night, thinking about my clients and their problems—but unlike the insomnia I had suffered after Adam's departure, this kind wasn't a nuisance. Working at Second Chance lit me from within. "Other than the finding someplace to live part, that actually doesn't sound so awful."

Felicia smacked a hand on her thigh. "That's the spirit. You let me know when you start looking for jobs, because I'll have a big fat recommendation letter waiting for you. A lot of people out there could use your help, Maggie."

Could they? Good. Because I was ready for them.

~

Felicia and I said goodnight, and I headed outside. Second Chance's driveway was reserved for clients, so as usual I had parked on a side street. The street I had chosen earlier that day was a dark, tree-canopied dead end; I had left my car next to an abandoned lot and across from a house that I had yet to see a single person enter or exit. It was not the kind of place where I would normally park, but the area was now familiar to me.

I had just approached my car and pulled my keys from my bag when a voice came vaulting toward me. "Lady!"

I spun around and saw a young man standing a few feet away at the edge of the abandoned lot.

"Can I borrow your phone?" asked the man. He had greasy hair and gray teeth, and he wore a strange expression, which I initially interpreted as distress. "I locked mine in my car, and I'm stuck out here in the cold."

On a ninety-degree day in July, I barely remembered what cold was, and the car the man referred to was nowhere to be seen. Yet my instinct was to give him the benefit of the doubt and say yes.

Then I looked at him again and saw that something in his eyes broadcast that I was in danger.

My heart was racing so fast I wondered if I, too, would have a heart attack. If I ran, could I make it the several hundred feet back to Second Chance before the man caught me? If I did, would Felicia still be there? Should I run to the house that seemed to be unoccupied, or try to find another?

"Smile," the man said as his eyes twitched. "I'm just asking for a favor."

And telling me what to do with my lips, I thought with disgust. I started for the street, but the man, anticipating my move, grabbed me by the wrist.

My galloping heart was threatening to breach my chest as his nails sank into my flesh. Did he want all the money I didn't actually have on me—or was he planning to take me to an underground bunker and rape and torture me? *Oh God,* I thought. Though it had been more than half a lifetime ago, I could still vividly recall the knife my client had held to my neck; I could almost feel Jack shifting in my womb and the simultaneous trickle of blood on my throat and urine down the side of my leg as I waited to find out if my child and I would live.

"If I was you, I wouldn't do anything stupid," said the man in a low voice.

If he were I, he would know that I did all kinds of stupid things, I thought suddenly. And some of them—not most, but some—worked out for me. I stared into his bloodshot eyes and, summoning what must have been the strength of every single one of my ancestors, screamed at the top of my lungs.

Whatever the man had been expecting, it wasn't my bloodcurdling screech, and he immediately loosened his grip. That was my cue: I ran toward the street and blessedly spotted two men walking a large German shepherd right in front of Second Chance.

"You ugly old bitch!" the man hollered, disappearing through the alley behind the house. "You're not worth my time!"

One of the two men walking the dog let me use his phone to call the police while the other stood guard with the dog. The man who had assaulted me was long gone when the police arrived, and I offered a shaky recollection of the event before they escorted me home.

When we arrived at Jean's, I could barely steady my hand to unlock the door, and even though the police searched the house quickly to calm me, I continued to tremble long after they left.

I had worked with many decent but desperate people early in my career—people who made bad choices because they were under the impression there were no others. The man who had assaulted me was hurting, for reasons that would never be known to me. Tomorrow I would try to wish him well. But on this evening, I wished I had stuck my keys right into his jugular.

Smile. I got into bed, pulled the duvet to my chin, and cried as the assault came flashing back to me. *You ugly old bitch.*

For a few minutes, I considered that maybe I would not return to Second Chance; I even entertained the idea that this attack, like the last one, was a sign indicating I should take a different direction.

Then I thought about what Jean had said about how bad things were simply bad things. I would continue showing up at Second Chance, though I would park somewhere else. And when I moved to wherever it was I was headed, I would pursue a career in social work. Because I would be damned if I let another person's bad choice dictate my decisions.

TWENTY-EIGHT

I was in the kitchen, making chicken shawarma from a recipe I had come across online, when Gita called. The timer on the stove began to chime as I picked up the phone, and I dashed across the room. “Okay, I’m here,” I told Gita after I had turned the timer off. “What’s the latest?”

“Nothing new here. But what about you? How are you feeling?” She was referring to the attack.

“Pretty good, actually. I’m still nervous, of course, but I’ve been parking right in front of the building when I volunteer, and I have someone walk me outside if I’m there after five.”

“I’m happy to hear that. Any decisions about your move?”

“Alas.” Jean returned in less than three weeks, and I had stopped looking for rentals. “The house is about to go on the market, though,” I said. My lawyer had told Adam’s lawyer I was ready to sell, and since the terms of the sale had been hammered out during the divorce proceedings, all we had to do was wait for an offer and agree to take it.

“Aww. I’ll miss your place. Remember, our invitation stands.” Gita and Reddy had told me I could stay in the apartment above their garage while I was figuring out where to head next.

"Thank you. At this rate, I may just have to take you up on that."

"I wouldn't mind if you did. So . . . I know you're leaving town, but how would you feel about going on a date before you go?"

"A date?" I said, staring at the pan of chicken that I had just pulled out of the oven. Even though I had halved the recipe, it was still far too much shawarma. "Have you been sniffing hair dye? I'm relationship kryptonite."

"I'm not talking about serious dating. Reddy has an old friend in Ann Arbor, and he just found out that he—Jeff is his friend's name—has been single for a while now. His wife died."

"And I get to follow his dead wife's act. Great plan."

"Oh come on, Toady. Reddy says he's a really good guy, and he's just getting ready to mingle again. He needs a solid first date—someone who will be gentle on him. Maybe you'll end up as friends."

I pulled a fork from the drawer and speared one of the chicken strips, which was still steaming. I took a bite; even piping hot, it was delicious. It wouldn't freeze well, though, and I probably wouldn't be able to eat it all before it went bad. But maybe I would bring some to Felicia tomorrow. "I don't know, G. I'm just settling into my role as Howard Hughes over here."

Gita laughed. "Stop it. Anyway, maybe this would help you figure out what you're feeling about Adam." She added slyly, "Or Charlie."

I bristled. "There's no point in feeling anything about him, now is there? It's over." Sure, every time I passed a tall, dark-skinned man I whipped around to see if it was Charlie. But I had not heard from him, nor had I reached out. For all I knew, he had already sold his house and left town.

"Mag-gie," sang Gita in her songbird lilt. "Our kids are finally out of the house, but we're still young, healthy, and hot."

I laughed in spite of my irritation.

"Let's face it: this might possibly be as good as it gets," she said. "Do you really want to spend the rest of what could be the best decade of your life alone?"

"Maybe I do."

"Are you trying to pretend I don't know you at all?"

She was right, at least somewhat. Try as I might, I would probably never thrive as a lone wolf like Jean. But I was beginning to think I was more like the coyote, which mated for life. I couldn't just switch partners on a whim.

"Please?" said Gita. "Do this one favor for me."

I sighed. Maybe going on a date could prove to me that I could spend time with a man without diving headfirst into a shallow relationship. Or maybe it would offer clarity on Adam, who was still sending his one-line emails and waiting for my response to his proposal.

I sighed. "If you really think it's a smart idea, I'll see if this Jeff person wants to go for coffee or something."

"You're the best, Mags. You won't regret it."

I told her I might, in fact, regret it—and if that was the case, she would, too. We laughed, and I hung up feeling grateful that my friendship with Gita had endured the changes in my life. Then I put away the extra chicken, fetched the book I had been reading from my bedside table, and went into the living room to be alone.

I met Jeff for dessert at a restaurant downtown later that week. He was early, and with his sandy hair and muscular build, more attractive than the picture Gita sent had suggested. His eyes lit up when he saw me, suggesting that he, too, was pleasantly surprised. "It's so nice to meet you," he said, shaking my hand.

"And you," I said. Over decaf and chocolate cake, Jeff told me he was an immunologist within the university's health system. He had lived in Chicago before moving to Ann Arbor a few decades earlier, and still visited often, so we talked about how the city had changed for better and worse. Jeff was a good listener, and curious; he asked me all sorts of things about Second Chance, and about my children and my move from Chicago to Ann Arbor. In turn, I asked him about how he had gotten into medicine, and about his daughter, who was studying anthropology at Yale.

And yet I had to consciously think about what I was going to say in order to propel the conversation forward. As I told Jeff about how I had met Jean, I realized that I had put so much emphasis on the physical chemistry that Charlie and I had shared that I had seriously discounted our emotional connection. Talking to him was effortless; we moved seamlessly from one tangent to the next, and I would come away from our chats feeling smarter, better—enriched.

"Any interest in getting a quick drink before we call it a night?" Jeff asked as we stood to leave.

I almost said yes, if only to be nice. I caught myself before the word escaped my mouth. It was not just about the alcohol; it was that I had no urge to disclose to Jeff that I wasn't drinking, or tell him what had led me to that decision. My heart was saying no.

I put my hand on his forearm. "I should probably get going, but this has been lovely."

There was a hint of melancholy beneath his smile. "It has been. But not lovely enough, I sense."

"I'm new to this, and taking it slow."

He nodded. "I understand. But if you ever feel like going to have a glass of wine, or maybe getting dinner, give me a call."

I told him I would, and we parted amicably, heading in opposite directions down the street. It was a clear, warm night, and the streets were congested. I had walked halfway down the block when I turned to see if I could spot Jeff.

I was strangely relieved when I realized he had disappeared into the crowd. But then I realized that was because I wasn't really looking for Jeff, but for someone else entirely.

TWENTY-NINE

One morning toward the end of July, I awoke with the understanding that it was time to make up my mind about Adam. Maybe I had dreamed something that led me to this conclusion, or perhaps I was enjoying one of the clearheaded thoughts that had become more frequent now that I was no longer drinking. It was a shame that I had not had another cogent thought informing me whether to take Adam back. All the same, before I left Ann Arbor, I needed to know if I was going home to my ex-husband.

So after having a cup of coffee, I sat down at my computer and wrote Adam a quick email requesting Jillian Smith's contact information.

He responded immediately, and though I was worried he might laugh at my request or call me insane, he had put her email at the top of his message. *Can you tell me why?* he had added.

Because I need to know a few things, and I think this is the only way to find out, I wrote back.

Then I emailed Jillian.

Unlike Adam, she waited two days to respond. But I wasn't worried she would tell me I was crazy, and I was not surprised that she agreed to get together with me. It made little sense for her to do so—but it was almost like I had known from the moment Adam told me her name that we were destined to meet one day.

Adam said you are just trying to get information. I hope that's true, she wrote.

It was, I assured her. And so, just a week before Jean was set to return, I drove back to Chicago for an overnight trip.

My first stop was Jack's new apartment. He had been offered, and had taken, the mail room position at the ad agency and had already moved in with his friend Miller. They lived on the ground floor of a row house in Pilsen. A burned-out shell of a car sat across the street, and I momentarily considered shoving Jack into my car and depositing him in the sterile and (slightly) safer suburbs. But the apartment itself was spacious and clean, and Jack had set up a drafting table near the window in his bedroom. "It's just for fun," he said when I inquired, and I had tempered my enthusiasm, even though my brain and heart had already formed a conga line. Though art had once been Jack's world, I had not seen him pick up a pencil or charcoal since college. Maybe he was finally starting to use the wings Adam was always talking about.

In Oak Valley, I said a preliminary goodbye to the house. It still contained some of my old furniture but was mostly filled with the belongings of the couple that had been renting it, and maybe that was why I had not felt sad when I walked through it. The renters had liked the place and neighborhood (and presumably, spending time with their grandchild) so much that they were considering making an offer on it. Linnea felt the house would sell fast, and I was glad about that.

I spent the evening with Gita, who touched up my hair and took me to dinner at our favorite Italian place. The next morning, I woke early to go walking with her, then showered, did my makeup, and put on my best blue dress.

"Are you sure this is a good plan?" asked Gita as I was walking out the door.

I thought about what Charlie had said about even the best-laid plans being unreliable. "No," I said. "But it's the one I'm willing to take a risk on."

~

Jillian Smith had agreed to meet me at a teahouse on Randolph Street near Millennium Park. I arrived early and took a seat near the window, hoping to get a glimpse of her before she saw me.

A young woman with a dancer's carriage walked in and glanced around. I expected her eyes to land on me with recognition, but she got in line to order. Then a woman with thin braids and a smattering of artful tattoos running up and down her right arm came rushing through the door. She looked nothing like the public policy expert I had in mind, but surely she could have made Adam feel youthful and alive. Yet she paid no attention to me as she ordered her tea, and left without a backward glance. Other people drifted in and out: a herd of teen boys, a middle-aged woman, two women who looked to be in their seventies. Jillian had agreed to meet me at eleven thirty, but my phone informed me it was almost eleven forty-five. Had I been stood up?

"Hello?" The middle-aged woman was standing in front of me. I wondered if she was going to ask to share my table, as people occasionally did when a café was crowded. I hated to sit in close quarters with a stranger, but as I glanced around, I realized there were more than a few empty tables available.

"I'm Jillian Smith," said the woman. "Are you Maggie?"

I almost fainted. Then I stood abruptly, sending my chair tumbling backward behind me. I turned around to pick it up, my cheeks burning. "Excuse me, sorry," I mumbled.

Only then did I allow myself to really look at her. She was short, with a lean build and no discernible curves. Her hair was red with some gray woven throughout. And her face—her face! We looked nothing alike, Jillian Smith and I. But with the fine lines in her forehead and around her mouth, the sunspots on her cheeks, and more than anything, the look in her eyes, which had surely seen far more than thirty years of life: she was me.

This was the woman who had made my husband feel alive?

"Hi," I said. "Thank you so much for meeting me."

"Sure." She looked as nervous as I felt. "Are you in the mood for tea?"

"Not really," I admitted.

"Me neither. Why don't we take a walk? We could head over to Millennium Park."

Perhaps this was a trick, and she was going to wait until we were sandwiched between tourists, then retrieve a weapon from her woven handbag and shank me before disappearing into the throng. But I agreed; after all, it had been my idea to meet in the first place, and in her khaki shorts and Birkenstock sandals, Jillian Smith did not strike me as the stabby type.

As we made our way toward the park, a man walking in the opposite direction jostled Jillian as he rushed past and continued on without apologizing. Jillian shook her head with disgust. "God. People are the worst." She glanced at me quickly, probably having realized that as Adam's ex-paramour, she could very well fall into the "worst people" category. But I found myself smiling in recognition, and without thinking to censor myself, I said, "Especially if you're a woman of a certain age."

"Isn't that the truth," she agreed.

"Adam said you were thirty," I blurted, recalling the uncertainty in his voice when he told me this. At the time, I thought he was hesitating because he was embarrassed. Lo and behold, he was lying. I wondered why, of all things, he felt compelled to fib about her age.

"I haven't been thirty in seventeen years," she said, dodging another man barreling at us. "He probably told you that so if you went looking for me, you'd find the wrong person."

That was highly likely. And yet her being younger than me, if only by seven years, was momentarily soothing. Then I realized I was still looking for reasons to justify Adam's behavior, when the point was not to rationalize it, but to understand it.

When we reached the park, Jillian pointed. "How about we walk toward the Bean?"

I nodded, and we walked in silence. We reached the great silver structure and stood and admired it for a minute. Then, without discussing our plan, we walked to Crown Fountain. The two towering fountains were lit with images of people's faces. A mix of children and adults frolicked through the shallow pool of water, sending its cool spray onto my skin.

"Why did you agree to meet with me?" I asked.

"Guilt," said Jillian, still staring out at the water. Then she turned and looked at me carefully. "I guess I wanted to meet the woman who Adam had spent most of his life with, too."

"Here I am. So you were crazy about him, huh?"

"Was and am, though it's over," she said wistfully. "I used to see him at the Starbucks around the block from my work—both of us seemed to take coffee breaks around the same time—and there was something about him that made me feel like I had to get to know him. I started chatting him up, and . . ." The color in her cheeks made her look like a child with a fever. "I didn't know he was married at first. He never wore a ring, at least not that I noticed. Later, I found out he sometimes forgot to put it back on after he worked out. It wasn't deliberate—though his flirting with me was."

The flirting comment stung, but I was fixated on her comment about his ring. When Adam and I had still been married, *I* had never forgotten to put my eternity band back on. Then again, I had stopped taking it off altogether, even when I was washing dishes or doing something that might damage it. Different actions, same sort of carelessness.

Jillian continued. "By the time he told me, we had already met for coffee several times, and I had fallen hard for him. Believe me, I knew it was wrong—not only the cheating, but also that he had waited to tell me he wasn't available. I guess love can make you blind."

"So you're not married, too?"

Jillian shook her head. "I was for a few good years in my thirties, and then after a few bad years, we got divorced. After that, I never wanted to marry again. But Adam . . . I was nuts about him. And he was nuts about you."

I laughed bitterly. "Right. So nuts he decided to cheat on me."

"Maggie, barring an act of God, I have the feeling you and I will never see each other again, and I know you want answers, so I'll cut to the chase. Adam was having a midlife crisis. I knew that from the minute he admitted he was married. He was attracted to me, for sure, and I was so crazy about him that I was able to pretend that he wasn't just spending time with me to boost his ego. Have you ever had an affair before?"

"No," I said curtly.

"Well, it's intoxicating. But Adam was already gone long before I allowed myself to admit that I was a cipher." She knelt and ran her hand through the water, then pressed it to her cheeks and her chest. "You should probably know that I don't regret it. I know that's awful, and it's mine to live with. But there was this period of time—after Adam and I began seeing each other and before I realized he didn't love me and never would—that was so magical to me that the rest was all worth it. Adam was smart and interesting and he made my life better, if that makes sense."

It did.

"I had never fallen in love with someone like that before. I'm glad I didn't die without knowing what that was like." She paused. "Why did you want to meet me, Maggie?"

I, too, bent to put my hands in the water, mostly because I needed a moment before I responded to her. I would never tell her that it was because I needed to see who she was, and why she had made Adam feel alive. Anyway, now I had my answer: she had looked at him with fresh eyes.

I stood and wiped my hands on my dress. "Adam asked me to come back to him—to remarry him. We divorced in January."

"I gathered that from you saying you were his ex-wife. I'm sorry."

"Right." A couple of young women were standing just to our right, pretending to talk but clearly eavesdropping. *Let them,* I thought. *Maybe they'll learn a thing or two about how not to make a mess of their lives.* "He said he loves me and will never hurt me again."

"And because he lied to you about other things, you needed proof that he wasn't lying about our affair," she said.

"Yes." We looked at each other.

"It's the truth," she said after a moment. "I wish it weren't, but it is. Adam seemed depressed about work and his father's death. At the end of our affair, if you can call it that—"

"You can."

She pursed her lips and nodded. "He started getting this deer-in-headlights look. I think he was scared half to death about what he'd done, and felt like he had to follow through, or then it all would have been for nothing. I don't think he ever actually stopped loving you; it was more like he set you aside in his mind and then felt like he had to stick with it."

Jillian reminded me of Charlie, the way she didn't hesitate to say what she was thinking. If we had met under different circumstances, she might have been a friend.

"Adam's a great man, Maggie," she said.

Yes, he is, I thought with a mix of melancholy and joy. He was fallible, but he was a good man.

"I hope this has been helpful," she added.

It was time for us to part, so I thanked her, and then she thanked me for being gracious, and I laughed and said it was gracious of her to call my setup gracious. Before going our separate ways, Jillian hugged me goodbye, which was at once strange and touching.

As I walked back to the train alone, I thought about what Jillian had said—how the magical times with Adam had made the pain of losing him worth it.

I knew the magic she spoke of. There was our first date at a Thai restaurant, where we had barely been able to eat, because we were too busy staring at each other over the table, or our honeymoon in Sonoma, when we spent hours in bed each day. Better still were the wonderfully mundane moments after we had settled into our marriage, like the way he would call me five minutes after leaving for work to say he missed me, or how he fell asleep with a leg slung over mine.

More than all of that, though, I had loved knowing I was not alone in the world. When Zoe screamed that she hated me at the top of her lungs, I had Adam to comfort me. After my mother died, Adam assured me that though she was gone, he was still there. He loved me more than life itself, he had told me, and I knew this to be true.

As I reached the L, I could hear a train approaching. I rushed through the turnstile and ran down the stairs, but it was too late. By the time I hit the platform, the train was pulling out of the station. As I waited for the next one, my mind returned to Adam.

For a long time, I thought he had left because of me, or at least because of a shortcoming in our marriage. But Jillian had confirmed that his decision to leave had largely been the by-product of his own internal crisis.

He swore he would never hurt me again, but to believe this was to believe he would never suffer another crisis of that magnitude. There were no guarantees; I understood that now. All the so-called proof in the world could not prove Adam would remain loyal and provide the new relationship he had promised.

Was a lack of certainty reason enough to turn down a second shot at the life Adam and I had spent three decades creating together?

THIRTY

There is something about struggle that changes you in irrevocable ways. I had spent more than a year waiting to feel like myself again, but as I packed my bags the day before Jean was to return from Italy, it occurred to me that I would never again be the version of myself that I had been searching for. Instead, the separation and divorce had reduced me to the very essence of who I was. As I passed before the antique mirror in Jean's bedroom, I understood that this reduction had not made me weak—though I had certainly felt that way at times—but far stronger, like a sheet of metal that had been hammered into a solid, unbreakable sphere.

I was glad to be leaving town this way, even if I felt ambivalent about my departure. I would miss Jean's house: her paintings and wacky survival novels, her yard and neighborhood, even the quiet. And I would miss Second Chance and Felicia, as well as the divorce support group, even if it had never felt the same after Charlie stopped going. I had not called him, though I'd considered it a few dozen times; after all, he knew I was taking off at the beginning of August, and he had not reached out to me. Our parting at the park had been final.

After I had packed everything but my toiletries and a change of clothing, I went outside to the small garden I had planted and called Rose.

"Maggie!" exclaimed Rose. "I'm so sorry about the other day."

"Oh, Rose. It's okay. You don't have to apologize." She was referring to the previous Sunday, when I had stopped to see her on my way out of Chicago. Our visit had started off well enough, but she had quickly grown agitated—I would say unusually so, but dementia was fast turning an unflaggingly polite woman into one who became angry at the slightest provocation.

"Maggie, what *is* this hellhole?" she had said, looking around with disgust as we sat on her sofa. At her neurologist's urging, she had just moved out of her apartment and into a single room on the opposite side of the building, which was a traditional nursing home. And in that moment, she didn't recognize where she was, which was precisely why her doctor had wanted her to move right away. Because of her dementia, the longer she waited to make a change, the harder it would be for her to adjust.

"It's not so bad, Rose," I had said, trying to soothe her. The room was spacious and decorated with some of her furniture. Nonetheless, it was still just a generic beige box with a hospital-style bathroom, and Rose's perfume could not mask the nursing home smell that permeated the air.

"It's a death sentence," she muttered. Then she had gotten up from the sofa and, with much effort, gotten into bed fully clothed, kitten heels and all. I had sat by her bedside for a while until she told me to leave. "There's nothing you can do for me, Heather," she muttered. "Go home."

She had mistaken me for the daughter-in-law she didn't like, and I had been crushed. And when I checked in a few days later, she was having "another bad day," she told me, and asked me to call another time.

Standing in Jean's yard, I was relieved to hear that Rose again sounded like the woman I had known and loved all these years. "Rose," I said, bending to pull a dandelion that had sprouted next to a tomato plant, "that's part of the reason why I'm calling. You had a really rough time that day. I'm not sure if you remember, but you got in bed with your shoes on and told me to leave."

"Oh my word. I hope you know I didn't mean it."

I yanked another weed and tossed it in the pile I had started at the garden's edge. "Of course I do. But I think you and I should have another conversation about your treatment plan."

She let out a long sigh. "Bad enough that I'm losing my mind, but to actually know it's happening is worse. I wish it had happened all at once. Like an explosion—so I never knew what hit me."

"I'm so sorry," I said quietly. My other mother, as I thought of Rose, was leaving my life, one stolen moment at a time. I bit my lip, then willed myself to say it: "Forgive me, Rose, but I have to ask you to please, *please* consider taking the medication your neurologist recommended."

"There's no saying if it will work," she said crisply, and I could just imagine her tilting her chin up the way she did when she felt she was right. "Knowing that, why would I subject myself to side effects?"

I bent down to pull another dandelion. "We all know it's not a cure, but if it meant even a few more happy days—just a little more joy—wouldn't it be worth it?"

She didn't respond, and I wondered if perhaps I had crossed a line. But then she said, "Okay."

I had been about to pull a ripe tomato from its vine, and I froze, my hand on the tomato's taut flesh. "Okay?"

"I'll try the pills."

I let go of the tomato and pumped my fist into the air. "Oh, Rose. Thank you. This is going to mean so much to Adam. It means so much to *me*."

"I'm glad," she said. "I just hope it works, at least a little."

~

Later, I stood in the kitchen, cutting one of the tomatoes I had picked while wrapping up my conversation with Rose. I salted a slice and took a bite. Its juice trickled down my chin, and I wiped it away with a dishcloth, savoring the sweet, acidic taste on my tongue. It was so much better than the hothouse tomatoes I bought at the grocery store. If I had known that earlier, maybe I would have started a garden in Oak Valley. Gardening, like traveling on my own and biking, was one of those things that had always sounded like a good idea but that I had never actually gotten around to.

Well, I was doing them now, I thought with pride, staring out the window at the plot that was overflowing with the tomatoes, cucumbers, summer squash, and chives I had planted.

It hit me, then, how many other things I could still learn and try. How many other chances I wanted to take, even if it meant risking failure. Rose had been right. On some counts, at least, there was still time.

After finishing the last bite of tomato, I wiped my face and washed my hands. Then I retrieved my computer from one of my suitcases, sat down with it at Jean's table, and began to write.

Dear Adam,

I saw your mother when I was in Chicago last weekend. I'm sorry to say that it did not go well. As her neurologist predicted, the move to the single room was confusing and upsetting to her. (She called me Heather.) Her dementia is getting worse, and even though I'm not her biological daughter, that is so damn hard to witness.

But when I called her this morning and discovered she was her old coherent self, I asked her—yet again—to consider medication. I explained how much it would mean to me and to you, and to my amazement, she agreed to give it a try. I believe she meant it and, provided she is lucid, that she'll remember agreeing to it. Could you please make an appointment for her to see Dr. Niall? I'll keep checking in with her, but it would help if you and Rick continue to encourage her.

I apologize for changing the subject abruptly, but there's no easy transition for this: I can't remarry you. Not now, and not in the future. I understand that you did love me even though you claimed otherwise, and I believe that you still do. I accept that your affair was a bad decision, and your leaving was a worse one. I know you regret both. I don't think I told you this yet, but I forgive you, fully and completely.

This email will hurt you, and that's the last thing I want to do. But I also want you to have a firm answer, so that you can move forward and find new happiness. I know that you will.

I'd like for us to be on good terms one day—if not friends, then two people who love their children enough to behave like they are. I've loved hearing about the changes you've made in your life, and I'm proud of you for having the courage to make your dreams come true. But I think we shouldn't be in contact for a while. I need the space and clarity to continue learning how to live without you. I don't know how long, but I'll tell you when

I'm ready to be in touch again. If there's anything urgent that you need to communicate in the meantime, have Zoe or Jack reach out to me.

Adam, you have given me love, my beloved children and our family, and many of the best years of my life. For all of that—and so much more—thank you. Please be good to yourself.

Love always,

Maggie

I closed the computer and exhaled. It pained me to turn down Adam and the new life he was offering. But it wasn't the absence of a guarantee that led me to say no.

It was the knowledge that I no longer needed a guarantee to be happy. I hadn't wanted to be alone. Now that I was, though, I knew that there was a whole new world out there waiting for me. And within this world happened to be a man whom I wanted to take a chance on. I wasn't sure if it was too late to take that chance, but like Rose, I was going to have to give it a go.

I ran to the bathroom to make sure I didn't have dirt on my face. Then I grabbed my sunglasses and a water bottle, went to the shed to fetch my bike and helmet, and set off down the road.

The late afternoon sun beat down on my skin as I biked, sending beads of perspiration rolling down the back of my neck and between my breasts. Still I pushed on.

I had traveled three miles when worry began to make its familiar trek through my mind. It was ridiculous to do this at this stage in the game.

The heat beat down on my shoulders as I hit the fourth mile, and I nearly had to walk my bicycle up the last hill. But I kept pedaling until Charlie's house came into view.

A "For Sale" sign with a "Sold" banner had been staked into the sloping front lawn. How could this be anything other than a literal sign I had waited too long? Charlie was leaving. He had moved on.

Yet I got off my bike, left my sunglasses and sweat-soaked helmet in the basket, and walked to the porch. I was about to knock when the door flew open.

"Maggie?" Charlie stood there staring at me as if I were a ghost. He had grown a short beard since I had last seen him, and was wearing a pale blue polo shirt. He looked even better than he had before.

"Hi," I said quietly.

Behind him, boxes were stacked throughout the house. "I was about to go out, and I saw you through the window," he said. "I would say it was the bike that tipped me off, but I'd spot your face from across Times Square."

Would he? In spite of all the cynical thoughts running through my mind, my heart began to swell.

"Sorry I didn't call first," I said. I had considered it, but I didn't want to have a conversation with him, even a brief one, over the phone. My mother had always said an apology didn't count unless you could see the other person's face.

"That's all right. I'm surprised to see you, though. It's been two months." He grimaced self-consciously. "Not that I've been counting."

"I—" I started, just as he said, "We—"

"Go ahead," he said to me as I said, "You first."

We both laughed. Then I took a deep breath. "I'm sorry. I shouldn't have left things the way I did. I was struggling over the situation with Adam, but that wasn't an excuse for leaving you hanging like that."

"I'm sorry, too," he said, putting his hand on my arm. "I should have reached out to you—at least to check in, if not to tell you I missed you."

"Why didn't you then?" I asked.

His eyes locked with mine. "A proposal from your ex-husband isn't exactly a small deal, and I didn't want to run the risk of influencing your decision. I hoped I would hear from you sooner, and when I didn't, I assumed you told Adam yes. But you're here . . ." He grinned at me, all dimples. "So maybe I was wrong?"

Minutes ago my limbs had felt leaden. Now every one of my nerves was buzzing. "You were wrong. That part of my life is over." I looked at him and laughed, even though I could feel tears pricking my lids, too.

"What is it?" he asked.

"I'm just . . ." I stammered, because I was not sure how to explain the joy I felt, having just realized that what I had mistaken for a tale as old as time was only a small part of a much longer story. "It's really good to see you," I said.

"And it's even better to see you," said Charlie, pulling me to him. Then he leaned forward and kissed me like he had been waiting months to do so. So I kissed him back to show him he hadn't been the only one waiting.

"Maggie," he said when we had parted, "it's almost August. Isn't your friend Jean coming home soon?"

I nodded. "Yes, tomorrow."

"So where are you headed next?"

I looked at the road in front of his house, and up at the vast blue sky, and then back at Charlie. "I don't actually know," I said. "Do you want to come?"

He smiled. "Yes."

What was I offering? I wondered as Charlie put his lips on mine again. I had no home, no actual destination in mind. And this man, who kissed me in a way that made me feel as alive as I ever had, might one day offer only the closed-lipped kiss of someone whose passion has gone missing.

But even if things with Charlie ended tomorrow, I would be glad that I had tried to find out what was possible for us. For today, I was just happy to be with him.

"Can I take you to dinner tonight?" he asked. "We've got a lot to discuss, and I have to tell you, I have seriously missed talking to you."

"I missed talking to you, too," I confessed. "And yes, dinner sounds lovely. But," I said, pulling my damp t-shirt away from my skin, "I should probably head home and shower and change."

"Why?" He grinned, sniffing me. "You smell good to me. Like a ripe peach."

I grinned back. "Do you want to pick me up?"

"Six thirty?"

"Perfect."

He looked at my bike, which I had left propped in the driveway. "It's crazy hot out. Can I give you a ride back?"

I thought for a moment. "No, I'll head back on my own."

"Okay." Charlie pulled me to him and wrapped me in his arms. "Maggie? I'm really glad you came over."

"I am, too," I said.

~

On the ride back, a deep sense of peace came over me. As I pedaled, the road before me faded and I was again with my mother. We were in her hospice room, and she wore a scarf on her head; her skin, which hung on her brittle frame, was almost gray. Though the doctor had not said as much, we knew these days were her last.

"Going to be soon," she rasped.

"Oh, Ma," I said, clutching her hands. "Are you afraid?"

"Course I am. Only a fool doesn't fear death, and even then he's a liar."

"You can hold on."

"Oh, love. No amount of holding's going to keep things from changing." Her voice was faint, her breath ragged as fluid pushed against her cancer-riddled lungs. The morphine helped her feel like she wasn't suffocating, but it put her to sleep for long stretches of time, and she loathed using even the smallest amount. And yet I was selfish: I encouraged her to ease her pain, because I thought maybe this would keep her with me a little longer.

I blinked back my tears and entwined my fingers in hers. "How lucky we are," I said, "to have had each other."

She smiled at me the best she could. "How lucky to be able to say goodbye."

"Not goodbye," I insisted. "Not yet."

I can't remember if she nodded, or if I have since filled in that detail in my mind. "It's just about time for me to go see what's next," she said. Then she unlatched her fingers and slowly placed her hand on top of my own—a gesture that reminded me that she was my mother, and on this matter, she knew best. "You're my heart, Maggie. It's been so very good, being with you."

This would be the last thing she would say; she slipped out of consciousness that afternoon and, three days later, passed out of this world and into the next.

The warmth of the sun on my shoulders felt like my mother gazing down on me. I pushed into the pedals and lifted my face to the wind, thinking about the time I had been given. If I, too, had only fifty-four years on this planet, it would have been too short. And yet it would have been enough.

For now, I had the good fortune of more chances to fail and succeed, more love to give and receive—more life. And while I didn't know what my future held, I would follow my mother's lead. I would summon my strength and go find out what was next.

ACKNOWLEDGMENTS

Thanks first and foremost to Tiffany Yates Martin, whose brilliant editorial guidance helped transform a sketch of a story into a novel. Tiffany, I could not have written this without you.

Jodi Warshaw and Danielle Marshall, it's such a pleasure to work with you both; thank you for bringing my fiction to readers. Thanks, too, to Gabriella Dumpit, Dennelle Catlett, and the rest of the Lake Union team.

Elisabeth Weed, I'm lucky to call you my agent.

Kathleen Carter Zrelak and Goldberg McDuffie, and Michelle Weiner and Creative Artists Agency, a million thanks for championing my work.

Shannon Callahan and Laurel Lambert, you're my secret weapons in writing and life. Thanks for reading draft after draft and keeping me afloat.

I remain deeply grateful for the support I receive from my friends and family. Thank you to Julie Lawson Timmer and Dan Timmer, Stefanie and Craig Galban, Jennifer and Jeff Lamb, Joe Lambert, Anna and Vince Massey, Stevany and Tim Peters, Alex Ralph, Sara Reistad-Long, Nicole and Matt Sampson, Michelle and Mike Stone,

Pam Sullivan, Janette Sunadhar, and Darci and Mike Swisher. Special thanks to Jennifer Lamb for answering my endless string of questions about social work.

JP, Indira, and Xavi Pagán, you give me a reason to write.

Lastly, thanks to my beloved grandmother, Patricia Pietrzak, who passed away before she was able to read this novel but who was with me for every page.

ABOUT THE AUTHOR

Photo © 2017 by Myra Klarman

Camille Pagán is the author of four novels: *Woman Last Seen in Her Thirties*, *Forever is the Worst Long Time*, *The Art of Forgetting*, and the #1 Amazon Kindle bestseller *Life and Other Near-Death Experiences*, which was recently optioned for film. A journalist and former health editor, Pagán has written for *Forbes*; *O, The Oprah Magazine*; *Parade*; *Real Simple*; *Time*; *WebMD*; and many other publications and websites. She lives with her family in Ann Arbor, Michigan. Visit her at www.camillepagan.com.